Abyssinian
(A Traveller to Henry's Court)

by Anne Stevens

Tudor Crimes: Book XII

Foreword

It is October, 1537, and Thomas Cromwell, the son of a sometime brewer, and drunken blacksmith, stands at the pinnacle of his political career. It has been a long, hard road from the tumbledown world of Putney to Whitehall Palace, but the commoner is now the beloved favourite of King Henry, and the first minister of England.

He overshadows even the Lord Chancellor, Tom Audley, and his reputation is such that grown men fear his summons, and children are frightened into obedience with the warning that 'Cromwell will come' if they misbehave.

Cromwell has steered the king through a traumatic divorce, the reformation of the church, the execution of Anne Boleyn, and his re-marriage to Lady Jane Seymour. It is now the twelfth of October, and the queen has given birth to the longed for son. Henry is delighted and, with unknowing irony, sees it as all being Thomas Cromwell's doing.

With Thomas Wyatt and Mush Draper, freshly returned from the war against the Ottomans, and his stalwart nephew Richard by his side, the Privy

2

Councillor feels that the Austin Friars plan is back on course. With his land reforms put before a docile parliament, and an English bible in every church pulpit, he can look forward to a prosperous future for both himself, and Henry's realm.

Rafe Sadler is established as a trusted advisor to the king, and Will Draper is Henry's valued Royal Examiner. Both men owe their elevation to Thomas Cromwell, and are in his debt. Whilst Rafe's devotion is unquestioned, Will finds himself in a constant struggle between love for the man, and disapproval of his methods.

Miriam Draper loves her husband, and looks upon Cromwell as a father figure. For her, the tension between the two men is heart rending, and she wants nothing more than a permanent reconciliation, and a prosperous, and quiet, life.

Whilst the former is possible, the latter is not. Reaching the peak of success is one thing, but for Thomas Cromwell, and his young men, the descent may be quite another.

1 **The Toledo Cortes**

The infrequently held *Cortes* of Spain are a tiresome intrusion into the running of the Holy Roman Empire, and can often create disharmony between the ruling dynasty, and the Roman Catholic church. This great parliament of 1538, held in the magnificent city of Toledo, is proving to be no exception, and royal wishes clash with religious needs on an almost daily basis.

"I am the Cardinal of Toledo, which makes me the primate of all Spain," the lean old man lisps into his wine goblet. "I am president of the royal council, and leader of the Cortes. Is this not so, Bishop Diego?"

"Of course, my friend." Diego Sanchez is, perhaps, the only man alive who has ever called Cardinal Juan Pardo de Tavera this, and it is not a word he uses lightly. The two men have progressed through the tiers of the Roman Catholic church in Spain for better than thirty years, and have outlived every other rival for two of the three most coveted positions available. "You are the most eminent man of the church in the whole of the Holy Roman Empire."

"Next year, Emperor Charles

will have to choose a new Grand Inquisitor," Cardinal Tavera says in an unusually high pitched voice which, together with his slight lisp, gives him an air of spoiled petulance that masks a character of the most steel-like determination. "Despite the silly games he plays with Anton Fugger, the emperor's banker is not capable of holding this great empire together. Only a man of God can keep Spain, and her Catholic empire on a faithful course."

"It is not doubted, Juan," Diego says. "The Cortes will back your move to bring the treasure of the New World under the church's sway, and block the Fugger influence. As Grand Inquisitor, you will have the power to send our people out into the world, and seek out any who deny the true faith."

"We must have stricter laws against the Jews, and those Muslims who think to continue practicing their heresy." The cardinal is Auditor of the Spanish Inquisition, and understands how the institution, set within the greater Catholic faith can be a most powerful medium for counter reformation. He also wishes to broaden the Holy Inquisition's remit, until he has the power to destroy anything, and any one, who seeks to deviate from the true Christian faith.

"The majority of the Cortes are in favour," Bishop Diego Sanchez replies. "They do not trust those Moors amongst us, who claim to be of our faith, and will welcome any restrictive action against them. Nor will the Cortes any longer accept the Jews amongst us … despite their apparent conversion to our faith."

"They must all be tested, Diego." The cardinal is in his late sixties, and is at that stage in life where his only satisfaction is in finding fault in others, and using his position to expose them, and turn them back onto the right path. "Let us not make the mistake of thinking it is only the Christ killers, and heretical Ottomans who need to be tested. There are those, within a short distance from us, who deny the word of God."

"We watch the Hanseatic League constantly, my friend," Bishop Diego says. "We do all we can to sway them away from the doctrines of the despised Luther, and agitate with the emperor to step up the war against this so called reformation. Men are fined if they speak against the church, and imprisoned if found with heretical tracts in their possession."

"Is it all enough?"Juan Tavera

shakes his head in answer to his own question. "Satan is perched on every man's shoulder, waiting for his chance to strike at the soul. It is not enough to burn the odd one, like the Englishman, Tyndale… though his death was a very great victory for the church. We must strike much harder. How are the arrangements going concerning the English?"

"Well, my friend." Bishop Diego Sanchez is confident that his latest scheme is coming to fruition, and sees a time, soon, when a great blow will be struck against the heretic, King Henry. "Secret letters have been despatched to our agents, and those who can aid us have been notified."

"Secrecy is of the utmost importance," Cardinal Tavera pipes. "The English must suspect nothing, until the blow falls… and it is too late."

"We do not use the usual channels of communication," his friend assures him. "I employ merchants, or travellers, to pass on cryptic messages, and they move about the trade routes of the continent unsuspected."

"No word of this must be leaked," the cardinal reiterates. "It must come as a devastating blow to the English. A blow from which they cannot recover. Afterwards, they will have no recourse but to return to the church, and renounce their disgusting heresy."

"Henry is a strong king, and will not wish his power diminished."

"Was not Herod a mighty king also?" The old cardinal almost cackles into his wine. "Was not King Saul humbled before the Lord our God?"

"Henry will not crumble." Diego has considered their plan from every angle, and knows the weaknesses, as well as its strengths. The English church has become strong since Henry cut his ties with Rome, and if the situation is allowed to continue, the new creed will become the rock upon which the protestants build their opposition to the Pope. "He will seek to make bargains, and refuse to ever bend his knee to His Holiness."

"Those are matters for the politicians to work out," the old cardinal says. "It is for us, as the Sword of God, to strike the blow which will ruin the English king's hold on his people. Are we sure that blow will fall?"

"I travel to London tomorrow," Diego Sanchez confirms. "My papers show me to be an agent of Emperor Charles, and orders all his loyal subjects to render whatever aid I might request of them."

"I fear for you, Diego." The cardinal sips at his wine, and squints at the document set out for him to sign. "This warrant from my office will not protect you from the English, if they suspect anything is amiss."

"It will see me across France safely," Diego says, "and it will show them that I am a man of great importance. It will impress the Imperial Ambassador in London."

"Ah, yes… this fellow, Eustace Chapuys… what do we know of him?"

"I have met him, once. He is a pompous little man, with a love of fine clothes, and rich banquets. His loyalty to the emperor is complete, but he is also a pragmatist. He will sail the course that suits him best."

"Then he can be bought?" The cardinal smiles, even as he says the words, for everyone, he muses, can be bought. "Is he *for* us, Diego?"

"He is a minor diplomat," Diego explains, "whose only worth is where he lives. His house lies adjacent to Austin Friars, the hub of Thomas Cromwell's great power. As the emperor's man, I will be welcome to stay with him… in easy reach of the Cromwell house."

"God smiles on us, my friend."

The cardinal dips his nose into his wine once more, and sniffs the heady bouquet. "Separated from our enemy by a garden wall, and able to watch and wait for the right moment."

"Thomas Cromwell is the guiding power behind Henry Tudor," Diego Sanchez says. "The king has raised him to the most pre-eminent of positions, and hangs on his every word. Was it not this Cromwell who brought about the estrangement between king and church? Was it not also he who forced through the divorce, and brought the Boleyn whore to the throne? In this way, Cromwell was able to force a break with Rome, and put vile protestant thoughts into the king's head."

"So clever ... so very clever," the cardinal mutters. "Then, the devil *is* clever. Now, Cromwell is printing off thousands of English bibles, and putting them in churches up and down the realm, so that the common people can read the word of God. These self same people were once loyal to the Pope, and must now be considered to be heretics. Once Henry recants of his blasphemous new church, we must bring them back to God ... with fire and sword, if need be."

"It is almost impossible to get

near Cromwell these days," the bishop says. "Once, he would walk amongst the people, shaking their hands, and distributing largesse, but his own men guard him closer now, day and night. That is why I have conceived so involved a plot against him."

"Yes, your mind is as sharp as a dagger still," the cardinal agrees. "To create a situation where someone can be put close to the man is clever, but to contrive for that person to be able to strike, and escape, is a wonder. It will work, will it not?"

"Thomas Cromwell is as good as dead," Diego Sanchez says with utter conviction. "He will welcome his assassin with open arms."

"To kill the dog is one thing, but to escape the wrath of his men is another," the cardinal sings in his falsetto voice. "It is important that such an escape is effective. There must be no-one left behind to sign confessions, or cast aspersions on Holy Mother Church."

"I travel to England tomorrow, and will return within the month," the bishop confirms. "Cromwell will be dead, and God's Instrument will be safe from capture, or revenge."

"I have given some thought to the method," Cardinal Tavera says, as he puts aside his drink. "Open the casket by your hand, my friend. See, beautiful, is it not?" Diego Sanchez gazes at the exquisite dagger, nestled on its velvet cushion, and nods his head.

"This is a holy relic," he says. "Its workmanship is not Spanish, is it?"

"No, it was sent to one of my predecessors, some three hundred years ago… by Conradin, then King of Jerusalem. It is claimed to be the dagger of Saint Longinus, who was the centurion in command at Christ's crucifixion. I have no reason to doubt the veracity of the claim, and consider this relic to have an amazing power. One prick of the blade, and Cromwell is a dead man."

"Then I shall take it with me, and see it serves its holy purpose well," the bishop says. The dagger is of oriental design, and has several gemstones set into its hilt. Diego Sanchez wonders, briefly, how a Roman soldier could ever afford such a magnificent weapon, but pushes the thought aside. It is enough that it is here, from the Holy Land, and sent by the last, true Christian King of Jerusalem. "Let its point find Thomas Cromwell's black heart, and consign him to the Hell he so richly deserves!"

Cardinal Juan Pardo de Tavera raises his hand and makes the sign of the cross at the bishop, then moves his lips in a murmured benediction. God, he knows, has chosen him from the rest, and has him marked for ever greater things. Through the power of God, he is to be raised to the greatest possible position, short of the papacy, and must use that power to unify the church, and rid the world of the heresy that clings to men's souls.

With Cromwell dead, England can be brought to heel, and the Holy Roman Empire can concentrate on bringing the far off Americas into the light of God. The Inquisitor's agents will scour the world, and destroy any hint of heresy.

"Go with God, my friend," he mutters to the bishop. "May your grand design come to pass, and may you bring King Henry back to the true church!"

*

"Are you Señor Chapuys?" The stocky Spaniard steps out of the shadows, and bows low to the startled ambassador. Chapuys' faithful servant puts himself between the two men, and drops a hand to the knife at his belt, but the little Savoyard touches his elbow.

"Peace, my faithful Alonso, this

gentleman addresses me in a Spanish accent. I am sure he is here as a friend." Alonso Gomez grunts, and steps back, but he remains with his hand in close proximity to his dagger.

"At your service, Ambassador Chapuys," the man says. "My ship docked but a few hours ago, and I come to pay my respects to a fine gentleman, for whom I have nothing but the deepest affection."

"I am pleased to hear it," Chapuys replies, somewhat pleased at the flamboyant flattery. "Might I have the honour of knowing your name, my dear sir?"

"I am Don Manuel Diego Alfonso de Granvella, a captain of the Imperial Guard," the big man says. "I am commissioned to seek you out, and place a letter into your own hand. It bears the official seal of the Bishop of Alghero."

"The Bishop of Alghero?" Eustace Chapuys ponders the title for a moment, then recalls a meeting some years before with a Spanish Sardinian cleric with an austere taste in clothes. "Then you must mean Bishop Diego Sanchez. Why would the fellow write to me after all this time… and in such an unexpected manner, Captain Granvella?"

"I am but the messenger," Captain Granvella says, and hands over the document. "I am charged to warn you that the contents are secret, and not to be discussed with anyone else. Good day, Ambassador Chapuys." The man steps back into the shadows of the narrow street, and is gone. Eustace Chapuys shakes his head and tucks the letter into his breast pocket for safe keeping.

"How peculiar," he mutters to himself, and Alonso Gomez wonders if it is some kind of a trap. He fears the letter contains incriminating information, which will hurt his master, or lay him open to arrest and trial.

"Burn it, sir," he advises. "Burn it, and claim it was lost... or never delivered. An ambassador will be believed before a mere captain of the emperor's soldiery."

"We are but a few yards from home," Eustace Chapuys decides. "I will retire to my study, and read this strange missive in private."

Gomez knows not to waste his time arguing, and escorts his master back, past the grand gates of Austin Friars, to the smaller house they rent next door. The ambassador shuts himself in his study, lights a long taper to see by, and opens the letter. It is, indeed, from Diego Sanchez, the Bishop of Alghero in Sardinia.

"Coming here?" Chapuys reads the short letter again, and still does not fathom any hidden meaning in it. It states only that Diego Sanchez, Bishop of Alghero, is travelling on the emperor's private business, and expects to stay with Ambassador Eustace Chapuys during his impending visit. "This is to be kept a close secret?" he asks himself, then sighs. Perhaps the emperor wishes to see how he is faring in England, and so sends this old acquaintance to spy on him, or simply that the bishop wants to be assured of a warm welcome in a hostile land, and writes in advance.

The ambassador ponders on what little he recalls of his brief visit to Alghero, and can remember nothing, save that the Spanish controlled town was small, unimpressive, and served up very poor food. In short, the place was a mosquito ridden backwater, hardly worth a visit.

Eustace Chapuys folds the letter and goes to put it in a drawer, then thinks better of it. The bishop's messenger insists that an air of great secrecy is maintained, and Chapuys thinks he might as well take the warning seriously. He holds the paper to the flickering flame of the taper, and watches as it chars, and then burns into nothingness.

*

"What is it?" Richard Cromwell asks the agent who has sidled up to him in a tavern. The man is little more than a beggar, but he has a keen nose for intrigue.

"Perhaps nothing," the man says. He is paid a few shillings to watch people for Cromwell, and report on anything out of the ordinary. "I saw the ambassador today."

"Which one?"

"The Spanish jack-a-dandy."

"Oh, Eustace Chapuys," Richard replies. "He is a Savoyard, despite working for the Spanish emperor. What was he up to that made your nose twitch so much, my malodorous friend?"

"He left his house with Alonso Gomez, to walk down to Whitehall Palace," the man says. "He usually sits in the long gallery, and bribes the king's doctors and servants for snippets of information. They tell him if the king slept well, or broke wind today, and he drops them a few coins. Only this day is different. He was met by another Spaniard."

"What Spaniard?" Richard is all

ears now, for mention of Spaniards is enough to awaken his keen interest.

"I do not know. He seemed a well set up sort of a gentleman, and he was armed with a brace of very fancy pistols."

"What transpired?" Richard Cromwell is interested now, and wonders what Chapuys is about.

"He gave Chapuys a letter."

"Yes?"

"And then he went off. I stayed with Chapuys, but he went back home."

"Do we know what was in the letter?"

"No, sir."

"What about the servant we have inside?"

"Of no real help," the agent says. "She says her master burnt something, but did not see what."

"So, Chapuys has a secret letter... and we are none the wiser," Richard Cromwell growls. "A fine piece of work, fellow!"

"I just thought..."

"Did you?" Richard shakes his head, and drops a coin into the man's hand. "Keep watch on his house, and let me know if anything else occurs. Understood?"

"As you wish, sir." The young

man pauses, as if loath to say too much. "What about the Spaniard. You do not get many of his sort roaming around London. Could he be a seaman perhaps?"

"That is a thought," Richard says. "Have a couple of the lads take a look down by the docks. If this fellow is still around, we might be able to find out what he is about."

"And after?"

"Whether we discover his purpose or not, see he has an accident."

"Fatal?" the lad asks.

"Are there any other sort?" Richard considers himself, and all at Austin Friars to be in a continuous war against enemies, both visible, and hidden, and sees any Spaniard as a threat. This one is delivering secret messages, and must be treated as a foe.

"Master Cromwell might…" The lad sees the look on Richard's face, and thinks better of what he is about to say.

"Just do as you are told," Richard snaps, "and let others do the thinking."

The lad slips away. He has his orders, and before the next night is done, the web of Austin Friars agents, set to watch over ports and harbours, will snare their unsuspecting prey.

2   The Church of Babel

As he rides through the neat, prosperous villages along the Tamar valley, Will Draper cannot help but compare them to the squalid settlements he has visited during his short progression from London. In his saddle bag he has a warrant from the king, instructing him, as King's Examiner, to investigate reported misdoings at several religious houses, and he and his companion are finally approaching their journey's end.

Three of the four accusations have proven to be malicious, and one has resulted in the closure, pending a full inquiry, of a small, but highly dissolute monastic house in Dorset. Will Draper's companion, Kel Kelsey, one of Cromwell's new young men, likens it to one of the better Putney bawdy houses, where every vice could be had for a few copper coins.

"What will them monks do now, Colonel Will?" the youngster asks, after a night of brooding. It is one thing to serve an eviction notice, and quite another to throw old men out of the only home they have known for decades. "Some of them have been in holy orders since my age."

"They must do as we all have

to," Will replies. He does not mean to sound so cruel, but the holy brothers have been keeping whores, and charging the villagers for blessings for years. The monastic house is not one that has known God for many years. The monks have chosen the wrong faith, and behaved in the way of any ordinary sinner. The reckoning, in the form of the King's Examiner, has finally arrived. Life can be short and brutal.

Will Draper understands this and has, long ago, resolved to make sure that life's hardships will not taint him, or any of those he loves. His birth, under a cloud of mystery, in a small northern village, is a world away from where he is now, and he thanks God for his good fortune as he plods along the frozen, rutted highway. If he must punish the odd wrongdoer in payment for his good fortune, then so be it.

He will never know if the priest who taught him to read and write, and often sent his mother and sister food in hard times, was his father or not, but the lack of this knowledge no longer twists into his soul. It hurt him when the kindly priest was replaced by a more worldly rogue, a nephew of the local baron, and he missed the old man greatly.

The new priest arrived with his woman, and started as he meant to go on, by charging his parishioners for even the simplest blessing. It was his sole desire to cheat his flock of their hard earned money, by selling them absolution, or charging them a fee for the utterance of the last rites.

"Colonel Draper... are you well?"

"Day dreaming, Kel," he replies. Moll, his old Welsh Cob needs no guidance by either hand or heel, and canters down the Plymouth road, unbidden. Kel Kelton, one of Thomas Cromwell's newer young men is riding beside him, on a more frisky bay gelding. "This talk of priests and monks made my mind wander. I was back in Ireland, fighting those phantoms, and screaming banshees again."

"The lads at Austin Friars tell the wildest stories about you, sir," the youth comments. "Why if half is true, you have led a most colourful life."

"Idle talk," Will says.

"But Ireland was true," Kel observes. "You have just told me as much. Master Richard says that there is a tale to be told about your German sword."

"Not much of one," Will tells

the lad, and sighs. It is a long, boring ride, in inclement weather, and young Kelton seeks only to pass the time. "I took a few men off into the forest, where we thought a local chieftain was hiding. We hoped to lure him out, when he saw how few we were, and it worked ... too well. He had a hundred warriors with him, and we were soon fighting for our very lives. My regimental commander, a fine rogue called Colonel Foulkes, came on with a company of muskets, and closed the trap."

"Did they flee?"

"No, lad. The Irishers never run away from a fight," Will explains to the eager young man. "They took two volleys into their flanks, and stood their ground. It was only when old Foulkes ordered our lads to charge with sword and pike that they finally wavered. As the battle was almost won, the chieftain... a huge brute of a fellow, came at me, screaming like a wild wood spirit. He swung at me, I ducked, and slid my sword under his arm. It went in about a third of its length, and snapped off."

"God's teeth!" Kel imagines the giant Irish chieftain wounded, and in a rage. "What happened?"

"He killed me." For a moment,

Kel Kelton is stunned by this revelation, then bursts into laughter. Will Draper unsheathes his sword, and hands it across to the lad, who grasps the hilt, and admires the beautiful workmanship. As Kel leans over in the saddle, his companion pulls a thin knife from his boot, and holds the point to the lad's throat.

"That was quick, for an older man, sir," Kel says, as the keen point scrapes his chin. "Is that how you did for your Irish lord?"

"Always have another weapon to hand," Will explains. "My sword broke, and he came in for the kill. It was his own stupidity that finished him. Afterwards, my colonel let me keep the fellow's sword. It is of German manufacture, but how it came to be in an Irish forest is a mystery." Will Draper slips the knife back into his boot, and retrieves his sword.

"As a King's Examiner, you should be able to solve the riddle," Kel jests. He is detailed to accompany Will on his latest task, by order of Master Cromwell, who thinks it will be experience for his new young man. "Was it after your time in Ireland that you came into Master Tom's service?"

"No, I was a bounty man, in Wales, for a while," Will replies. "It paid well, but the life was hard and cruel. I set off to find adventure, and found Tom Cromwell instead. You know of Cardinal Wolsey, and how he met his end?"

"Master Tom speaks of it, when he has had a couple of drinks," Kel confirms. "Cardinal Wolsey was my master's master, and he came to a bad end."

"It was I who brought the news," Will explains. "Cromwell took to me, and offered me work. We have had our ups and downs, but knowing him has advanced me to where I am now. I am the Chief King's Examiner, with a dozen men at my command."

"Once, when you had spoken harshly with Master Tom, his nephew called you '*a son of a priest's whore*', and Master Mush was almost for cutting his throat over the insult. They shouted back and forth, until the bad blood was drained away, and that was that. It is always how Austin Friars men settle things, I'm told. They trust one another… and no one else. Is it true?"

"About the bad blood?"

"No, sir… about the priest." Kel frowns, as he struggles with his thoughts. "I was found, you see."

"Another unsolved mystery, young Kel," Will mutters. "For it is a wise man who knows his own father."

He recalls how the kind old priest was so cruelly usurped, then sent to a Welsh parish, and how badly the new man behaved towards his flock. The new priest was the bastard son of a nobleman in Yorkshire, who had been given the parish to keep him from under his father's feet. Even the lowest of the Baron's did not like to be reminded of their indiscretions, and a bought parish was a cheap option for a sinful lord.

Father De Forest arrived in the village at the height of the sweating fever, and locked himself away in one of the church's tied cottages, with a woman he had picked up in Lincoln, and who he claimed as his housekeeper. A few days later, Will's mother died, and within hours, his sister followed. The priest was sent for, and demanded his fee. So he paid him with his last few pennies, and had him mumble his badly flawed Latin over the new graves.

Will Draper had already decided to leave the village. There was war in Ireland, he'd heard, and willing young men were needed to enlist in King Henry's new army. It would be a new beginning. The priest would stay behind, and continue to prey on those given into his care, and the thought worried young Draper.

God, Will thought, moves in mysterious ways.

In the night, he crept into the priest's house, cut his throat, and retrieved his money. Escape from Purgatory was not to be bought with a few coins, he decided. It was the violent death of that priest, by Will's own hand, that drove him to Ireland, where he learned his soldiering, and honed his ability to look beyond the obvious. He came back to England with a worldliness he would never have had as a village boy, but it was his meeting with Thomas Cromwell that catapulted him into a life unlike any he could have ever hoped for.

"A wise man indeed," Thomas Cromwell's young man agrees, "for I know not who my father was, and my mother left me on London Bridge, to be cared for by any poor soul foolish enough to take me in."

"How come you to be called Kelton then?"

"I was found by a travelling tinker, and handed in at St. Ethelberga's church, by Bishopsgate. The priests took me in, and marked down that I was a foundling, brought to them by the tinker, who called himself Kelton. I ran off almost as soon as I could walk. They wanted to make me into a priest."

"I doubt the life of an ordained minister would have suited a lad like you," Will says. "You seem like the more boisterous sort to me."

"I've never been to war," the youth says. "Though I know how to kill men, well enough." He refers to an ambush, some months before, when he and Richard Cromwell had defeated a dozen rogues on the road to Lincoln.

"Richard tells me you fought like a raging fury," Will says. "I almost ran away from my first fight."

"What, you?" Kel laughs. "The king thinks you to be the bravest man in England... save for his own self, of course."

"Let the king think what he may," Will replies, "for it is his country, after all. The king's laws, and the king's way. All made up for him by *your* master."

"Grief, sir... but are you still annoyed at my poor old master?" Kel is a street urchin, who has been lucky enough to catch Cromwell's eye, and he is grateful for it. In many ways, his early life matches that of his more illustrious companion. "He but asks the favour... you need not grant it."

"I know that." Will is annoyed

because he is doing Cromwell's bidding again, and can see no reasonable way to refuse the man. "He makes it sound so simple. 'Fine day, Colonel Draper', he says, and I agree. Before long, he is speaking about bibles, and how reasonable it is that every church in England has one. Now, I happen to think this is an excellent idea, as does the king, my dear wife, and every scoundrel at court. Of course every church must have a copy of the new bible, I tell him, and he is so glad I agree with him. Agree? Agree to what, I think, and it is too late. 'Dear fellow … it is so small a matter that I am almost loathe to ask … but' … there is always a but… 'for the king's sake… and to avoid a scandal' … and I am trapped once more."

"You make it seem such a wicked thing he asks of us," Kel Kelton says. "It is only a small matter of delivering a bible to a church in Plymouth."

"I doubt it will be that easy," Will Draper complains. "Why does not Master Cromwell simply send them a bible? This new translation is licensed for use. Why, the Matthew Bible is already on most of the pulpits in England. Archbishop Cranmer has set the price at ten shillings, and expects the priest and his poor parishioners to pay for it."

"Ten shillings?" Kel marvels at so heavy a book being so reasonable a price. "The good folk of Plymouth will be happy to pay up. To refuse would be a stupid thing to do."

"Refuse the new bible?" Will groans inwardly. He is beginning to realise why Cromwell sends him to do the job. "What do you know, Master Kelton?"

"That the sky is above me, and the road below," the youth replies, with a smirk on his face.

"I could cut your throat, and claim it was some outlaw gang," Will says, with a small, cold, smile. "You are sent with me, to report back. That is obvious. What does Cromwell think might happen?"

"The Church of Saint Anthony of Padua is unlike any other church in England," Kel confesses. They are only a mile away from the town, and it is too late for the colonel to turn back now. "Do you know of this fellow?"

"No, and I wonder why he should come to English shores, when he is plainly an Italian," Will growls. "Tell me, lad, and I might let you keep both ears."

"Anthony of Padua is the patron

saint of sailors, and travellers," Kel says. "The church still uses the old Latin form, because its congregation are mainly sailors from around the world, and travellers from afar. The minister argues that as they often only speak Portuguese, Spanish, French or Italian, it makes sense to use a common tongue. It seems that most of these strangers know a little vulgar Latin."

"The king demands we use the English bible," says Will. "If we allow one church to refuse, the rest might rebel against his authority."

"Just so, Colonel Will." Kel sees the profile of the busy port on the horizon, and urges his gelding into a trot. "Master Tom needs someone with *authority* to make this erring minister see reason."

Will Draper sees it all now, and understands why Kel Kelton is riding along with him. The King's Examiner is there to argue and convince, whilst Thomas Cromwell's new man is there for quite another reason. The king's minister is using him again, and forcing him to play a part in something that is both underhand, and immoral.

"How long have I got to convince this minister?"

"Whatever do you mean, sir?" Kel asks, with wide eyed innocence.

"The reverend gentleman will see the way clear."

"A day... two days?" Will is not to be put off, and Kel Kelton sees that he must explain the way of things to the colonel.

"Two days," he says. "After that, I fear the Reverend Craven is likely to meet with an unfortunate accident. It is hoped that his replacement is a man of better sense, and that he will start using the new bible without further ado."

"Have you no qualms about it?" Will Draper asks the question, but already knows the answer. The lad is a Cromwell man, to the core. Cromwell has made him. Cromwell, with the gift of a few kind words, and the odd coin or two, has given him a purpose in life. Like Richard, Mush, or Rafe Sadler, he is now a devout Cromwell man ... to the very end.

"I have sat around the table at Austin Friars, and listened to tales about you," Kel responds. "You helped to bring down Queen Anne and her brother. You had Malatesta Baglione poisoned, and you have killed countless enemies of Master Cromwell. Why now, when you have your wealth, and your fine wife and big house, do you seek to judge me, sir?"

"I do not seek to judge you," Will says. "Your immortal soul is your own damned business. I shall speak with this man of God, and put him on the right path. As for his precious church … let them speak in a thousand tongues… but they must read in English."

"This minister is a stubborn fellow," Kel Kelton says. "It might be beyond your skills to make him listen. I am here to help."

"You are here to kill a man," Will replies, sharply. "I cannot believe Cromwell would stoop so low as to use a mere boy for so wicked a scheme."

"Do not blame Master Tom," young Kelton tells his furious companion. "He but chose you for this mission. It was Rafe Sadler who doubted your ability, and mentioned his worries to your brother-in-law. Mush then told Richard Cromwell, who decided to send me along, just in case."

"Then Master Thomas Cromwell can say his hands are clean," Will concludes. "Murdering a priest, even a bad one, is not the way, Kel. Trust me, I know!"

*

"See how he smiles at me, Thomas?"

"Wind," the Duke of Norfolk

mutters to Suffolk, and the baby Edward, heir to the throne of England, duly confirms the comment with a loud belch.

"He has a good pair of lungs, sire." Thomas Cromwell is horrified at how casually Henry holds the seven day old infant on his lap. "Perhaps if you were to let me take the weight ...?" Henry relinquishes the young Edward, and Thomas Cromwell slips the child into his own arms with practiced ease. "The fellow is as heavy as a cannon ball, and favours his mother about the eyes... if I might so comment, sire."

"My son is lucky to have so able a minister to watch over him as he grows," Henry says. "I am not immortal, Tom, and if anything should ever..."

"Enough, sire," Cromwell chides. "You are younger, in spirit than any man in court. Do not speak of death so readily."

"But if..."

"Edward will be a fine Prince of Wales, for many years to come," Thomas Cromwell says. "Then, when God ordains it... he shall become king. I still cannot believe how fate has worked its way. Edward has loving uncles, and I will continue in my duty, until I too am called. Now, our little

Edward is sucking at my thumb. I fear we must relinquish him to his wet nurse."

"Of course. See they look after him well, Tom." Henry is struggling with some inner turmoil, and Cromwell wonders what it might be. A legitimate son is born, at last, and all should be well in the king's closed world.

"What is it, Henry?" Cromwell uses the given name sparingly, and only when he needs the king to open his heart. "What concerns you? You know I can be trusted."

"I would have you stand as a godparent to Edward," Henry confesses. "Ned and Tom Seymour, and Bishop Gardiner and Cranmer, spoke against you."

"Against me?" Are they flexing their muscles so soon, he thinks, "How so, dear friend?"

"They remind me of your low birth, and say it is not meet to link you with the child so closely."

"They are right," Cromwell replies with a wry smile. "Your Majesty does me great honour by even thinking of it, but he must have greater men pledged to him. Bind Norfolk and Surrey to the boy, and have them swear an oath to protect him. Let Ned and Tom be appointed guardian, should you ever … forgive me, now I speak of death."

"You speak wisely, as always, Tom," Henry says. "How can I ever thank you enough for your honest advice? You might consider becoming a lord. It is not so bad a thing, though the current lot are a scurrilous band."

"If I am to remain honest, then do not make me into one of them," Thomas Cromwell urges. "The nobility have their place, Henry, but you must continue to employ clever men, no matter what their birth. Stephen Gardiner, Bishop of Winchester, is a bastard by birth, but has risen high on the strength of his tenuous relationship to the Tudor family. Cranmer has his own ideas and might suggest his own man for the honour. You know, of course, that he is patron to the Attorney General, Sir Richard Rich?"

"What of Audley?" Henry is out of touch with court politics, because of his concern for Queen Jane, during her pregnancy. "The Chancellor was Rich's master."

"Cranmer is here for life," Cromwell explains, "whilst poor Tom Audley can be replaced at any time. Rich is no fool, and knows when to switch horses."

"God's teeth, Thomas," Henry

growls. "Cranmer suggested Rich, and said he would be a goodly choice. Ned Seymour spoke about Heneage as a fine fellow."

"The Groom of the Stools is indeed a fine fellow," Cromwell replies with a sly smile. "His wife is mistress to Ned Seymour, and he seeks to bribe the man into compliance."

"And Rich?"

"Sire… if you do not hang the rogue, he will become Lord Chancellor one day… and we will all wonder why. Do not advance the man any further. Look to those who have nothing to gain, and love you well."

"You mean men like Rafe Sadler, and Colonel Draper," says the king. "Good, honest fellows. You have set my mind at ease, Tom, and I am grateful. I shall choose some reliable godparents, rather than let my son be used for political or personal gain. Let me reward you."

"I wish for nothing, sire."

"You have become my new Wolsey," Henry says. If pressed over the cardinal's death, Henry has convinced himself that he was blameless, and about to restore the man's fortunes. Cromwell is stung every time his old master is brought up, and decides to exact some small recompense.

"Grant a royal patent to the Draper Company," Cromwell says. "Give them the royal warrant to send an expedition to the northern parts of the New World."

"To seek gold?" Henry's interest is aroused, and Cromwell knows he will get what he wants.

"Or something more precious," he says. "The Spaniards, the Flemish and Portuguese reports speak of vast forests stretching a thousand leagues, and of great beasts, covered in fur."

"A hold full of timber hewn in the New World is hardly worth the effort," Henry complains.

"Of course not," Cromwell says, and springs his idea. "What if the Draper Company took shipwrights across the great sea? Those men could find a safe harbour, and name it for you. Port Henry, or King Henry's Land might be appropriate."

"Ho!" Henry grins at the sheer audacity of the idea. "That will put the fox amongst the chickens, Thomas. François is named *after* his country and my new country shall be named *after* me. My fancy is for Henry's Land.

"An excellent suggestion, sire. These men would use their skills to build great ships. Instead of shipping back the timbers, we have a steady supply of war ships coming to English ports. Within ten years, we might be building a dozen men o'war a month."

"So many?" Henry sees a problem. "This will all cost a great deal of money. I know the Draper Company will stand the initial outlay … as you have told me… but where is their profit?"

"Why, in furs, my dear friend," Cromwell explains. "Four Draper ships will set off, and a year later, return with holds full of pelts. The fur market is brisk, and the Muscovites have a virtual monopoly on the trade. We will undercut the Russians, and find a ready market in France, Flanders, Spain and the German states. One cargo of furs will bring us in as much gold as a ship could hold, and with less outlay. No miners to dig for the ore, and no chance of losing a ship to corsairs. The Great Harry is the best gunned ship on the seas."

"That is *my* ship, sir!"

"Which the navy will lease to the Draper Company," Cromwell says. "They will pay all running costs, and reimburse you for any damage or loss."

"Then all the ships will be from my navy?"

"Of course. Why should Miriam

Draper spend money building merchantmen, when she can hire them, for half the cost?"

"Will that cover our expenses?"

"Comfortably, Your Highness."

"How do I benefit?" Henry asks the key question, and expects to be well rewarded for the use of nothing more than his name on a warrant, and the loan of some war ships.

"At first, the crown will take a cut of the furs," Cromwell says. "Then, once the ship building is under way, we will be offered them at a fraction of their real worth. Think, sire … a hundred double decked war ships, each armed with sixty four English made cannon. The Spaniards and the French would have to surrender the seaways to us."

"I like it," Henry says. "See it is done, my friend. Now, do we have any other business?"

"The queen, sire?"

"Oh, what of her?" Henry asks. It is the first time he has thought of her since the moment his son was born. "Is she well?"

"Tired, sire," Cromwell says. "The doctor says she must have complete rest."

"Doctors… ha!" Henry turns, and starts to walk away. "Pray inform

Her Majesty that her husband is pleased with her… and invite her to a ball I shall be giving the day after tomorrow. I trust she will be recovered enough by then to perform her royal duties?"

"Sire… I fear Queen Jane might not be well enough," the minister continues. "If you would only speak with Doctor Theophrasus?"

"The Jew?" Henry nods his head. "I do not need advice from a clever witted Hebrew, Master Cromwell… even one who can prove he is a Cornish born Christian. Tell Jane I shall see her anon!"

*

"The Church of Babel," Will Draper says, as they rein up their horses outside the grey stone building. It is a late Anglo Saxon rectangle, with a stubby tower at one end, and its doors stand open as if ready to welcome all comers. "Let us see if we can find Reverend Craven at his prayers."

The Reverend Craven is not at prayer, but at dinner. He is a tall, lean looking fellow, with a hooked nose, and small, black eyes, and an enviable appetite. He is just slicing himself a thick round of smoked ham hock when his housemaid, Lucy, makes an appearance at his elbow.

"Visitors come, mastuh," the girl mutters. She is about fifteen, with a wide, toothy mouth, and a comely figure. Her skin is a light brown colour, and she struggles with English, which is her second language. "Them's got horses, and are gen'muns!"

"Still yourself, my dear girl," Arthur Craven says, as he dabs at his lips with a cloth. "Pray, beg them to present themselves to me here, where I can offer them some repast."

"Masuh bin eatin'," young Lucy informs Will Draper, "an' he say you come an' eat. Folla me, gen'muns."

"Is she what they call a *neygra*?" Kel whispers, and receives a shrug from his companion. Will Draper is used to the olive skinned Spaniards, and knows that Moors are black as ebony, but he has never seen one in the flesh.

"Ah, gentlemen... to what do I owe the pleasure of such fine company?" The priest gestures to the empty chairs at his well laden table. "Sit. There is enough for us all. The ham is a particular favourite."

"Reverend Craven, I am Colonel Will Draper, the King's Examiner, and this is ... my servant, Kelton. I have come on the king's business."

"You have come at a most opportune time," Craven says. "A gift from God, you might say. Now, what is this important business of the king's which involves a poor man of the cloth?"

"The new bible, sir," Will says. He cuts himself a piece from a cold leg of lamb, and gestures for Kel to help himself.

"Thank you, most humbly... master," Kel says, and snatches up some bread and cheese. He has been cast in the part of a servant, for the moment, and must support the colonel's lead.

"You may eat it in the kitchen quarters, lad," Will says, and waves Kel away. The young man realises that he is being given leave to look about the place, and bows himself from the room.

"A surly young fellow," Craven says. "He scowled at you, sir."

"He is new," Will says. "I must beat him more often."

"That will only teach him how to lie, and hide his feelings from you," Craven replies. "You should follow the old maxim... that a good master makes for a good servant."

"You counsel me to turn the other cheek, father?"

"I am not a 'father', Colonel

Draper," Craven tells him. "My church is independent. That is to say, Saint Anthony's is not under the dominance of any other ecclesiastical order. My correct title is, therefore … Parson Craven."

"You use the Bishop of Rome's Latin bible."

"It was already here when I was ordained," the parson explains. "God, I assure you, does not mind what language his word is heard in. My flock are from about the world, and many cannot speak much English."

"And they all come to you?" Will Draper shakes his head in disbelief. "What of all the God fearing Plymouth folk?"

"That is for them to say," the parson says with a shrug. "For the nonce, I am content with my flock as it is."

3   The Letter

"Wassa lookin' at?" Lucy asks as she lifts a cauldron from the kitchen fire. "Yus eyes'll stick dat ways, boy."

"I've never seen a *neygra* girl before." Kel cocks his head on one side, and studies the nut brown skin, and thick, coarse hair. "Are you a Spanisher then?"

"Bless, no," Lucy giggles. "Master Rev'ren say I'm half white, half Moorish, and half mule." Kel smiles at the description, and ignores the mathematical impossibility of the mix. "I was left on the church step by one o' dem sailors."

"As a baby, you mean?"

"No... 'bout three years gone," Lucy explains. "My massa was a Portugee gen'mun... an' he lost me to a Lascar over some cards. I guess the Lascar was done fed up o' feedin' me, an' here I am!"

"Then you are not a true *neygra,*" Kel decides. "My friend, Mush has seen Moors, and Turks... and he says they are all colours from white to coal black. Master Richard tells me that real *neygra* people are from a place called Africa."

"Nev' bin there," Lucy replies. "My Portugee used to sail along the

Barbary shores, but we never landed. He said they was not so 'siptable. I learned my Portugee an' my English from him, an' my God speakin' from Rev'ren Craven."

"He sermonises in Latin then?" Kel asks.

"Lor' but he speaks in anything them wicked sailors will listen to," Lucy explains to the nice looking white boy. "He damns them all to Hell, in ten diff'ren languages. You should hear him wailing into them Godless Scots. He curses 'em with blazing hot Hellfire. You have a girl?"

"Sort of." Kel Kelton is keen on the cook's daughter at Austin Friars, but she wants him to be *someone* before she will consider him as a suitable suitor. "There is a girl, who I am fond of, but she is a chaste one."

"You want to bundle with me?" Lucy asks. "The Rev'ren don't care for it, overmuch, an' says it's a mortal sin outside wedlock, but I *like* it."

"Here?" Kel glances over his shoulder, as if the devil was going to jump out at him.

"Sure, its warm enough," Lucy says, and slips out of her linen shift. Her body is golden brown, and as beautiful a thing as Kel has ever seen before. "Wa'sup… you not know how, boy?"

"How much do you want?"

"How much?"

"Yes... London whores charge from a penny, right up to a couple of shillings."

"Do they now?" She giggles at this, and twirls about in front of him. "An here's me, givin' out a free portion!"

*

"You must have an English bible in your pulpit," Will Draper says. "It is the law, Parson Craven."

"I have studied Thomas Cromwell's law," Craven says, and spits out a piece of gristle. "It says that an English bible must be available for all to read, or to be read from. It does not exclude the presence of other texts. If I so wish, I could have a Hebrew scripture, or a Latin bible in my pulpit... so long as the English one is there also."

"Well... yes," Will Draper sees the man knows his law as well as any at Austin Friars. "Though why should you?"

"The good people of Plymouth never come to pray in my church," the reverend says. "It is because I tell them how they will burn in Hell for their puerile sins. The Earls of Devon and

Dorset refuse to listen, because I tell them the truth. Instead, they go to St. Andrews at Sutton Hoo, or keep their own tame priests."

"Then your church is always empty on Sundays?"

"No, it is always full... for every service... every day of the week," Craven tells the King's Examiner. "Ships come into this harbour from all points of the world, and their crews are foreign to these shores, and our way of speaking. They are Germans, Poles, Muscovites, Barbary traders, Portugee pirates, Italian merchants, and wild eyed Scots. They come from France, and Flanders, or even further a field. Some even come from the *Americas*."

"Where is that?" Will cannot place the name. "*A merry cuss* is an odd sort of a name."

"An odd sort of a place too, I believe," the parson says. "It is the Genoese name for the New World."

"I see, and the common tongue is Latin?" Will Draper is beginning to see that the parson is not trying to be rebellious, but wants only to pass on the word of God.

"Many of them know it, and if not, they know the sound of Latin because of their own priests... poor, misguided Roman Catholics... and are comforted by the droning noise of it. The Lord's Prayer, spoken in English, means nothing to them."

"Very well," Will Draper says. "The answer is simple. The English bible goes into the pulpit, on open display. You must read from it at least once during each service... but may make the individual blessings in Latin. I am sure that will satisfy Master Cromwell."

"A most amiable solution," Craven says, little realising that his easy agreement has saved his life. "I shall start tomorrow, but for now, I must relate a strange story to you... for I am at a loss as to how I should react."

"You wish to consult me on a matter that affects the king's law, sir?" Will Draper has had a good meal, and thinks he must now give advice on some petty local matter concerning sheep, or land boundaries. "I must warn you that I am an investigating officer, and not a qualified lawyer."

"I doubt any lawyer could help."

"Then you seek the advice of an old soldier," Will tells him. "I hope I am able to help."

"As I say... it is beyond my poor wit, sir." The parson fills their glasses again. "Last month, I was handed a sealed letter, by a Lascar, fresh in from a voyage. I questioned him, as best I could, but he had no English, and spoke a poor sort of Portuguese. Lucy was able to help me in my discourse."

"What could he tell you about your mysterious letter?" Will is intrigued, and suspects something of great interest is about to unfold.

"The fellow told me he had been given the letter, by someone who had it from a great lord in Tangiers. I was quite surprised that it had been through several hands, and the seal remained intact, but my Lascar friend explained that each courier along the way had been sworn to his duty. I took this to mean that some kind of oath was involved, but could get nothing more from him on that matter."

"Most peculiar," Will prompts, "but what of the letter he delivered to you... I assume you opened it?"

"Yes, of course. I read the contents with some dismay. It seems that an embassy is on its way to visit England, and this letter was a forewarning of the event. The letter is addressed to '*The High Lord of Albion*', and the Lascar knew of no one grander than I. The young fellow claimed to have heard me preach on a previous visit, and been told I was a great man hereabouts. He could tell me nothing more, other than that it had been placed into his safe keeping by his captain, just before the man died of fever in the Bay of Biscay. I pressed for more information, but all my Lascar could tell me was that his captain had been given the missive by another fellow. I presume it was this 'lord' in Tangiers, or one of his agents."

"You have this letter still?" Will is intrigued. Any official foreign embassy is usually arranged well in advance, by emissaries from both sides. Tangiers is a Portuguese outpost, and they already have a diplomatic agreement with England. For some far off lord to simply write and announce his coming is strange indeed. The parson stands, and crosses to a cabinet by the window. He opens a drawer, and takes out a neatly folded piece of vellum.

"What is this?" Will tries to decipher the few words on the outer cover, and fails. "Arab...Muscovite? I do not know why, but it seems familiar to me."

"It says 'to the High Lord of Albion ... or words to that effect... in ancient Hebrew. Though it could just as easily say 'great ruler' or simply 'king'." Craven carefully unfolds the document, and lays it down flat on the dining table. "The tongue is most alien to our own," he says, as if addressing a room full of Oxford scholars. "Whereas we might be able to recognise French words, and their similarity to our own... the original Hebrew is a difficult, and confusing language to read. See here?"

Will looks, and sees that there are two, almost identical ciphers next to one another.

"They look alike," he confesses.

"Yet mean two different things," Craven explains. "It is a beautiful, and subtle language."

"You speak Hebrew?" Will asks the man of God, but he is not overly surprised. His own wife, and his brother-in-law are both fluent in the ancient language, having been raised by their Jewish grandfather.

"Hebrew, quite well... also Arabic, French, Spanish, Italian, Latin, and a few oaths in Gaelic."

"What does it say?"

"The start is a salutation to the High, or the Great Lord of Albion... an ancient name for Britain... and the main text seems to be about the King of Kush wishing an alliance with us."

"Kush?" Will has never heard of the place.

"There was an ancient kingdom of that name, I believe," the reverend explains. "Though we call it Abyssinia now."

"Master Thomas has spoken of the place," Will muses. "He says it is beyond Barbary ... even beyond the Ottoman lands, and that the Portuguese, foolishly, lay claim to it."

"The Portuguese wish to convert the country into Christians, and exploit their wealth, more like." Craven frowns. "Might not this embassy be coming to seek King Henry's help?"

"Why send letters in so obscure a fashion?" Will thinks there is something odd about this, and presses the priest for a more concise translation. "Do they name their king, or even state in which season they will come?"

"My oral Hebrew is better than my grasp of the written language, sir," Craven confesses. "Though I can confirm that Kush and Abyssinia are one and the same. There are legends about a fabulously wealthy kingdom, peopled by a race of black Jews, who fled persecution from the old kings of Rome, and became followers of Jesus Christ."

"Old, fanciful tales."

"Old tales that turn up in many cultures," the lean minister says. "Chaldea, the Phoenicians, the ancient Greeks, and even modern men like Erasmus, mention the old story."

"How is this letter signed?"

"That is the most amazing part," Craven says. "The seal claims to be that of *Prester John*, the ancient ruler of the Abyssinian Empire."

"How can that be?" Will has heard the name mentioned in old legends, from a time before the fall of the old Romans. "He would be over a thousand years old now."

"How many Henry's have ruled us over the years, sir?" the priest asks. "Can it not be that this fellow is Prester John the ninth, or tenth, and that *Prester* is a title, rather than a name?"

"Perhaps," Will concedes, "but why would so mighty a ruler come all this way?"

"He does not." The minister points a thin finger at a spot on the document. "Here, see… the letter says that a *Nah-seekh* will come unto us and bring … I know not what this part says… and also *Prester John's* friendship."

"*Narseeker?*" Will frowns at the unfamiliar sounds.

"It means something like 'earl' or 'duke', but the implication is that our visitor will be a son of the king."

"When?" Any foreign embassy means the chance of advancement, and the hope of being able to do down an enemy. The king, and Tom Cromwell will be most happy with this news.

"The letter does not say. I think it was entrusted to some lord, who passed it into the hands of a traveller to our shores. I suspect it has been through many mishaps, until it came to the hands of my poor Lascar, to whom I gave a silver sixpence piece for his trouble."

"Then we are no further on," Will concludes. "The letter has gone through many hands, and this prince and his entourage may also have fallen into enemy hands. From Abyssinia, he must travel through Ottoman and Moorish lands, or sail along the infamous Barbary coastline. The chances of him ever reaching England must be…"

"He is here."

"Here?"

"In Plymouth." The reverend is smiling like a fool, and almost jumping up and down. "The letter came a week ago, and I thought to send it to London… but news came to me that a

King's Examiner was to visit. So, I awaited your arrival. Then, just this morning, a ship made land, just down the coast. It flies a yellow flag."

"Then it must not dock." The yellow ensign is commonly used to warn of plague, or some other disease aboard, and no ship flying it can sail into a harbour.

"There is no plague," Craven admits. "A crewman came to me this morning, with news. The Prince of Abyssinia is aboard, and seeks an audience with King Henry. I did not know what to do for the best, so told the fellow to return to his ship, and have the yellow flag run up. The prince can sit awhile, I thought, until your arrival."

"Do you know the ship?"

"It is the Santa Juanita, out of Cadiz," Craven says. "She is a regular visitor to Plymouth; a small merchantman, whose master takes on any cargo for gain. I suspect this Abyssinian prince has hired Captain Bolivar to bring him to our shores."

"He must have paid well to get any ship's master to run up a yellow jack," Will Draper says. "When can I meet with this fabled Prince of Kush?"

"On the next high tide," the priest explains. "Now you are here, I can pass you the responsibility, and wash my hands of the matter. The yellow flag will come down at dawn, and your man shall dock by noon tomorrow. You are most welcome to stay here for tonight. I can find you a bed, sir... and your servant can curl up in the kitchen."

"An admirable idea, sir," Will says. "I will have my lad unpack your marvellous new bible, and place it in the pulpit."

"What would you have done had I refused it?" the gaunt priest asks.

"Nothing," Will replies, with a smile, "but Master Kelton has orders to cut your throat if you are unwilling. You have made a wise choice."

"So much trouble over a simple bible," Craven says, and fingers his scrawny neck. "Why, not one man in ten can read in Plymouth. I could tell them that God is a boiled turnip, and they would not know any different."

"Is that not why all Englishmen should be able to read?" Will asks, and the parson nods his head at the statement. "Then you are for emancipation of the poor starving wretches?" he says.

"Let every man be able to read and write. Teach them how to count. Make them free. Then try and get them to do a day's work, sir," the parson chuckles. "Just you try, by God!"

*

Lucy is dressed again, and Kel Kelton is just fastening his doublet, when Colonel Draper appears in the kitchen door. He takes in the scene, and suppresses a smile. She is an unusual, and attractive girl, he thinks, and in his younger days he would be as keen as young Kelton.

"The matter is settled," Will says to the young man. "Your trip was unnecessary, thank God."

"Oh, I could not have done it, sir," Kel lies. "My one hope was that good sense would prevail."

"You lie well," Will replies. "You will fit in very well at Austin Friars. God help you."

"You begrudge me that which you have?" Kel Kelton cannot see beyond the fine clothes, and obvious wealth of the man who once sat at Cromwell's right hand. "Is there no room at the inn for one such as I, colonel?"

"We sleep here tonight," Will Draper says, coldly. "I have the spare bed, and you must make yourself comfortable by the kitchen fire. I trust that will not be too great a hardship for so ambitious a young man?"

"If I must," Kel mutters. He is already beginning to feel some guilt over how easily he has forgotten his beloved Maisie, but is excited by the chance of spending more time with the generous *neygra* girl. Another night of unpaid for love will suit him well, he thinks.

"You must don your finest clothes on the morrow," Will Draper says as he leaves the kitchen. "For you are to meet a royal prince!"

*

Thomas Cromwell is trembling with anger. Were the object of that anger … the king … to be present, the royal minister doubts he would be able to keep himself from striking the man in the face.

"This is … *too* much," he spits out. "Can the man be so blinded by his own self esteem that he fails to see the damage he is causing?"

"Calm yourself, my dear, sweet man," Queen Jane says in her most soothing of voices. "Come, sit by my side, whilst we have these precious moments, and let your anger subside. Poor Henry knows no better, and can think only of his marvellous heir. My son Edward has dazzled the king."

"He is a fine child," Cromwell says. "When I look into his eyes, I see his mother, and when I hold him in my arms … I think of how I have held you, my love."

"Then do not threaten those special feelings by losing your temper," Jane advises. "Even Henry will wonder why you champion me so well. Let him have his way."

"It will be too boisterous," Cromwell complains. "Adolphus says you should rest."

"Dear Doctor Theophrasus is a kind sort, and seeks to be overly coddling, my dear. I need only make an appearance at Henry's ball, then slip away. I dare say the king will have other distractions?"

"Lady Jane Rochford flirts with him, of course," Tom Cromwell says, "though only at my instigation. She keeps him in a lighter mood, when his leg is troubling him. I think he has it in his mind to stray, now he has a son."

"So much for love," Jane replies, with a gentle smile. "I have fulfilled my part of the bargain, and must hope my brother, Ned, keeps his word. He has sworn, and under oath, that I might marry whomsoever I wish, after …"

"Hush. Do not say it," Cromwell takes her small hand in his, and squeezes it. "Let it remain an unspoken wish."

"Then you would have me?"

"Of course." Cromwell has thought it through, and thinks he can see a way to make it work. Ned and Tom Seymour crave wealth and power, yet are no match for his own cunning. If he promises them enough, they will gladly let their sister remarry wherever she will.

"A widow with a child?"

"The King of England," Cromwell says. "Edward will make a fine king, but he must have strong regents to help him rule. Why not his loving mother, and his 'fatherly' old minister?"

"I would tell the world that you *are* his father."

"How could we... honestly, my love?" Thomas Cromwell has his lawyer's hat on, and knows that the ambiguous nature of the child's beginning clouds the issue. When he first lay with Jane, she had already been with the king, and either man might be the true father of the prince. Besides, any such declaration would mean death for them both. "If only for our child's sake... you must remain silent, my dearest one."

"Then you are sure ... in your heart?" Jane can feel tears coming, unbidden to her eyes.

"Of course," Cromwell replies. "I feel it when I look at him."

"If only…"

"Enough. There must be no talk of Henry's health, or any idle wishing." Cromwell sighs, "Above all, the king's jealousy must not be aroused. Treason is always lurking in the shadows, my dear."

"I must dress soon," Jane says. "Henry wishes me at his ball, and I will not let him down."

"Would that he might let you be at your ease," Thomas Cromwell concludes. "After an hour, I will think up something that will allow you to slip away."

"Dear Thomas… so sweet… so loving."

"To the end," Cromwell says. He stands, kisses her hand, and bows himself out of the room. As he leaves the royal chambers a half dozen ladies-in-waiting scurry in like mice, and start to flutter about their charge.

"The blue silk, madam?"

"Hair up, or down, My Lady?"

"Will the king come a calling tonight?"

"Yes… up… and no," Jane replies to the torrent of questions. "My Lord will be drinking well into the night, and I fear he will be too tired. Besides, the doctor says I should abstain for a month or two. So, no men in my chamber tonight."

"Would I had a man to fill *my* private chamber," one of the ladies says slyly, and the others laugh at the rather coarse jest.

"Master Cromwell is single," Lady Sarah says, and this causes even more laughter. True, the queen is never to be left alone with a man, they think, but Thomas Cromwell does not count. He fusses about Jane like a mother hen, and treats her like the kindest of uncles. "Or we might start listening to poetry."

"You sow!" This is from Tom Wyatt's latest conquest, and is directed at her predecessor in his bed. "Master Wyatt has a golden tongue."

"And an impressive cod piece," Queen Jane says. "Now, can we return to our duties, ladies? I dare say most of you have a story to tell about that lewd fellow, but remember what befell the last woman he immortalised in verse."

"Anne Boleyn was nothing but a *putain*, according to my father, and he is a gentleman of the Royal Society of Heraldry," one girl chirps up. "He says she dishonoured the king with her wicked ways. Thank God the king has a faithful queen now, My Lady."

Yes, thank God, Jane thinks. Thank God that her secret is safe, and all she must do is outlive a debauched old man with gout, who drinks too much. That she will, one day, be with the man she really loves sustains her, and arms her against the times ahead.

4 The Blackamore

From the lych-gate of the church it is a gentle down hill stroll into the heart of Plymouth. The town is a harbour, a cluster of cobbled streets, and a defensive position that is less than a fort. Four poorly built towers are connected by low walls that would hardly withstand a serious attack.

Will takes all this in, and will put it in his report to the king, which will pass through Thomas Cromwell's hands first. The minister will read about how ill prepared the town is, and instruct masons to strengthen the ramparts, and have a dozen of the new iron cast cannon mounted to face out to sea. He will also note the colonel's concern about the lack of a garrison in a town that is visited by so many foreign ships.

"How would you go about taking this town hostage, Master Kelton?" Will asks as they walk. "Let us pretend you to be a wily Spaniard, or a Barbary pirate."

"There are only two cannon on the walls, and neither covers the harbour," Kel replies. How many ships have I got... and how many armed men?"

"You would mount a frontal

attack?"

"Two ships. One frigate to stand
off, and pound the battlements, and a
second to sail into the harbour, and put
men ashore. I have seen only a token
number of military men. I suspect the
harbour master employs a dozen
fellows, just to keep order amongst the
drunkards. About a hundred men could
take the town, but they could not hold
it, once the yeomanry are alerted to the
assault. A thousand men would be here
within a couple of days."

"Then say I am no pirate, but a
Spanish general, charged with invading
England?" Will asks. "Say I have thirty
ships, and five thousand troops?"

"Then I would say Plymouth is
in trouble," Kel observes. "I might lose
a few hundred men, but I could hold
out against a force of yeomen until the
cows come home. Henry would have to
raise the city garrison, and bring down
every cannon he has locked up in the
Tower of London."

"Which would take a month."
Will shakes his head. "If it were I, one
ship, decked out like a merchantman
would suffice. My sailors would come
ashore, unopposed, and be able to take
the key points without a musket being
fired. Then I would land my army, and
march on London. Every Roman

Catholic in England would cheer, and rally to the enemy."

"You mean Norfolk," Kel says, shrewdly. "He has about ten thousand men at his disposal. Then there are the Poles to think of. I believe they too would turn on Henry."

"Cromwell teaches you well," Will says. "I hope he reads my report, and acts. You must also warn him to strengthen Plymouth, for it is our soft underbelly, and it waits for a dagger thrust."

"Do you think this prince you speak of is dangerous?"

"He is an unknown," Will says. "He comes here in strange circumstances, and he comes to knock at the back door, rather than the front. Still, we shall see what he wants soon enough."

"The parson says we will see the merchantman from the Hoe. It gives a fine view across the Sound and we should see where he ties up to discharge his cargo," Kel says, and gestures towards the sloping headland. The turf of the open area has been cut away, to reveal the white limestone beneath. "Parson says the white cut out figures are meant to be two giants, called Gog and Magog, who once lived in these parts."

"Heathen rubbish," Will mutters. Then he sees a ship, riding high, and watches as it slips into harbour, almost unnoticed. "Here is our visitor, Kel. Let us hope he has not brought ten thousand Abyssinian soldiers in his retinue."

"You think…" Kel frowns, and stares at the ship. "She is riding too high in the water," he says. "I doubt she is even laden."

"Most unusual," Will says, more to himself than to anyone else, but the softly spoken words stick in Kel's mind. "Did you sleep well enough?"

"Not much, I …" The young man stops, and almost bites his tongue. "That is to say…"

"That is to say you spent the night swiving your little black girl," Will concludes. "What will poor little Maisie have to say?"

"Christ on His Cross, Colonel Draper, do not jest with me so," Kel replies. "Maisie has a vicious temper, and is as like to knife me, as kiss me on my return."

"Jest?" Will Draper puts on a puzzled expression. "I do not jest, Master Kelton. Why should I keep quiet about your fling? It will make a good story around the kitchen table at

Austin Friars."

"Sir… you would ruin me with the girl, for a jest with the other lads?"

"I would."

"I beg you…"

"You would do better to bargain with me," Will says. "I am open to offers."

"Money?" Kel asks. He has made a few pounds, but nothing near enough to silence a wagging tongue.

"Respect."

"I do respect you, Colonel Draper, as God is my witness."

"Yet you accept secret missions behind my back," Will tells him. "You would go against my wishes, and keep secrets from me."

"I was ordered to."

"Then let me make it clear, Master Kel," Will explains. "If you ever try to deceive me, or interfere with my own plans, I will speak with your beloved Maisie."

"I see. You seek to misuse me, sir." Kel replies.

"No, I seek to make you sure of your loyalties, when under my orders," Will says. "I expect loyalty from you. I will never ask you to do harm to Tom Cromwell, or his plans, but I will not be used again."

"Very well," Kel says. "I was a

fool to keep it from you. I beg your pardon."

"Very well, we will speak of it no more," Will tells him. "Now, let us meet the Santa Juanita's passenger. I doubt he will be hard to find."

*

The colonel's small jest proves to be only too true. As they reach the quayside, a tall black man appears on the gangplank. He is easily as tall, and well built as Will Draper, and looks to be of a similar age. He wears a pair of Turkish pants, which puff out around his calves, and a rich purple silk shirt. He has a turban wrapped about his head, and a fine woollen cloak over his broad shoulders.

He surveys the dilapidated harbour, and his gaze settles on Will Draper, who has on his best doublet. The man considers for a moment, then advances down the narrow plank, to the cobbled quayside. He walks straight over to Will, and touches a hand to his forehead, as if in greeting.

"You are the King of Albion?" he asks, in faltering English, and Kel Kelton sniggers. The handsome black man cocks his head on one side, and drops a hand to the enormous sword hanging at his waist. Will steps between the youth and the visitor, and offers him a low bow.

"I am the King's Examiner, sir," Will says. "Do I have the honour of addressing a lord of Abyssinia?"

"Ah, yes... you say Abyssinia... I am Prince Ibrahim of Kush," the man replies. "I have come many miles to visit your famous king. We have little knowledge of your land, and thought it ruled by a great Richard... who smote the Saracen from the walls of Jerusalem."

"Richard the Lionhearted," Will says. "An ancient king, sir. We are ruled by King Henry now, who is the eighth one of his name. And your master, sir?"

"My father is Prester John of Kush," Ibrahim says. "He is the thirtieth of his line. I shall be the thirty first. Is your king in his castle?" Will sees the black man is looking over his shoulder at the meagre towers behind him.

"No, Your Highness," Will replies. "My King is a great man, and has many castles. He lives in London, not Plymouth, and we must journey for almost a week to reach him."

"Then the stories are true?" The prince smiles, and shows off a set of great, white teeth, "Albion is a mighty kingdom?"

"One of the mightiest," Kel puts in.

"Your slave is most forward," Ibrahim says.

"He is … my servant, sir," Will explains. "What of your retinue?"

"All gone," the prince replies. "I set out with more than a hundred men, and ten chests of treasure for your king. We fought our way across the great plateau, and sailed around the coast of Africa, beset with pirates and slavers. I lost a few here, and a few there, until I came to a remote place on the southern coast of Spain, where wild Moors attacked us. My bodyguards stood their ground, whilst I, and a single loyal servant managed to slip away."

"A sad tale, sir," Will gestures towards a nearby tavern. "Might you wish to take some refreshment, whilst we talk further?"

Prince Ibrahim, son of Prester John, High Lord of Kush does not need a second asking. He follows Will and Kel into the rough sailor's tavern, and silence falls over all those inside.

"A Blackamore!" the landlord says, with a happy grin. "That will bring us good luck, and no mistake. What would you have, gentlemen?"

"Some of your best wine, and

food. What have you ready?"

"Cheese, bread, and some pickled cucumbers?" the man offers, and Will nods his agreement.

"See we are not disturbed." He ushers his new guest over to an empty table, and a nearby sailor lurches to his feet.

"Hey … we don' wan' nah *neygra* in …" He slumps back into his chair, and Kel waves the weighted leather cosh to and fro at his drinking companions.

"Any more for anymore?" he asks, and is met with utter silence. He nods, and slips in beside the prince. "Your pardon, sir, but, you being a Blackamore, makes you a strange sight, even for these honest Plymouth folk."

"Yes, I often wondered how people became less black as I travelled. The Moors are almost the right colour, and the Spanish are lighter skinned, but you white faced creatures are most odd to my eyes. What drains you so?"

"God knows," Kel mutters, and decides to leave the talking to Will. The idea that he might be a black man, drained of colour, has never occurred to him before now, and he becomes lost in thought.

"So, your entire retinue are lost?" Will asks. He has no intention of making any further moves until he knows the full story.

"I escaped the battle with the Moorish robbers," the prince explains, "along with my personal servant. Together, we made our way to more Christian parts. For a month, we waited in Seville, hoping some of my followers might have survived the last battle, and followed us, but to no avail."

"Your English is very good." To Will's ear, it is as if the man has been taught by a Cambridge scholar. His words are precisely chosen, and pronounced well.

"I was taught by the wisest men in Kush … or Abyssinia, as you very white people call it," Prince Ibrahim explains. "I am fluent in the Holy tongue, of course, but Hebrew seems not to be widely spoken outside my world. I was also taught to speak Latin, and several of your tongues. English was the hardest to master."

"You speak it well."

"I speak it like a well educated foreigner," the black prince replies, honestly. "From Seville, I went to Cadiz, where I hoped to take ship for Albion. It was there the Spaniards arrested me. They feared me, you see, and thought me to be a spy, working for the Moors. It took many days for me to convince them I was a follower of Jesus Christ."

"How did you manage that?" Will Draper asks. "The Spanish Inquisition seldom releases any of its victims."

"They brought learned men to question me about Christianity, and I was able to prove my faith to them. In the end, they decided to accept my story. I told them I was a pilgrim, on my way to visit various holy shrines. They released me, but my servant had not fared so well. Because he could not speak anything but his mother tongue... Hebrew... they took him for a Jew, and they tortured him to death. I was alone. The Santa Juanita was the first ship I could get to ... Enga-land, as you call it."

"A cruel story, sir," Will says. "Your letters of introduction only arrived a few days ahead of you, and we were not expecting so grand a visitor. We must journey to London with all speed, where my king will be pleased to greet you."

"I have nothing left to give him," the Abyssinian says. "He will think the men of Kush to be a poor sort."

"King Henry has no need of

treasure," Will says. "He will wish to speak with you about your far off land."

"That is good news, sir," the prince replies. "Might I now trouble you for your name?"

"My pardon," Will says. "I am Colonel Will Draper, the King's Royal Examiner. It is my duty to protect His Majesty, and look into anything that he thinks of worth."

"Then you come to see if I am of worth?"

"No, sir, I came to Plymouth to deliver a bible," Will tells the curious black man. "We have a new English bible."

"In English?" Prince Ibrahim seems to be concerned at this, and seeks some clarification. "How can there be anything but the true word of God, as written down by my ancestors, the twelve tribes of Israel?"

"We used to use the Latin version," Will explains. "Hebrew is not a welcome language in England. Now, Latin is also frowned upon. Our king thinks we must all read the word of Our Lord in English. That way, every man can understand, and glorify God."

"Oh?" The prince picks up a piece of grey bread, and stuffs it in his mouth, as if stifling a laugh. He chews, and nods his head at this piece of information. "The Spanish priests promise Hellfire to the people, and spend all their time burning heretics, Muslims and Moors. We choose to follow the true word. We try not to lie, nor do we covet our neighbour's oxen. We avoid killing where we can, and have no need for adultery. In Kush we have enough wives for all of our needs."

"You have many wives,?"

"I have four, which is considered to be a goodly amount," the prince confirms. "My father has eleven, but keeps them in a separate palace."

"Wise man," says Will.

"Just so. Prester John is wise. It was he who decided to send me to Albion. In our tradition, the men of Albion are a fierce warrior race; great giants who expelled the Romans. My father seeks such an ally for the great war to come."

"War you say?" Will's heart sinks. Why can these fellows never turn up wanting a peaceful time of it, he thinks. "With whom?"

"Portugal."

"The Portuguese are our friends."

"Because they fear you."

"That has something to do with

it, but Henry will not go to war with them, unless he has a very good reason."

"What if he knew why they suddenly wish to take over my country?" the prince asks. "Might that change his mind?"

"It would have to be a very good reason," Will says, honestly. Henry is all for twitting the French, and small, profitable forays across the sea, but he is not likely to send an army to Abyssinia. "Even Englishmen would struggle to get past the Ottoman hoards."

"Diamonds, and gold."

"Ah... how much?" Will senses a shift in the conversation, and wonders if the Abyssinian prince thinks he can bribe the king with a few thousand pounds in bullion, or some glittering rocks.

"More than any man can imagine," Ibrahim says. "It has always been our secret, ever since King Solomon's time, but now, the foreign devils have learned of it."

"Of what, sir?" Will asks. "You must have facts for the king, not fairy tales about some biblical fellow."

"King Solomon came to Kush, and found the diamond fields on our high plateau. Precious stones litter the ground in all directions. He filled a dozen chests, and marched down to the sea with his army. Upon his return to Israel, he chose to claim he had found a fabulous mine, whose location was to be his secret."

"What then?" Will finds the story enchanting, but it tells him nothing of any substance.

"Solomon died, but imparted the secret to one of his high priests. The story was passed down, and known to my ancestors, who fled Israel at the time of Christ. We settled in Kush, and the secret became ours. We sought out the diamond fields, and found them. We also found rich veins of gold running through the high plateau land. Prester John the First knew that we would be visited by enemies, if this ever came to light. We kept it a secret, and harvested only enough treasure to keep us in comfort."

"And you now want to tell us about it?" Will asks.

"Horse shit," Kel mutters.

"I have no choice," the prince says. "The secret is out. The Portuguese know, and intend invading our country. Once they have the gold mines, and the diamond fields, they will be richer than Spain, France, and your Enga-land all together. What price your precious alliance then, Colonel Draper?"

"What you say interests me, sir," Will tells him. "Your story must have a wider audience. When we reach London, I will use all of my influence to get you an audience with the king."

"This Henry is a great warrior?" Prince Ibrahim asks.

"The greatest," Will says. "There is a story that tells of how he once routed twenty thousand Frenchmen, almost single handed.

"How is such a feat possible?" the Abyssinian asks.

"I cannot say," Will tells him, "but I do know that the battle was won... and that is what you want, is it not... a winner of battles?"

"My father can raise fifty thousand warriors, but they have nothing but spears, and swords, against cannon. Do you have any cannon?"

"Not personally," Will replies with a smile, "but the king has several hundred. He also commands a great fleet of warships."

"If God grants us victory, my father will fill two of your largest ships with gold and diamonds," the prince promises.

"Then eat up, and let us make plans for the trip back," Will says. "They will love you at court!"

5 The Way of Things

Rafe Sadler skirts the melée of hangers-on who fill the outer court, and edges past the Duke of Norfolk, who is busy arguing with Suffolk about who are the worst enemy, the French, or the Scots. He is clear of the outer court fools, and hurrying down the long gallery, when a familiar voice calls out to him.

"Pray, slow your pace, Rafe, lest my lungs burst trying to keep up." Tom Wyatt, who has just slipped out of Lady Wenscott's chambers is alongside him, and eager to know what is afoot. "You have the air of a man about to deliver bad news. Tell me, old friend."

"I must find Master Cromwell," Rafe replies, without slowing his pace. "Have you seen him?"

"If he is not with the king…" the poet ponders. "Try the rose garden. He is always skulking about there, when he has the time."

"Of course!" Rafe veers to the left, and breaks into a brisk trot. He passes two guards, who recognise him as Henry's new favourite advisor, and snap to attention. "Master Cromwell?" he snaps, and one of the two points.

"By the fountain, Sir Rafe," he says, bestowing a title not yet granted.

"He is reading a book … and it is *not* a bible!"

Rafe continues, and comes upon his old master. Cromwell is seated on the rim of the fountain's stone bowl, with an open book on his lap. The Privy Councillor glances up, and smiles.

"Rafe… this is a pleasant surprise. We so seldom meet these days. You must come to dinner one evening. Bring your lovely Ellen with you and…" His voice tails off, as he sees Tom Wyatt coming on behind. "What is it?"

"Master Tom, I found you as quickly as I could."

"In God's name, what is it, my boy?" Cromwell can see disaster in the younger man's eyes. "Is the king unwell?" Rafe shakes his head, and spits, to moisten his mouth.

"The king is safe," he says. "Doctor Theophrasus bade me find you, at once. The queen is…"

"Dear Christ, man… is she dead?"

"No, sir." Rafe's eyes are filling with tears. "The doctor bids me tell you that… she bleeds. You must come to her chambers, at once."

Cromwell leaps to his feet, and the book, a translation of the Arthurian legends, crashes to the floor. He looks to see which is the quickest way, and breaks into a fast walk.

"Does the king know?"

"He is out with his hawks," Tom Wyatt says. "I doubt he will be back until supper."

"What happened, Rafe?" Cromwell cuts across the outer court, and brushes people aside. "How could this be?"

"The king kept Queen Jane late at the ball, and it tired her," Rafe explains.

"I sent word for her to be brought to her chambers."

"The king dismissed the messenger, and insisted she stayed by his side. Poor Jane was up until past the midnight hour," says Rafe. We finally had her brought away, and I saw that her ladies put her to bed. Then, an hour ago, she felt unwell, and we sent for Theophrasus at once."

"That was for the best," Cromwell says. "What then?"

"She was in some pain, and her nightdress was spotted with blood. The doctor said it was the strain, and she must keep to her bed," Rafe continues. "Then she began to bleed much more. The doctor sent me to find you, and bid you attend. I think he fears what will happen if the queen takes a turn for the worse."

"It must not be," Thomas Cromwell is in tears. "Not now. With the king content, at last… it is her time. Dear God… is it a punishment?"

"Punishment?" Tom Wyatt is still with them. "What ever could the poor sweet thing have done to deserve God's punishment?"

"Nothing… she is blameless," Cromwell replies. "I am not thinking what I say. Pray God she is well."

They reach the queen's outer chambers, and find a half dozen ladies, sitting at their embroidery. There is an air of worry in the room, and one of them is quietly sobbing.

"What news?" They all look up, and he sees that they know nothing. He steps towards the queen's door, and Sir John Russell makes as if to bar him. Cromwell raises a fist, and Tom Wyatt catches it in his hand.

"Sir, this is not seemly," he says. "Sir John is doing his duty. None may enter without permission."

At that moment the door opens, and Adolphus Theophrasus emerges, wiping his hands on a linen cloth. There are some blood stains, but hardly enough to worry about.

"The queen is resting," he says

to Cromwell. "There was a heavy bleed, but it has ceased for now, and I think she will be well, providing she rests, Last night could have killed her, my friend."

"T h e r e   w i l l   b e   n o reoccurrence," Thomas Cromwell says. "I shall see to that. The lady is too precious to … to us all, to take the risk."

"Does King Henry have a care,
now he has his rightful heir?"

The words drift over the gathered men, and Rafe Sadler looks about to see if anyone else has heard the scurrilous little rhyme. Sir John Russell looks shocked, but will say nothing. He is a Cromwell man, ever since the affair of the jewels, and he will stay silent. The doctor merely sniffs, and smiles wryly. Cromwell seems not to have even heard, and is scowling towards the inner court doors.

"Are you quite mad, Master Wyatt?" Rafe whispers to the poet. "I know you do not value your own life, but to utter such treasonable…"

"Of course he does,
all filled with pain,
King Hal shall worry
for his poor Jane." Tom Wyatt continues the couplet, and smirks at how easily he has disturbed his stiff

necked friend. "Poor Henry. How he would weep, if he lost another wife under such cruel circumstances."

"Enough," Cromwell snaps at him. His melancholic cloud has passed, and he sees that there is much to attend to, if he is to keep his promise. "Rafe, see that tonight's festivities are cancelled. Queen Jane is not to be disturbed."

"The king will not tolerate it, Master Thomas," Rafe explains. "He wishes to frolic about like a youth again. Refuse him his pleasures, and his temper would know no bounds."

"I shall speak to His Majesty," Cromwell says. "Now, if you love me, do as I bid. Cancel tonight's ball at once, but do not let Henry know what is afoot."

"Ho!" Tom Wyatt does a fine impersonation of the king's favourite exclamation. "Methinks Master Cromwell has a nefarious scheme in mind. How might I help, sir?"

"Ride to Dover as fast as you can," Cromwell says.

"And then?" Tom Wyatt feels a surge of pleasure as he expects to be part of some clever mission.

"Take the first boat to Utopia, and stay there for a year or two," Cromwell concludes.

"Ah, I see. You do not wish me to be privy to your machinations."

"I want you to stay at home for a month or two," Cromwell says. "Write some nice poetry, and stay away from court. If Henry is angered, he looks for someone to blame, and you are an easy target, my friend. Spend time with your wife and child. How is the boy?"

"Hm… that is to say…" the poet stammers, and does not wish to admit how scarce is his knowledge of either the boy, or his mother.

"Go home, Tom," Rafe tells him. "Master Thomas is right."

"Very well. In a few days. Send for me, if I am needed," the poet says.

"Thank you." Cromwell considers sending Mush Draper with him when he leaves, but he is far too valuable a man to spare just now. "Come, Adolphus, we must seek out the king!"

*

Thomas Howard, the third Duke of Norfolk, and Lord High Steward of England, is in his sixty fourth year, and the advancing years are doing nothing for his temper. Having just quarrelled with Charles Brandon, Duke of Suffolk, he seeks to find an ally against his despised enemy,

Thomas Cromwell.

"Good day to you, Ambassador Chapuys," he says to the slightly built Imperial representative to Henry's court. The Savoyard tries to avoid the odious fellow's company at all costs, but sees that, on this occasion, he is cornered.

"Your Lordship," Chapuys replies, with a low bow. "Are you keeping well, sir?"

"Well... oh, yes... I am keeping well, Master Chapuys." The duke sidles close up to the emperor's man, and drops his voice to a whisper. "What does your master think of the king's good news?"

"You mean the child?" Chapuys shrugs. "I wrote at once, of course, but doubt the news will reach my master until tomorrow at the earliest."

"I dare say his nose will be out of joint?"

"His nose?" Chapuys has not heard the expression before, and wonders what the duke can mean.

"Out of joint." Norfolk says it louder, as if he thinks by raising his voice the foreigner will understand. "Upset. Not happy."

"Ah, I see." Chapuys smiles, and shakes his head. "The emperor will be pleased for the king. He has longed for a son, has he not? Now, he will be content, and less likely to harbour thoughts of military expansion."

"You think so?" Norfolk grins. "Then you do not know the king, sir! Now he has a son, Henry will want to expand his realm."

"Why do you tell me this, sir?"

"To warn you."

"Against what?"

"Against Cromwell, of course," Norfolk replies. "He urges Henry to build more war ships, and demands that the leading nobles keep troops at the ready. Why would he do that, sir?"

"To fight the Scots?" Chapuys answers, with a slight smile on his lips. "Or he might wish to conquer Ireland at last."

"Or the New World."

"I think not," Chapuys says. "The emperor would be disquieted at any such action. Master Cromwell is not so stupid."

"Cromwell is power mad," Norfolk says. "Do not make the mistake of thinking him to be a friend. He had Queen Katherine removed, did away with my niece Anne, and led England away from Rome. Now he forces his English bible into every pulpit in the realm. The bloody man is a real danger."

"My Lord, I am the Imperial Ambassador to the court of your king," Chapuys explains. "I have no power over Master Cromwell, and I cannot influence your king's foreign policy. What do you expect of me?"

"Write to Charles, and warn him." Norfolk has his own plan and, in his arrogance, expects this odd little man to fall in with it at once. "Tell him Cromwell seeks to build an even bigger navy, and wishes to take his gold mines from him."

"What action do you expect him to take?" Eustace Chapuys says. "The emperor has strong fortresses in the New World, and many war ships sailing back and forth. Any move against us would result in war. Not just in the New World, but across Europe."

"Tell your emperor that I have warm feelings for him, and that I have many doubts about this new English church. Like him, I look to the Pope for religious guidance."

"He will be pleased."

" T h e n   w e   h a v e   a n understanding?" Norfolk smiles, and holds out a hand. "Cromwell is the enemy?"

"I really do not think we should clasp hands in such a public place, my dear Lord *Norfook*," Eustace Chapuys says with utter disdain. He always pronounces it as *'Norfook'*, even though he has learned of his mistake some time before. The duke has to grate his teeth, and accept the seemingly unwitting corruption of his family title. "It is not seemly that we appear too friendly."

"Leave it to me," Norfolk growls. "I need only know that the Emperor Charles looks favourably on it, and I will see to the rest. I bid you good day, Master Ambassador!"

Eustace Chapuys is loyal to his master, yet loves Thomas Cromwell almost like a brother. He stands in the outer court, and ponders over the strange discussion he has just had. His servant, who is never far away, loiters in a close by alcove. Chapuys crosses over to him, and they fall into whispers.

"You heard?" Chapuys asks.

"Every word, sir," Gomez replies. "The duke seeks to draw you into some mischief, and you must be careful."

"He seeks to turn me against Cromwell, and intimates that he would have England become Roman Catholic once more."

"A fool's dream," Alonso Gomez whispers back. "Master Cromwell has things too well arranged.

The only way the duke could win out is if Cromwell was gone."

"There have been attempts," Chapuys mutters. He is aware of a recent assassination attempt on his friend, which went awry more out of good fortune than diligence. "What if *Norfook* seeks to have Cromwell killed?"

"He is too well guarded," Gomez says. He is a ruthless killer, as well as a bodyguard, and he knows how these things are arranged. "Anyone who struck at Master Cromwell now would be dead a moment later. Who would sacrifice himself so readily?"

"Then what does Norfolk think will happen?" Chapuys is a political sort, and finds it hard to see into the darker corners of any plot which involves murder. "He warns me that Cromwell is dangerous… and I already know this. He seeks the emperor's support, presumably if Cromwell falls, and he returns to power. What does he know, Gomez?"

"That Cromwell will fall," the servant offers. "If I were told to bring about the emperor's demise, I would know not to try assassination. Instead, I would remove those who support him."

"How so?"

"I would pick off his supporters, until he stood alone, and then move against him."

"Norfolk seeks to isolate Cromwell," Chapuys says, "but how would he start?"

"Sadler, the Drapers, his nephew... or the young men who run his offices at Austin Friars," Gomez says. "Lop off each branch, and the tree will wither away."

"Then anyone might be at risk." Eustace Chapuys wishes to speak with Thomas Cromwell, but he has just gone in to see the king, and it may be hours before they can speak. "How do I protect them all?"

"Put those you can on guard," Gomez explains. "Then we must protect those we cannot warn in time."

"I will go to Draper House at once," Eustace Chapuys decides. "Once Miriam and Mush are warned, they can send messages to the rest. Though Will Draper is not at court."

"Where is he?" Gomez asks.

"Plymouth, for the king." Chapuys says. "It seems a priest down there still uses the Latin text. Cromwell ordered him down there, after the king spoke to him. It seems someone whispered in the king's ear."

"Norfolk?" Alonso Gomez

suggests. "He uses the king to isolate Draper. The roads are dangerous in the West Country... full of outlawed Welshmen, and Cornish cutthroats."

"Then we must send word."

"Send me," Gomez says. "A fast horse, and a bag of silver is all I need. If I ride hard, I might reach him before he starts back to London."

"Do it," Chapuys says. "If all we say and think is a nonsense, then no harm is done. If we are right … then God give you wings, Gomez!"

Gomez bows, and takes the proffered purse of silver. He is not a man to cross, and he has fought for Spain, against the French, and against a wide selection of men who would do him wrong. Now in his thirtieth year, he is employed by Eustace Chapuys, and is as devoted to him as others are to Cromwell. He will do his duty, and try to warn Colonel Draper, a fellow soldier whom he admires.

"Three days, sir," he says. "If I am not back by the Sabbath, you must hire a new servant." Eustace Chapuys nods his head, and almost reaches out to pat the man on the shoulder. To lose so fine a servant would sadden him, but to lose him would mean that Will Draper has also come to some harm.

"Stay safe," Chapuys says.

"And you, sir," Gomez replies. He considers warning his master to be on guard, but against whom? He has his eyes and ears, just like Cromwell, and knows that strange things are afoot. Just that morning he has discovered that a Spanish gentleman's body has been pulled out of the dock, and that an accident is ruled out by virtue of the expertly cut throat. "Trust no one, until my return."

*

"What is this?" Henry is deciding, with the Master of the King's Wardrobe, what to wear at the evenings ball, and is annoyed by the interruption. "Thomas… can it not wait?"

"Not for a moment, sire." Tom Cromwell waves the Master of the Wardrobe away, and bows to the king. "I have Doctor Theophrasus with me. He has some worrying news, and you must hear it at once."

"Then speak… but hurry along, sir." Henry is bored with doctors, and their worries about the health of his queen. His son is well, and that is all that concerns him just now.

"Your Majesty, I have had bad news from a reliable colleague in Cambridge. It concerns the sweating sickness." Henry almost gasps in horror. He has a mortal fear of the sickness, and recalls previous outbreaks of various plagues. "It seems a mild form of it has struck in the town. So far it seems to kill only one in five."

"Dear Christ... one in five?" The king swallows hard. "Will it reach London?"

"I fear it is already there, sire," the doctor says, "and may reach us here at Hampton Court at any time."

"What can I do?" Henry demands. "I am the king, and I must be kept safe ... for the sake of the realm, you understand."

"Your lack of fear is most admirable, sire," Theophrasus replies. "It is hoped that this early warning will be of help to us. The sickness is carried from person to person by bad air. You must avoid large gatherings."

"I am to be at a ball tonight." Henry loves pageantry, and is loath to miss out on an event where he can flirt with ladies, and drink himself into a stupor.

"Sire ... one breath of this bad air might be enough to lay you low," Thomas Cromwell says. "With so many people in attendance..."

"Of course, you are quite right." The king sees it is the only safe thing to do. "We will abandon the ball, until we know more of this sickness."

"Might I induce Your Majesty to take a potion I have with me?" the doctor asks. "It is a rare, and expensive concoction. A distillation of ancient Chinese herbs, and rare crushed spices from the Indus. It will help fight off any sickness."

"Let me smell it." Henry takes the proffered vial, and sniffs at it. "Dear God, but it smells like a rutting stag. Must I drink it?"

"For the good of the realm," Cromwell says, sternly. "You must live, no matter what befalls the rest of us."

"Is there not enough for the rest?" Henry asks. Cromwell sighs, and shrugs, to show that it is too rare, and too expensive.

"Alas, sire… it is the way of things."

Later, as they leave the inner court, Cromwell asks what was in the amazing potion. The doctor looks sheepish, and explains that it is nothing more than honey, vinegar, and a touch of valerian extract from his garden.

"It will help the king go to sleep," Adolphus Theophrasus says. "He will awaken in a day or so, and be relieved that the sweating sickness has completely passed us by. In the meantime, Queen Jane will get her rest, and be excused any more of these ridiculous public appearances."

"Thank you, my friend," Thomas Cromwell says. "I could not have deceived him without your help."

"I trust you will not mention it, should you ever be arrested, Thomas," the doctor replies, seriously. "I am far too old to be lodged within the Tower of London."

"Henry shall never know."

"If he ever wakes," the doctor says with a mischievous twinkle in his eye.

"My God... how many does that happen to?" Cromwell asks. "This is the king we speak of, my friend."

"Oh, perhaps one in a hundred might succumb," Adolphus Theophrasus replies with a chuckle in his voice. "It only ever kills those who are obese, or drink too much."

"What?" Cromwell is appalled at the prospect of having helped poison the king, until he sees the hint of a n amused smile playing about his friend's lips. "O, you wicked fellow," he says, and laughs at his own gullibility. "You, wicked wicked old rogue!"

6   Easy Coin

Walter Tall is a short, stocky fellow, and his comrades, of course, call him Tall Walter in jest. He allows their small discourtesy because he knows each and every one of them fears him. He is an ill born Staffordshire man, whose mother kept him until he was old enough to work, then sold him to a master brick maker in Chester. A couple of years of hard work soon convinced him that his future lay in a far less demanding profession.

By the age of twelve, Walter was an accomplished cutter of purses, and at the age of fourteen, he killed his first man in a fight over a girl. He fled Chester, just ahead of the magistrate's men, and disappeared into the wild Welsh marches, where he joined up with a roving gang of thieves, and waylay merchants.

The work was not hard. Twenty men in hiding could easily stop, and overpower, single travellers, or block the road and take a coach. Walter Tall learned fast, and moved up the ranks fast. By the time he is twenty-four, he commands a band of twenty-five men.

"On your feet, lads," he calls, and bodies begin to shake themselves awake all over the clearing. "There is work to do."

"It don't feel right," Jakey No Lugs says, for the tenth time that week. "We should stick to the forest. Why bring us all this way into Devon?"

"Easy coin, No Lugs," Tall Walter says. "We are paid good money, just to camp about these parts."

"For a week now," Jakey says. He has the misfortune to have been taken stealing a lord's sheep on two occasions, and has paid with an ear each time. A third offence would mean the rope. "Who is our mystery benefactor?"

"I told you. The fellow is the man of a gentleman, who is the man of a lord," the gang leader explains. In truth, he is not sure who he works for at the moment, but an advance of thirty shillings has soothed his curiosity. "We are bid to keep ourselves in readiness, and await word."

"Word of what?" Jakey asks. "This fellow pays well for nothing, I fear. Are we to go against the king's army for our money?"

"No, we are going to make easy coin, my friend," Walter says. "Two travellers coming on the London road, wanting their throats cut. What could be simpler?"

"Rider!" The voice comes down from a high tree top, and Walter crouches down. No Lugs follows suit, and their men, in various stages of waking all lie still. It is early morning, and the sound of hooves galloping can be clearly heard.

"One man," the lookout hisses.

"It might be our messenger," Walter whispers. "Keep under cover, until we know better." The horse comes on, from the way of London, at a steady gallop, and shows no sign of slowing.

"Do we take him?" Jakey No Lugs asks, and Walter Tall shakes his head. Why spoil the chances of success by waylaying a single rider?

"Let him ride by," their leader says, and Alonso Gomez passes through the valley of death unmolested. The Spaniard keeps up a steady gait, and looks neither to the left nor the right as he rides towards Plymouth. He is a keen reader of signs, and notices that there are no birds in the copse to his left.

Men and horses hidden away, he thinks. He has been riding hard since the night before, and knows it would be fatal to slow his pace just now. With luck, the concealed band have not already struck, and Colonel

Draper still lives, somewhere on the road ahead.

"Looked like a Dago to me," the lookout calls, once Gomez is out of sight. "I doubt he had two pennies to rub against each other, but the horse was a fine one."

"Forget him," Walter Tall calls back. "Our prey will earn us a fat purse, and little effort." He knows his victim is some court official, and expects him to be easy meat. Thirty men, coming on at a rush is enough to put fear into any man. The fellow is to be killed, and robbed of all he has. Any companion is to meet the same fate.

"Rider!" Walter Tall smiles, and kneels down again. The chances of two riders passing in so short a time are slight. This must be his man, with the money, and his final instructions.

*

Gomez is some fifteen miles from Plymouth, and is beginning to fear he has missed his quarry, when he breasts a low hill, and sees three horsemen on the road ahead. He kicks his heels into his mount's flanks, and the tired beast sets off down the slope.

He is still a couple of hundred paces away when the three men spread out, and put a dozen yards between themselves. The Spaniard smiles then.

This is a soldier's way, he thinks. Widen your front, and lessen the target is an old adage, and Gomez is convinced he has found his man.

"*Señor*, we are well met!" The Spaniard reigns in his mount, and stops before Will Draper's own mount. "You remember me?"

"Alonso Gomez, the servant of Ambassador Chapuys," Will Draper says, and nods to the newcomer. "This is an odd chance meeting, is it not?"

"Not by chance, *Jefe*" Gomez replies. "I have no papers, but I am sent on an urgent mission... to find you, and warn you of my master's suspicions. He fears that the duke has..."

"Which duke?"

"Norfolk, sir," Gomez explains. "He seeks to intrigue with Ambassador Chapuys, and has suggested that the Cromwell party might be pruned down with a few assassinations."

"That bastard!" Will Draper thinks at once about his wife's safety, and wonders what the old devil has in mind. "I must..."

"No, sir!" Gomez catches at his reigns. "Señor Chapuys is a most loyal friend. He commands me to tell you that your family are being watched. He will also alert Cromwell to the plot."

"You thought to warn me?"

Will glances towards his companions. "I am in company, Señor Gomez, and safe enough."

"Three miles behind me, a war party awaits your coming," the Spaniard explains. "From the tracks, I would number them at twenty-five or even thirty. They kept under cover as a passed, so must be up to some mischief. I suggest we turn back."

"What is it?" Prince Ibrahim rides closer, and Alonso Gomez appraises him with a cunning eye.

"You are not from these parts, brother?" he asks in Castilian Spanish. The Abyssinian shakes his head, and replies in the same tongue.

"I am not, friend. Though your own tongue is not native to me either. I am from Kush… or Abyssinia, as these Englishmen call my far off land."

"You have come a long way for a fight, sir," Gomez replies, in English. "We must find some stronghold Colonel Draper, or be overwhelmed."

"There was an inn," Kel Kelton says. "Back down the valley away. It is a low place, but it has four walls, and a door we can bar."

"Then let us retrace our path," Will says. "How are these fellows armed, Gomez?" The Spaniard can only shrug, and explain that he did not have the leisure to count their swords and pistols.

"Back home, we do not yet have muskets aplenty," Ibrahim says. "Prester John owns a few, of course."

"Here, any rogue with a few pounds can buy a pistol and shot," Will tells him. "We must wait and see what will come against us. How much powder have we, Kel?"

"Two pistols, and enough powder and ball for a dozen shots apiece," the young man replies. "I was not expecting to face an army, sir!"

"I have my musket, and plenty of lead shot," Alonso Gomez puts in. "Now, may we ride?"

*

"Well, what is it?" Walter Tall is on horseback, and struggling to keep his mount under control. They have come upon some fresh hoof prints in the muddied road, and Jakey No Lugs is examining them with care.

"Three riders, coming this way," he says. "Then one meeting up with them, and then all four of them going off that way."

"That blasted Spaniard!" Walter curses. "He must have seen us, and given warning to our prey. No mind, he will die with the others."

"Who is it, Walt?" his right

hand man asks. "Who do we have to kill for so much money?"

"Some courtly fellow."

"No, not for fifty pounds," No Lugs says. "Enough to buy a house and five hundred acres… for some slack jawed cockscomb?"

"Colonel Will Draper, the King's Examiner," Walter Tall hisses at him. "There… does that make it any the better? He is warned now, and we must give chase. If he reaches Plymouth, we are done for, and must run back to our Welsh forest." He spurs his horse into a gallop, and the rest of his troop follow. They ride on, down the length of the valley, and come to where the coast road adjoins the London way.

"Look!" Tall Walter stands in his saddle, and stares ahead, to where an inn straddles the road. It is an old building, made of stone, and with only narrow slits for windows. At some time someone has added another floor, made from wood, and furnished the upper story with larger windows. There is a rough lean to attached to the inn, and some tired horses stand inside it.

"They seek shelter at the inn," Walter tells his men. "We will surround the place, and corner our quarry."

"What if they are armed?" one

of his men asks.

"Then we might lose one or two," Walter replies. "Equal shares, lads. There is enough gold to set us all up."

"Might we not trick them out?" No Lugs says. "Tell them we mean them no harm?"

"Would you believe that?" Walter says, and they all laugh at so lame a thought. "Let us get at them, before the local yeomanry hear we are abroad. You two, cut a strong trunk, so we can batter at the door. No Lugs, take three men, and fire your pistols through the window slits. Long Tom, you and some others climb atop that shed, and onto the roof. Hack through the thatch, and drop down on them."

"No quarter, Tall Walter?" a weasel looking rogue asks as he dismounts. "What of the innkeeper and his family?"

"Kill them all," Walter Tall replies. "We need no witnesses of this day's work."

*

"Innkeeper, where are your family?" Will Draper's sudden presence makes the fat hostel owner shake with trepidation. He shakes his head, and points across to a dirty looking little girl who is tending the fire.

"My servant, sir," the man says. "I have no family... since the last sweating sickness passed by."

"Very well. There are men coming. Bad men. They intend killing us all." Will draws his pistol, and lays it on a nearby table. "Can you load a pistol?"

"I can, sir," the man replies. "I will recharge you, as you demand. Shall I send the girl away?"

"Too late. Have her hide herself."

"Anyone upstairs?" Kel dignifies the rough made ladder to the upper floor with the name of stairs.

"No. I never have guests, unless it is the goose fair." The man rummages in a drawer, and brings out a wicked looking meat cleaver. "Rob Stanley, at your service, good sirs."

"Colonel Will Draper," Will says. "You would fight with us, sir?"

"I will not let these rogues have it all their own way," Rob Stanley replies. "Besides, I was a Cornish yeoman before I took on this place. What are my orders, sir?"

"Reload, as you may," Will says, "and use your chopper to good effect if you can." The man nods, and tucks the murderous cleaver into his belt.

"Eve, stay under the table, and out of our way," the innkeeper says. He does not add that, should they lose, she might be the last to die. "Say your prayers, girl."

"Buggery to that," little Eve says, and picks up a long roasting fork. "Anyone wants me, they'll get this up them!"

"Riders... dear Christ on the Cross... there are ... thirty or more of the bastards, sir!" Kel cries.

"Your odds, Master Kel," Will says with a grin. "If you can manage a dozen, I shall do for the rest, eh?" In truth, the odds are not good, and they are trapped inside an indefensible old building, but Will knows that fear is contagious, and he must not show it.

"A wager, Colonel Will," Kel replies. "I lay ten shillings that I kill more than you. What say you?"

"Done, and I hope one of us is around to collect on the bet," Will says.

"Bastards!" Rob Stanley curses. The men have dismounted, and spread out in a wide semi circle. "They mean to charge down my door." The innkeeper turns a heavy table on its side, and pushes it against the door, just as the first charge starts. Two men carry a short, thick length of fallen tree trunk, as wide as a large man's fist, and go to ram it against the door. Two more flank them and cock their big pistols.

Walter Tall is watching with satisfaction, but his smile turns to a look of horror as a demonic creature appears from the shambolic lean to. The creature, is huge, as black as the devil, and is screaming out some terrible cry. The men with the ram are seized with terror, and try to run, but the monster sweeps down his great curved sword, and strikes one of them dead.

The second man runs, even as the black devil falls on one of those carrying a pistol. The man's scream is cut short, as his head flies from his shoulders. At that moment Will Draper pushes a pistol out through one of the slit windows, and fires it into the fourth man's face. He falls backwards, and the devil's creature runs for the inn's door. Kel pulls the table aside, opens the door, and admits the Prince of Abyssinia.

"By God, but that was well done, Your Highness!" Will Draper cannot hide his pleasure at how well the ruse has worked. "They are three down, and have lost a brace of pistols."

"Most enjoyable," the prince replies, hardly able to regain his breath.

"Now we are more evenly matched."

"A Blackamore?" Rob Stanley raises a hand, as if to rub the black skin, but a scowl from Ibrahim deters him. "You are welcome sir, but I feared the devil was coming to call."

"I am Prince Ibrahim of Kush. In my land, we call him *Shaitan*, and his skin is red, like blood," the prince says. "Have you any of your English beer?"

"I shall fetch you your fill, My Lord," little Eve says. She has heard the black man named as a prince, and wishes to stand close to him. She fills four mugs with strong beer, and serves it to the men. Kel smiles at her, but she is not interested in anyone but the marvellous Prince of Kush.

*

"What was that?" No Lugs is shaking with fear. Three of their men lie dead outside the inn's door, and the others are shocked into silence.

"Have you never seen a damned *neygra* before?" Tall Walter says. "They left him with the horses, and we fell for it. Now they are all locked inside, and we can finish them off."

"They have pistols."

"So have we," their leader replies. "Let us fire at the windows, and creep around the sides. If we can get close enough, we can fire the thatch. Once that is blazing, they will either burn, or rush out onto our waiting swords and pistols. Yes?" He turns, and glares at his men. One nods his agreement, and the others follow suit. They will give him one chance, before choosing another leader.

Walter Tall senses this, and decides to throw them all into the attack. At the height of the fighting, he will take to his horse, and gallop off with the gold. With fifty pounds to spend, he can ride to Suffolk, and become a gentleman farmer.

"Make up torches," No Lugs commands. "Who has tinder?" Three men raise a hand, and go off on their mission. "Right, those with pistols, aim at the window slits, and the door."

A half dozen men cock pistols, and discharge them. The heavy lead balls hit the stonework, and one penetrates the door, and lodges itself in the replaced table top. One of the attackers staggers, and falls to his knees. He topples over and Walter runs to him. He sees there is a neat hole in his back, and he looks about to see where the shot might have come from.

"Be wary!" he cries, even as another man cries out, and drops his pistol. He staggers away, clutching at his shoulder, and more men are turning to seek out the enemy from behind. At that moment the three pistols inside crack, and another of the attackers yelps and grabs at his thigh.

"Now, lads," Walter shouts. "Now or never!" In response several of the men run to their horses. With the enemy also at their rear, they have no stomach for the fight anymore. "You dogs... you scum!" He raises his fist, and rants at the fleeing men, even as others make for their own horses.

"It is over, Tall Walt," his lieutenant says. "To horse, for God's sake!"

"Fifty pounds, and fifty more... if we kill one man," their leader says, and heads turn. A hundred pounds, between those who are left is not to be sniffed at. Eighteen men turn, and charge at the front door of the inn. The leading pair throw their shoulders at it, and it gives. The next two throw themselves against the flimsy door, and it falls inwards, pushing aside the table behind.

The first four are inside, and another fourteen, their blood up, push to follow them in. There is a pistol shot, and the sudden clash of steel on steel. The first man in pulls an axe from his belt, and meets Rob Stanley's wild charge. The two men go down to the floor, in a welter of arms, legs, and deadly edges.

Will Draper runs his sword through another, but he is replaced by two more. Kel Kelton tackles another with his sword, and a dagger in his left hand. The man is an old hand at close quarter killing, and blocks his thrust. He cannot get in a return stab, so drives his sword hilt into the young man's face. Kel staggers back, blinded by the blow, and waves his dagger, to ward off a killing strike. None comes.

The girl, Eve, picks up the heavy pan of water she has been boiling on the fire, and throws it over the nearest assailants. Kel's attacker screams in pain, and Kel take advantage of the moment. He thrusts his sword into his throat, and twists. A great spurt of blood sprays over both Kel, and the girl, and the man falls down, clutching at the fatal wound.

Will Draper is fending off two men with sword and dagger, but he has little room to work in. The innkeeper staggers to his feet, and holds up the severed head of his foe. He is crazed with fury, and throws himself at Will's attackers. The cleaver sinks into an unsuspecting shoulder, and a man screams like a pig going to slaughter.

Will drops under the second fellow's guard, and sends in a killing thrust. The man's mouth fills with blood, and he sinks to his knees. At the door, men are still piling in, but there are cries of dismay from outside. Alonso Gomez, who has been concealed in the woods with his musket, has arrived. He falls on the besiegers from behind, and works his dagger with deadly proficiency.

He draws his knife across the rearmost man's throat, opening it up from ear to ear. Almost before the man is dead, Gomez stabs another between the shoulder blades. The fellow cries out, and twists sideways, pulling the blade from the Spaniard's grasp. He curses, and draws his sword.

The Spaniard steps back, and slashes back and forth, cutting open backs and arms, as they present themselves. Three men fall under his sword, and a fourth turns, and comes at him. Gomez is forced back by his attacker, who is taller, and more skilled with the sword. He fends off three smart attacks, and fumbles for the spare knife he keeps in his sash.

Walter Tall sees the Spaniard's move, and presses home his attack. Gomez finds the knife's hilt, and goes to pull it free, when he stumbles, and falls backwards. The leader of the gang sees his chance, and leaps over the fallen man. As he does, he slashes wildly, and opens the Spaniard's arm. Once clear, he runs for the horses.

There is the sharp crack of a pistol, and Walter feels the lead ball hit him in the left buttock. He staggers on a few paces, then falls to one knee. Men are running, and he expects the death blow at any moment. Instead a surly looking young girl comes to him, and smacks him across the head with a heavy wooden serving tray. The blow knocks him sideways, and he slips into unconsciousness.

*

"How have we fared?" Will Draper asks.

"Better than they, sir," Kel Kelton reports. "The innkeeper is sorely wounded though, and will not last out the hour. He killed two of the fellows before he fell. I have counted eleven dead, and four more wounded, and taken prisoner."

"The prince?"

"He killed his share," Kel says. "As for the Spaniard… I think he did for five, before he went down. His arm is cut to the muscle, and he might not have the use of it for a while. We must pray it does not fester before we reach a doctor."

"What of the prisoners?" Will asks.

"We have their ringleader," Kel says. "He was the one you shot in the arse. Little Eve laid him low with a wooden tray. She also saved my life."

"If she wishes, she may come with us," Will says. "Miriam will find some work for her."

"Yes, sir." Kel frowns at the thought of the prisoners. "Three or four of them are only slightly wounded. Are we to hang them?"

"Not without trial," Will tells him. "As for their leader... he shall go to the Tower of London, for questioning."

"I could find out everything here, if you would but let me," Kel says. "The man is already in fear of his life."

"No. It is not proper."

"Proper ... they tried to murder us." Kel cannot understand why the colonel finds the law to be so important.

"What if some great lord decided you had wronged him?" Will explains. "What if he pronounced you guilty, and hanged you, before trial? Then what if we found you to be innocent?"

"We *know* he is guilty."

"That is what the great lord would say... were it not for the laws of England." Will slaps the hilt of his sword. "This is not the way to settle things, Kel. A man crosses you, so he dies ... or you die. The law makes us all equal. The man who cannot draw his sword and win, has recourse to the law. Our fellows shall live, until that same law says otherwise."

"Well said, Colonel Draper," the prince says. "Besides, if these men are not too badly hurt, they will make most valuable slaves."

"We do not make Englishmen into slaves," Will says.

"No?" Ibrahim shrugs his broad shoulders. "My father has a thousand slaves. He would take their leader, and give him back to God, in some ingenious way. Once he buried a miscreant up to his neck in the soil, and painted sweet nectar on his face. The red ants came, and ate his face from the bone. It was only after they bored through the eyes, and into the brain that he stopped screaming."

"Dear Christ, what had he done?"

"He ... *fodido*... with one of Prester John's wives.," the prince explains, and illustrates the fact with a

118

thrust of his hips. "Not my mother, you understand?"

"We should send Thomas Wyatt to your country as our ambassador," Will says. "That might just about cure his licentious ways."

"This Enga-land of yours is a most dangerous place, Colonel Draper," the prince says. "Might we get on now, and I can speak with your king?"

"To offer him riches beyond avarice, no doubt" says Will. "I fear any further delay would lead to my ruin. The king does so love to hear about great battles, fought against enormous odds. When I tell him how the Prince of Abyssinia stood shoulder to shoulder with two Englishmen, and a Spaniard, he will want to hear the whole tale. We might embellish it… but God alone knows how!"

*

"Is the king awake yet?" Thomas Cromwell fears that his friend Adolphus Theophrasus really has miscalculated his valerian potion, and that the king will never wake up.

"Not yet," Sir Thomas Heneage replies. "Though I have stood by his bed, and coughed."

"Coughed?" Thomas Cromwell almost laughs out loud at the absurdity of this. "Can you not shake him?"

"Shake him?" Heneage, who is Master of the King's Stool, and therefore very close to the king, is horrified. "That would be a most unseemly thing to do, sir. I cannot touch the king, without his express permission."

"Dear Christ, Heneage... you wipe his arse, and empty his piss pot for him," Cromwell curses. "The king must be awakened."

"He is tired."

"He has been asleep for thirty six hours," the angry minister snaps. "No man can be that tired. The Imperial Ambassador awaits him, and the French fellow too. They will be insulted."

"That is not my fault," Heneage says. "I dare not wake him."

"Sir, do you deny Master Cromwell access?" Tom Wyatt asks. He has been hanging about the outer court, hoping to catch Henry's interest in a new saucy poem he has written.

"I must."

"Then how do we know the king is well?"

"He is snoring, sir."

"Sir John!" Tom Wyatt calls. He turns to Sir John Russell, who has come along to see what all the commotion is about. "Are you not the king's personal messenger?"

"I am, sir," the man agrees.

"How is your presence announced?"

"By a flourish, of course, Sir Thomas," Russell replies. Tom Wyatt is now knighted, and must be treated like a real gentleman.

"A flourish of trumpets?" the poet says. "Then pray leave the chambers, and return... not forgetting your flourish!"

"The king will..."

"The king must awaken," Cromwell says, and waves for Russell to get on with it. The young gallant steps outside the outer chamber, and steps back inside. The three royal trumpeters, take their cue, and raise their instruments to their lips. The flourish reverberates about the huge chamber, and courtiers appear from every direction.

"Now then, my dear Heneage, perhaps you might see if the king is awake?" Cromwell asks, his voice dripping with sarcasm.

Heneage bows, and slips into the king's chambers. A moment later, he re-appears, followed by a well aimed silver candlestick, and a bellow of rage. The trumpets, blown so close to the royal apartment, have penetrated through the king's deep sleep. Tom Cromwell sees how they all cower, and steps into the inner chamber.

"God's blessings, sire," he says, as Henry lurches from his bed. "The sweating sickness has passed us by, unscathed... and Your Majesty is fully recovered."

"Recovered from what?" Henry feels his own forehead, and presses two fingers to his dry throat.

"Overwork, sire," Tom Cromwell says. "Doctor Theophrasus says that the strain of your new son's arrival, and the weight of the crown has fatigued you. His potion has worked better than hoped for. Not only did it protect you from the sweating sickness, but it also gave you some much needed rest."

"Oh... well, I do feel rather rested," the king admits. "What day is it?" He scratches his belly, and breaks wind. "Where is Heneage?"

"Close by, sire," Cromwell says. "Shall I send him in to attend you?"

"Yes, give me a quarter hour, and I will be ready."

"There are only a couple of short audiences scheduled, sire," Cromwell says. "The French ambassador wishes to whine about wine tariffs, and Eustace Chapuys craves a moment of your time."

"Ha! Little Chapuys, who speaks in French, yet thinks in Spanish," Henry says. "Though I do recall he once jousted at one of my tourneys."

"He fought against Colonel Draper, and another gentleman, before you vanquished them, sire."

"By God's Holy Cross... yes. Draper almost had me, but was not quite my equal. Poor Chapuys tried to intervene, and took a thump for his pains."

"Yes, sire. He may be a Savoyard, but he possesses the honour of an Englishman."

"You like him?"

"I trust him, sire."

"What does he wish to tell me?" Thomas Cromwell shrugs his shoulders, and shakes his head. A mystery is more likely to appeal to Henry's nature, and guarantee a royal audience.

"He claims that it is for your ears only, sire."

"Ah, a secret," Henry says, and he rubs his hands together. "I so love secrets."

"Then I might have them

standing by, sire?"

"No, tell the Frog bastard to bugger off … but do it a little more politely," Henry decides. "Whine and wine … very droll, my friend. I care not for trade tariffs. You see to it for me, Thomas."

"As you wish, sire." Cromwell bows low, having just been told he may handle the imposition of new taxes on French wine. It gives him scope to squeeze more from an enemy, whilst keeping the import duty on Portuguese wine low. Whilst this does not benefit him, it will be a great help to Miriam Draper, whose company buys almost half of the Portuguese grape harvest each year. "I shall advise Ambassador Chapuys of your wish to see him."

"Good show," Henry says, and he breaks wind again. "Where in suffering Hell's name is Heneage?"

7   The Prediction.

The wharf, which once fronted the old Draper house, has been added to, and extended in both directions. It now stretches for over eighty yards, and has a dozen mooring points, each of which has a boat tied up at it. Over thirty men and women are unloading some of the channel cogs, and reloading onto the smaller skiffs that ply their trade up and down the Thames.

"Chelsea?" Miriam shouts, and Peggy Downs waves, to show she is ready to cast off. "Big Jim, see to Peg. Help her unload at the market, and come back here for another load.

"M'am." The big, slow moving old fellow ambles off.

"How are those cheeses, Lou?"

"Only one salt damaged," Lou replies. "Though we could still pass it off as fresh, if we…"

"No. I deal fairly with my customers." Miriam knows that this way of working will bond the poor people of London to her, and ensure they come back again, and again to her market stalls for their provisions. "Send it to the kitchen, and have them put it outside the front gate with some hard bread. Perhaps the beggars might have a taste for free salted cheese."

"Yes, Mistress Miriam," Lou responds. She has been with the Drapers for just over a year now, and knows a good position when she sees one. "Though they are choosy these days, ever since you started giving them meat in the free broth."

"We must feed the starving," Miriam replies.

"Some of these beggars are hard pressed as to where to go for a handout," Lou persists. "Master Cromwell does a finer breakfast, but you are more generous with your portions. I swear, mistress, I might be better off out of your service. You would feed me as well as you do now, and I need not work!"

"And this irks you, girl?"

"It does, mistress," the young girl says. "Can we not set the women to sewing shirts, or embroidery for their food, and put the men to bottle washing, toting goods, and other such labour?"

"They cannot embroider in the streets," Miriam says.

"There is the warehouse off Sidney Street," Lou says. "Mistress Beckshaw says the rent is…"

"Ah, Pru has put these ideas into your head," Miriam says. "I hope she has done her sums correctly."

"The rent is two pounds a year. We could let the women folk sleep there, and charge them a penny or two a week. This would come from their earnings."

"From the embroidery we do?" Miriam smiles, for it is an idea she has pondered for herself. How to keep the poor busy. "How would that work?"

"We buy in all our embroidered linen from Antwerp," Lou explains. "We pay tuppence three farthings for every yard piece, and another penny farthing to have it embroidered. If we buy in the plain washed linen, it would cost us tuppence a yard. Our girls would embroider it for a penny a yard. That is…uh…" Lou is not good with reading or counting yet, but is getting there.

"A quarter increase in my profit," Miriam concludes. "Very well, Lou… see to it."

"Me, Mistress Miriam?"

"Yes, you. See to it all, and use my name if there are problems," Miriam Draper says. "You have thought it through to a goodly end, and you will be able to take fifty or more poor women off the street. Now, where is Pru?"

"Counting House, m'am," Lou

says, with a happy smile. "*The Wild Rover* docked at Harwich this morning, and she is tallying up the bill of lading."

Miriam sees that her business interests are being well looked after, and she has a pang of jealousy that these women, whom she has hand picked, can do the job as well as she. It is a short walk to the counting house, where the day's income is tallied, and banked safely. The tallying floor is occupied by a half dozen clerks, all men, who tot up Miriam's wealth on an hourly basis. In the cellars of the old converted house there is a room with thick walls, an iron bound door, and four armed guards.

"Good day, Mistress Beckshaw," she says as she comes in out of the cold autumn day. "How is your husband, John?"

"About the king's business in Coventry," Pru replies. "He shall be home the day after the morrow. How are you, my friend?"

"Well. The children are healthy, and Will is…"

"Come from danger near, to danger dark," Pru says. "You must come to dinner soon."

"What was that?" Miriam sees that the strange phrase has been uttered without Pru's knowledge. It is the odd foreknowledge that grips her now and then. "Come from danger near, to danger dark... what ever can you mean?"

"Pardon?" Pru blinks, and stares at Miriam. "Have I said something to upset you, my dear friend?"

"It is nothing," Miriam tells her. "If Will was ever in danger, would you see it for me?"

"I do not know," Pru says. "These things come to me as they may, and I can do nothing but utter them."

"Of course," Miriam says. She watches as the clerks scratch away at their ledgers. In less than six years she has gone from being a market stall girl on London Bridge, to mistress of a vast mercantile empire. With the grand house, a fine husband, and healthy children, she wonders how long she needs to go on. "How much is all this worth, Pru?" she asks.

"It varies, from day to day," Pru says. "One day a ship comes in, and the next day ...one sinks... or you buy an orchard, and its yield is lower, or higher, than we thought. The best I can say is this... you are richer than the king. You are even richer than Master Cromwell. With the profits from the

Corfu adventure added in, the Draper Company will yield about two hundred thousand pounds over the next twelve months. Then there is the income from the markets, which brings in another fifty thousand. Your vintners trade earns you about twenty five thousand. Then we have the…"

"Enough," Miriam says. "Have I enough to cover the coming venture to the New World?"

"The outlay will be about twelve thousand," Pru advises. "If the venture fails, you will owe the king about a hundred thousand for his lost warships. If it succeeds, you will be richer than the Emperor Charles."

"If it succeeds." Miriam ponders events for a moment then asks the important question. "Can you see that far?"

"Rarely," Pru Beckshaw tells her mistress. "I *knew* John was coming for me, and I had a feeling about the last time the sweating sickness came to London, but it is rare to see so far ahead. Master Cromwell once asked me about the king's future, but I knew not. I used to dream about Queen Jane… and *saw* her with a son… but those dreams have stopped, and I see nothing about her now."

"Then we must rely on the

fates," Miriam says. "I have told Lou that…"

"Yes." Pru turns to a page in one of her ledgers. "Here are all the costs, and an indication of how we might profit. I doubt the company will make more than thirty pounds a year, but it will help many poor people. I will help her, as she asks."

"Mistress Draper, come quickly!" One of the clerks is agitated, and waves to her from the door. She sighs, and goes over to see what is upsetting the fellow. On the outer wall, beside the door, someone has lime washed a crude sign.

"What is it?" Miriam asks. The figure is freshly daubed, and the lines are running, and blurred, but she can make out what it is meant to be. The clerk shakes his head, and tries to back away. "Tell me… what does this mean?"

"I do not know, mistress," the fellow lies.

"Paint it out, at once." Miriam turns on her heel, and sets off in the direction of Austin Friars. Thomas Cromwell will know what to do, she thinks, as she remembers the last time she had seen such a sign. It had been painted on the door of her grandfather's house in Aachen … a crude five pointed star … to signify the presence of a witch.

*

"Your Royal Highness, may I present you with this small gift from my master, in the hope that it finds favour with you?" Eustace Chapuys snaps his fingers at the two men who have followed him into the king's presence with a heavy burden. The quicker of the two takes hold of one corner of the dust sheet, and twitches it aside.

For a moment there is complete silence. Henry stands up, despite his aching leg, and walks up close to the portrait. It is of him, but somehow a little younger, and a little leaner. The king examines it closely, then nods his approval.

"Holbein?" he asks.

"An admiring contemporary of his, sire," Eustace Chapuys replies. "Though the fellow's touch is almost as deft as the master's, Hans Holbein is unsurpassed for his sureness of touch, and purity of style. The emperor means this to show you how he still thinks of you." The message is a clear one to Henry. Charles, the Holy Roman Emperor reasserts his friendship, and still sees the King of England as a powerful monarch.

"We are pleased," Henry says. "I shall hang it in my Privy room. This is the king's most intimate chamber, and displays how highly he thinks of the gift. Every time he eases himself, the emperor shall be looking on.

"The Emperor Charles also wishes me to convey his continued *support* for Your Highness," Chapuys says, and Henry's ears prick up.

"Support?" he asks. "Does your master envisage some coming trouble, *M'sieu* Chapuys?"

"Not at all, sire," the little Savoyard replies with a thin smile. "He merely wishes you to know that his support for you, and for your chief minister is absolute."

"Just so, sir." Henry contemplates this statement, and waves a hand to signal that the audience is at an end. The moment Chapuys bows himself out of the throne room, the king calls for Cromwell, and informs him of what has been said.

"He said *support*, sire?" Thomas Cromwell purses his lips, and fiddles with the cuff of his new lace shirt.

"He did." Henry frowns at Cromwell's consternation, which confirms his own interpretation of the short conversation. "He actually looked me in the eye as he said the word!"

"Oh dear," Cromwell says. "He looked you in the eye?"

"Damn it, Tom... stop questioning me," Henry snaps. "What does it mean?"

"That Charles thinks you to be under some sort of threat," his minister tells him, "though I cannot imagine from which quarter the threat is perceived. Reginald Pole is a small threat... but he is abroad. The Scots are too weak to threaten your realm, and the northern rebels are done with. Your Majesty is surrounded by those he trusts."

"Just so... then what is the nature of this threat?"

"Perhaps the emperor fears you losing me?" Thomas Cromwell muses, and watches the king's face crumple into horror.

"Lose you?" he cries. "By God, no. You are my right arm, Thomas. Who would dare... ah, I see. There *is* one who hates your position. Tom Howard would drag you down from your high office, if I let him."

"Your Highness assures me of his love for me," Cromwell says. "You would not see me fall."

"I would not."

"Then perhaps the old Duke of

Norfolk means me some harm?"

"I would hang him."

"Then he might seek to bring down those close to me, so that I am weakened, and thus fail in my duty. Chapuys knows something, sire. I know the fellow, and he would not speak unless ... unless he had proof."

"He thinks Norfolk to be a traitor?"

"No, sire, not treason," Cromwell says. "The act would be against me, not the crown."

"I shall let it be known that to hurt one of yours is to strike at me," Henry fumes. "Norfolk *will not* meddle in my affairs!"

This is what Cromwell has hoped for. Norfolk has shown his hand to Chapuys, and the little man has warned his friend. The king's declaration will frighten the duke from his vengeance, but the Privy Councillor hopes that it is not too late for Will Draper. Alonso Gomez has ridden off to the rescue, and Thomas Cromwell can only hope for the best.

*

"Why are there no ditches around your villages?" Prince Ibrahim asks. "In Abyssinia our dwellings are enclosed by either a wall, or a ditch. It stops other villages raiding for slaves."

"We do not raid one another," Will replies, as they ride.

"No, we raid the Scots, and they raid us," Kel Kelton adds.

"Crazy Englishmen," Gomez mutters. His arm is bound tight with a linen bandage, which the girl, Eve has applied, after rubbing a mixture of dung and animal fat onto the small wound. "If you and the Scots became one, you could conquer the world!"

"Why do not the Spaniards and the Portuguese join forces?" Will asks.

"We hate one another," Gomez admits.

"If you Spaniards defeated them, they would not be after my poor country," Ibrahim says. "Instead, I must come calling on my cousin Henry for help."

Cousin. Kel smiles at the idea of old Hal being related to this noble looking Blackamore. They are as alike as fire and water, and the Abyssinian is taller, handsomer, and a much better fighter than the king.

"King Henry helps those he likes," Will advises. "Let him see your nobility, and dazzle him with stories of your travels, and he will be a most loving friend. Bore him, and your mission is doomed almost at once."

"When will we come to your

London?"

"Before nightfall," Kel Kelton says. "We will be over the bridge, and safe abed before the watch calls midnight."

"What is this bridge?" Ibrahim asks.

"London Bridge," Alonso Gomez answers for his English friends. "It is a wonder to behold, sir. It links the north of the river to the south, and its span is over seven hundred paces. There are houses and markets built upon it, and I often wonder why the whole lot does not fall down into the churning water."

"Are there no boats?" Ibrahim asks.

"Plenty, for a penny a piece," Will says. "We could take the flat ferry from Southwark, across to the Draper's Landing. Tonight, we will stay at my house, and attend court on the morrow."

"You own your own great house, and moorings?" Ibrahim asks, somewhat taken aback. "Are you a very great lord then?"

"No, I am but a soldier, sir," Will replies. "My wife owns the house, the landing stages, and the ferry."

"Your wife?" Ibrahim laughs out loud. "Back home, the women are there to serve us."

"That is the way here, also," Kel says with a smirk. "The colonel lives a confused life, and his wife rules over him!"

"As will your Maisie," Will says, lightly, and the young man blushes and falls silent.

"Do you have a wife, Master *Go Mess?*" Eve asks. She has just buried one master, and must find another quickly. She does not like the thought of working for the colonel's wife, who sounds like a strange sort of a woman.

"*Go- mez,*" the Spaniard corrects. "Not I girl. My life has been too full, and too dangerous for marriage."

"Oh, then you must use whores?" Eve asks. Gomez grins. The girl is sat up behind him, and is clinging on to his waist.

"A man must do what he must, girl," Gomez says.

"You should find a nice girl. One who can sew and cook for you," Eve says. "We English girls know how to warm a man's bed, sir!"

"How old are you, child?" Gomez asks her.

"Fourteen, or fifteen," Eve guesses. "How old are you?"

"Older than Methuselah," he responds.

"Then you should hurry and wed," Will jests.

"A man must marry," Ibrahim says. "How else can he have strong sons to guard his goats, or go hunting with. Do you have lions in Enga-land, Colonel Draper?"

"Only in the Tower of London," Will tells the amazed prince.

"They live in towers?"

"The king's zoo is lodged within," Gomez says. "I once paid a penny to look at the beasts."

"You must take me there, one day," Eve says, and clasps her arms about the Spaniard's waist all the harder. "After we are married."

"I have not asked, girl!" Gomez has fought French knights, and Iberian bandits, but he does not know how to defend himself against a simple village girl. "You presume too much, and must let me be. What if I do not wish to be wed, or do not find you pretty enough?"

"Then why would you let me ride with you?" Eve replies, with incontrovertible logic. The Spaniard can see what she means. The girl is not unattractive, and she seems willing enough. Eustace Chapuys would welcome her into the household, and expect nothing in return but a little light housework.

"We shall see," Alonso Gomez mutters, and Eve smiles into his broad back. The battle, she thinks, is won, and her immediate future is assured.

*

"In England, it is the sign of the witch," Thomas Cromwell says, as he studies the drawing Miriam has done for him.

"My people use it in their Cabalistic magic," Miriam tells her benefactor. "It means many different things."

"Here... it means only witchcraft."

"Why daub it on my wall?" Miriam fears that her Jewish antecedents are coming back to haunt her, and that she and her family must flee the country.

"It is not aimed at you," Cromwell tells her. "Norfolk is feeling restless, and seeks to do me some mischief. The king will not allow him to act against me, so he strikes at my people. This is meant for Prudence Beckshaw."

"Who knows about her gift?"

"Her curse, more like," Cromwell says. "Norfolk has his

agents. If they have heard something, it is an easy matter to cast doubts on the girl. Once charged with witchcraft, there is no going back. Uncle Norfolk is a wicked old fool, and might seek to ruin Pru, simply because she is one of our own."

"If the priests become involved, she might well be burned at the stake," Miriam says. "What can we do for her?"

"Send her to oversee the new manufactory you have opened in Chester," Cromwell says. "Once out of sight, Pru's 'gift' will soon be forgotten. I have arranged for the king to warn Norfolk off, and things should soon return to normalcy."

"Let us hope so," Miriam Draper says, "for I have no wish to see my friends pay for your indiscretions." The words are harsh, and spoken in haste. She knows that court politics are very involved, and dangerous to dabble in. The old duke fears for his place in the king's affections, and is striking out like a wounded bear.

"Calm yourself, Miriam," Tom Cromwell says. "All will be well." He cannot put it into words, but he promises himself that, should Norfolk persist, he will bring him down. Failing that, he thinks, the man must meet with some unavoidable accident.

"Mistress Beckshaw tells me we are worth over a hundred thousand pounds," Miriam says. "Can we not simply retire to the country, and live out our days in peace and comfort, Master Tom?"

"Oh, they would let you go, my dear," Thomas Cromwell agrees, "but I am like a great stag. The lesser beasts in the herd fear the powerful Hart, and cannot allow him to live."

"We could live quietly in Antwerp, or spend our days by the canals in Bruges," Miriam persists.

"And what of Will?" Cromwell's question silences her protests, and she clenches her small fists in frustration. "He was once a poor village lad, and he thinks only to progress himself. Peasant to soldier of fortune… to King's Examiner… then to… what?"

"Will loves me, and would live wherever we needed to," she says. "He can serve the Holy Roman Emperor, just as well as Henry."

"I doubt it. In a year or two, Henry will need a new man to act as General of the King's Army. Norfolk is old, and cannot even manage his naval duties. Your husband will be knighted, and elevated to an unprecedented position of power."

"Why would the king do that for a commoner?" Miriam asks. "Especially one who has a Jewess for a wife."

"Henry knows he has another fifteen or twenty years left, at the most," Cromwell explains. "He will wish to make one last great impression on his realm. Most men would endow a university, or give a fortune to the poor, but Henry will want a huge victory."

"He would go to war, out of vanity?" Miriam cannot understand men, or their lust for killing. "Against whom?"

"Oh, that hardly matters," the Privy Councillor says. "It might be France, or Spain... or the Scots. Yes, the Scots. With all the great soldiers retired, or already dead, Will would have the sole command. He would have thirty thousand men, and two hundred cannon at his back. No man could resist."

"Will has had enough of war." Miriam says it, but doubts that he would shun so much glory.

"Will cannot refuse. A knighthood and an army," Cromwell concludes. "Then, if he wins... an earldom. Move your fortune to Antwerp, Miriam, but do not expect your man to follow any time soon"

"Then I must stay, and see what comes."

"A great storm," Thomas Cromwell tells her, "and for those who can withstand it ... the greatest prizes of all. Your man might be the Earl of Arundel... or Duke of..."

"Utopia?" Miriam pulls her cloak about her shoulders, and stands, as if to leave. "My precious witch *saw* something today, Master Tom, about my husband... and I cannot guess what it means."

"What was it?" Cromwell asks.

"Oh, something about coming from a near danger, to a danger dark." Miriam Draper shrugs, and steps out into the cold courtyard. "I shall send one of my girls over with some of the latest batch of spices for your cook. *The Wild Rover* is safely back from her run to Genoa and Lisbon, laden with fine produce."

Thomas Cromwell calls for one of his lads, and bids him escort Mistress Miriam back to Draper House. He watches her as she sets off for the riverside mansion, and ponders on all she has said to him. It seems, from Pru's prediction, that Will is returning to London, having overcome some difficulty, but he cannot think what a *'danger dark'* might mean.

The nature of foreseeing the future is that it must be shrouded in some mystery. Does 'dark', Cromwell muses, mean 'great' in this context, and that the danger is on a national scale?

Perhaps 'dark' means sinister, and the danger involves some form of evil as yet undisclosed, he thinks. He is still pondering the question when Sir John Russell comes calling at his door. The fellow has ridden up from Hampton Court, in record time, and bears a message from the offices of the king.

"Take Sir John's horse, lad!" Thomas Cromwell shouts, and two urchins dart forward to obey. The king's special messenger is out of the saddle, and bowing to Cromwell in one fluid movement.

"Master Cromwell... I have news from Hampton Court Palace, for your ears alone."

"What is it?" Cromwell asks. These days, everything... even the most trivial happening... seems to be urgent, and for Thomas Cromwell alone to be able to solve it.

"May God forgive me the news I bring this day," Sir John Russell says, and Thomas Cromwell's heart twists in his chest.

8 At Draper House

The cellars of the great house by the river are surprisingly damp proofed, thanks to Miriam Draper's clever master builder. The foundations are dug out from the heavy clay, and a double brick lining keeps the underground chambers relatively dry. The vaulted ceilings are high enough for a man to stand upright, and wooden racks fill over half of the huge space. It is the ideal place to keep wine, and Will Draper enjoys showing his extensive cellar off to anyone interested enough.

"Six thousand bottles, and over two hundred kegs," he tells the Prince of Abyssinia. "My wife imports wines from Iberia, France and Italy. Choose your poison, sir."

"My poison?" The tall black man looks horrified at the suggestion, and Will smiles as he realises how his small jest has been misunderstood.

"I mean, choose what you wish to drink," he says. "I jest, of course, when I call it poison."

"Ah, a jest." The prince nods his head, and picks up a dark brown flask. "Then this shall be my poison, Colonel Draper."

"Dark rum," Will says, as he reads the waxed paper tag tied around the bottle's stubby neck. "It is a fiery concoction, from the New World. I hope you have a strong head, sir."

"We drink *Masara*, a strong corn brew," Ibrahim replies. "I am sure it is more powerful than any drink from the Americas."

"We shall put that to the test," Will says. "Might I prevail on you to call me Will? For we have fought side by side, have we not?"

"As you wish… Will." The prince considers for a moment, then touches his right hand to his heart. "Then you must call me Ibrahim, in private. When I meet your king, I think my full title would sound better. Prince Ibrahim of Kush sounds better… yes?"

"Of course." Will picks up a second bottle of the strong rum, and leads the way back up to the ground floor. The prince is most admiring, and confesses that Draper House is every bit as grand as Prester John's palace.

"You have many slaves?"

"Servants," Will says. "About twelve house staff, and another hundred and fifty who work for my wife's company."

"When will I meet this magical wife of yours?" Ibrahim asks. "She sounds like a veritable goddess. In my land, women are kept in their place."

"Pray, do not express that thought to Miriam," Will tells the prince, "or we may have to eat in the stables!"

"Has Miriam ever met one of my kind before?" Ibrahim asks. "Might she not be frightened at the mere sight of my magnificence?"

Will Draper thinks the prince is in for an awakening when he meets his wife. Miriam trades with everyone, from Arabia to Muscovy, and knows what it is to be considered different.

"Miriam is a Jewess," he says. "Though we do not shout it abroad. English law does not treat God's Chosen lightly. She can speak Hebrew, and will know more about your people than anyone else in London... save Doctor Theophrasus, who has travelled as far as Baghdad and Egypt."

"Then I shall have friends about me," Ibrahim says. "I can speak Hebrew with your wife, discourse on the course of the Nile with your doctor, and tell your king wonderful stories of my land. I hope he is interested enough to help my cause. Prester John is under threat from the Portuguese, and that can mean nothing good for Enga-land."

Will takes his guest into the great hall, and bids him sit in the chair nearest the roaring fire. The serving girls have stoked it up with cords of wood, and placed two goblets on a side table. He draws the stopper from the first flask of rum, and pours out two large measures of the dark brown liquid.

"Let us raise a glass to your father," Will says.

"And to your king," Ibrahim replies. He swallows the rum down in two gulps, and smacks his lips. "A most excellent drink, my friend. Let us now drink to your dear wife... and to my own... and speak of when I might visit your King Henry."

Miriam Draper has been met at the front door by one of the servants, and appraised of the fact that a '*great heathen*' was with the master. She throws off her heavy cloak, and enters the great hall. The tall Blackamore turns as she comes in, and his face breaks into a wide smile.

"Ah, Miriam... we have a guest. May I name to you His Highness, Prince Ibrahim of Abyssinia?"

"*Sholem Aleichem.*" The prince touches fingertips to his heart, and lips. May peace be upon you, he says, and Miriam responds without a thought.

"*Aleikhem shalom.*" And upon you be peace, she responds, and curtseys, to the imposing Abyssinian.

"You speak Hebrew well, my lady" The prince says, and seems delighted at this turn of events.

"A few words," she replies.

"Which you pronounce perfectly," Ibrahim replies. "Your husband has told me your secret."

"Then it is no longer a secret."

"My lips are sealed, Mistress Draper."

"I see my husband has opened our finest rum for you," Miriam says, and ignores the implication of what he says. "Might I hope for your presence at dinner this evening?"

"Prince Ibrahim will stay the night," Will tells his wife. She digests this unexpected news, and nods her compliance.

"I must warn the cook that we have a guest, and I shall have Joan prepare some chambers at once."

"I must apologise for this imposition, mistress," Ibrahim says. "Your husband has taken it upon himself to introduce me to your king."

"You are welcome, sir," Miriam tells him. "I fear we were dining alone tonight, so there will be no clever company for you to have discourse with."

"You have great lords visit

you?" Ibrahim asks.

"The King of England called here once … to use our privy," Miriam boasts. "Then we have had the Duke of Norfolk, Suffolk, and the Duke of Cumberland. Bishop Gardiner would often eat with us, and the Holy Roman ambassador is a family friend."

"Then we must ask Eustace to dine with us tonight," Will says. "He is always fine company, and I owe him a favour."

"Yes, I heard," Miriam tells him, rather coldly. "Had not Señor Gomez come to your aid, I would have been dining alone tonight."

"Now, now, my love," Will replies. "Prince Ibrahim was by my side, and he is worth any ten of the king's men. I shall send young Adam to invite the ambassador, and apologise for the short notice. He might also find your brother, and invite him to our table."

"Mush is not good company, since he returned from the island of Corfu," Miriam says. "My brother came home with a new mistress, Your Highness. A most fearsome young Venetian girl, with a temper to match her beauty. My idiot brother neglected to end it things with his old mistress, and finds himself torn between two passionate women."

"In Kush... I mean, in Abyssinia... there would be no problem," Ibrahim says. "He should marry them both, for that is the honourable thing to do."

"The English are not so open minded, sir," Will tells his guest. "Mush keeps Lady Mary Boleyn on a farm in the Sussex countryside, and his little Venetian beauty, Isabella, at Austin Friars."

"They do not know of each other?" Prince Ibrahim finds this amusing, and his laugh is rich and deep. Miriam marvels at the man's easy charm, and is reminded of Will, a few years back, and of Tom Wyatt, who is still a wily charmer.

"Tom Wyatt is still in court," she says, without thinking. "Perhaps Adam might also invite our poet friend?"

"And Richard," Will adds. "You will like Richard, Ibrahim. He is the strongest man in London, and will want to arm wrestle with you."

"Then it seems we are to have a veritable feast," Ibrahim replies. "With so many fine Englishmen, and Ambassador Chapuys for company. I foresee a fine evening ahead."

"Oh!" Miriam has just recalled Pru's prediction from that morning. A dark danger to come... and Prince Ibrahim could not be any darker. "We might also ask Pru and John Beckshaw."

"Then poor cook must cater for nine," Will says. "Unless you wish to invite Norfolk and Suffolk?"

"I like Charles Brandon," Miriam answers, "but the Duke of Norfolk grows more unpleasant with each passing day."

"This man is the king's councillor?" Ibrahim asks.

"He wishes it were so," Will says, and gives a brief description of the man, and his perfidious ways. He finishes by guessing Norfolk to be behind the attack on the Plymouth road.

"Such a fight!" the black prince declares. "I seldom get to kill quite so many men in one day."

"It is a bad, and wasteful habit," Miriam jests, "killing men."

"In the Kingdom of Kush, Prester John has very many enemies," Ibrahim explains. "I am his eldest son, and must guard his life. If a councillor conspires against him, or some treacherous lord tries to take the crown, I have the right to take his life."

"Does it happen often?" Miriam asks.

"No more than once or twice a month," the prince says, "but there is the matter of the families too. If I kill a man, I must also kill all of his male relatives, for fear of revenge. Last year the prime minister rebelled... and he had seven sons, eight brothers, and forty five nephews."

"Dear God," Will mutters. "You will be right at home in King Henry's court!"

*

Miriam must raid her store cupboard at short notice, but still manages to lay on a fine feast for her dinner guests. She has a half dozen freshly trapped hares for a stew, and a haunch of venison that has been hanging for three weeks to make a fine second course. A dozen roasted chickens, and a brace of wild geese will supply the side dishes, and an array of custard pies and spiced buns shall end the meal on a sweeter note.

Whilst Ibrahim and Will continue to sample the rum, she arranges everything with a deft hand. Each place setting has a pewter plate, and silver forks... a new French innovation ... are set beside them.

"Keep the wine flowing," she

says to Silas, her steward, whom she has drafted in to wait on table. Make sure the food arrives hot, and do not let the girls chatter."

"Yes, mistress," Silas says glumly. It is going to be a long night, he thinks, and he has been up since dawn. In the distance, a lone bell begins to toll, then another, and another. Soon, it seems as if all the churches in London are at bell ringing practice.

"Is it a saints day today?" Miriam, who is not a Christian, asks, and the old servant shakes his head. On saints days, Mistress Miriam allows for an even more generous meal for the servants, and tries to ease their workload, so that they might visit church.

"Crispin is tomorrow," he says. "It was on Saint Crispin's day that the old King Hal did for the French at Agincourt. It is not celebrated as much as it once was. Today is but Saint Crispin's Eve... that bein' the day *before*, as it were."

"Then why do the bells ring?" Miriam sighs, and dismisses it from her mind. The Christian church is beyond her understanding, with all its saints days, and special services ... yet it does so little to feed the poor, or provide work for honest working men.

"Those are tolls, not peals," old Silas says with a knowing nod. "That be *Passing Bells*, my lady." and trundles off about his own business. Miriam shrugs. In her faith there is little time for overly elaborate ritual, and the worship of the one God is treated as a duty rather than like a series of feast days.

There is much to do, she thinks, and the guests will be arriving soon. A few minutes later, and a servant knocks. He is sent from Austin Friars, with excuses from Richard Cromwell. He cannot leave home at this time, and must beg Miriam's forgiveness. The messenger knows nothing more, and takes a penny for his trouble.

"Richard is kept away," she tells her husband, who frowns at the news.

"Why?"

"The messenger does not know."

"How odd. Richard never shuns a meal here," he mutters. "I must send Adam out again, and ask if I am needed at Austin Friars."

"Oh, no Will," Miriam begs. "Not tonight. We are to have guests. What will I tell them if you are not here?"

"Tell them that I am..." His word s trail away as Eustace Chapuys appears at the door behind Silas, who insists on announcing him in a stentorian voice.

"Forgive my early arrival," the little Savoyard says, after the old man bows himself out, "but I thought you might not have heard the terrible news."

"What is it?" Will jumps to his feet, and Ibrahim follows suit. "Pray tell me, sir!"

"It is the queen," Eustace Chapuys says, with tears welling in his eyes.

"Is she unwell?" Miriam understands the vagaries of childbirth, and wonders if she is sickening for something.

Ambassador Chapuys shakes his head, and fights to say the loathsome words: "Jane is dead!"

*

Thomas Cromwell hears the news from Sir John Russell stone faced, and asks a few questions. It seems that, after he left for London, the queen complained of tiredness, and retired to her chamber. A short while later, she called for help.

"The foreign doctor came at once," Russell explains, "but could do nothing to stop the bleeding. Her Majesty declined swiftly, and left us shortly after. It was the doctor who bid me ride to tell you the news. Soon, all London will be in mourning for so dearly loved a lady."

"What of the king?" Thomas Cromwell does not care, but it would seem odd if he did not ask, and his power for self preservation still functions.

"Raging about, smashing things, and demanding of God the answer to his question." Russell is almost sneering with contempt.

"Which was?"

"Why does this happen to me?" Russell knows how easily Cromwell can find out the truth, so does not hide it from him. "He bemoans his ill luck with women, and fears he is doomed to a life without an *honest* wife."

"He thinks God kills his wife to punish him?" Cromwell smiles, then spits onto the fire. "Poor Henry. My heart bleeds for him, and for his lack of an *honest* woman in his life. What of little Prince Edward?"

"Ned Seymour has the boy," Russell says. "There were those who would have stopped him, but he was armed, and had a half dozen roughs with him. He claims Henry will not want to be reminded of the mother by the child."

"Does he, by Christ!" Thomas Cromwell thanks the man, and bids him return to Hampton Court Palace at once. "The king will have need of you, my friend. If he asks after me, you must tell him I am arranging matters in London, and will be there, by his side, on this Monday coming. Is that clear, sir?"

"It is, Master Cromwell," Sir John says. "I hope you know I can be trusted to look after your best interests?"

"I do, sir, and should it be necessary, I shall call on you," Cromwell replies. Russell reminds him very much of Will Draper, when first they met, but has the advantage of being able to overcome his scruples, when required.

As the man takes his leave, Richard Cromwell steps out of the kitchen, with a half chicken in his hand. He shrugs at his uncle's frown, and explains himself.

"I was ready for dinner at Miriam's, uncle, when Russell came with his tragic news. I have sent my excuses, and am ready for your instructions. The morsel of chicken will keep me going until breakfast."

"Poor Jane," Cromwell says. It is only now, after the initial anger with Henry, that what has happened begins to affect him emotionally. "I should have been there with her."

"How would that have helped?" Richard has no knowledge of how much his uncle loved Jane Seymour, and wonders at the depth of emotion he is showing. "You are not a doctor, Uncle Thomas."

"And you are no genius, nephew," Cromwell replies with a sigh. "It seems that poor Edward is in the grasping hands of his uncle."

"Ned… not Tom," Richard guesses. "Tom Seymour is a braggart, and a man of loose morals… not a clever man. It will be Ned's idea to acquire the Prince of Wales, and raise him. He will argue that Henry is too grief stricken to manage."

"Just so." The old Thomas Cromwell shrugs off his own secret grief, and emerges once more. "I have been idle for too long, nephew. It is time to ensure all of our futures. Prince Edward must not stay with the Seymours, for they hunger far too much for real power. Where would Ned take the child?"

"Not too far," Richard says. "He has a new manor house in Esher, on the edge of the Hampton Court parklands. "I believe he purchased it from old Boleyn."

"You believe?"

"I know." Richard corrects himself, and is happy to see his uncle's wits are restored. He has not been the same man since Henry wed Jane Seymour, and has been delegating far too much work of late. "He paid three thousand Brabant ducats into a Bruges bank."

"Ah, old Boleyn is putting something away for his old age," Cromwell says. "May he live to enjoy it."

"I could always arrange…"

"No!" Cromwell does not want Anne Boleyn's father to be quietly killed. "Let him live, and remember how he condemned his own children to death. That is his punishment. Now, how do we return Prince Edward to the fold?"

"That is an easy matter," Richard tells his uncle. "Ned Seymour has few servants with him, and no more than six hard men to do his bidding. When next he goes hunting with the king, I will have a few of our lads call on his home in Esher, and bring little Edward away."

"Without conflict, mind," Tom

Cromwell warns. "The child is precious to me, and must not be hurt. Have him taken back to his nursery at Hampton Court Palace, and leave a half dozen sturdy lads to watch over him. I shall explain things to the king, and they will be made welcome."

"Yes uncle."

"Now, what about this strange foreign prince Will Draper has brought back with him… is he important?"

"He is the son of the Lord of Kush," Richard says. "I have it from Chapuys' servant. He claims to be richer than… well, anybody, and begs an army of the king."

"God's teeth, but that will keep Henry amused, until the funeral," Cromwell snaps. "Very well, let Rafe Sadler know about it, and he can arrange an audience at some future date. I have no time for such nonsense at the moment. Norfolk has tried to kill Will Draper, and seeks to stir up trouble over Pru Beckshaw."

"John Beckshaw is Will Draper's man, not ours, uncle," Richard protests. "Why should we help his wife's friend?"

"Because we do not need hysterical witch trials all over England," Cromwell explains. "Nor do we want the king to get involved in

Miriam Draper's business. If he suspects how wealthy she is becoming, he might also remember that she is a Jewess."

"That would not bode well for any of us," Richard says. He has several investments with Miriam, and does not wish to see his growing fortune damaged in any way. "What do you wish me to do?"

"Nothing too difficult. Miriam is sending the girl to Chester for the next month or two. Until she leaves, see she is guarded, and kept safe from persecution."

"Very well... and what about My Lord Norfolk?"

"We lack proof." Thomas Cromwell is constantly aggrieved that those lords who are closest to the king cannot be brought to book. "If I press too hard, Henry will excuse them, and our own relationship with the king will be bruised."

"Then let us turn the trick on him, uncle."

"What trick do you speak of?" Cromwell already knows what to do, but is pleased to see his nephew is beginning to think in a proper manner. "What would you suggest is the right course of action in this case?"

"The Duke of Norfolk seeks to

cut away the very roots of Austin Friars," Richard Cromwell states. "Let us oblige him in a similar way. He has a young mistress, stewards, agents, and confidants. Might we not thin *them* out a little?"

"A sound enough idea... but not a bloodbath, nephew."

"As you wish, Uncle Thomas." Richard bows, and retires to make his plans. He equates a bloodbath with the sacking of a small town, and the slaughter of many thousands, so the parameters are set wide indeed.

*

"The repast, as usual, is excellent, my dear Miriam." Eustace Chapuys has eaten a little of everything, but cannot make any real inroads into the venison. Tom Wyatt is in a mood, Mush is nowhere to be found, and Richard Cromwell, an eater of massive proportions, has made his excuses. "I only wish I had not come with such terrible news."

"The poor girl," John Beckshaw says.

"A motherless child must find a true father," Pru mutters.

"The king will prove to be a most goodly parent to the child," Will says. "Prince Edward will be well taken care of."

The handsome black prince smiles to himself, and ponders what the pretty wife of John Beckshaw says. Does any man know his true father, he thinks... even a royal prince? He helps himself to another of the delicious custard pies, and glances over at Miriam Draper. There is something odd about the woman, and he marvels at her great beauty, and at how fluent is her Hebrew, despite her hardly ever using the tongue these days.

"Sir?" Miriam has caught him admiring her, and offers him some more wine. He nods, and holds out his goblet. As she pours, their eyes meet, and he sends her a clear message. If it can be done, his eyes say, then he is agreeable to a private moment. She colours up, and sets her lips into a tight line. The answer she sends back is a resounding 'no'. Prince Ibrahim simply shrugs, as if to tell her that it is her loss.

"Let us hope you have better luck with the king when you meet," Will says. He is no fool, and sees how Ibrahim has been looking at his wife. Under other circumstances he would demand some satisfaction from the man, but it is bad form to run your sword through a royal guest.

"There is no offence intended," Ibrahim replies, with a slight smile. "In

Abyssinia, I have free choice of any woman I want. Your English customs are still very foreign to me, so I must apologise to you, Colonel Draper.

"A danger dark," Miriam Draper says to herself, and starts to slice into a huge fruit pie. "Now, who is for a slice of Russet apple tart?"

"Ah... if I must," Eustace Chapuys says, and they all laugh.

"You are quiet, Master Wyatt," Pru says. "You will not be long away from court... for your master will have need of you one day."

"I have no master," Tom Wyatt replies. "I am a gentleman, Mistress Pru, and answer only to the king."

"And God," Will says.

"Well... yes."

"And to your father." Eustace Chapuys adds. "So, you are answerable to no-one... save Almighty God, the king, your father, and any man you owe money to?"

"A good point," the poet says with a grin. "That does lengthen the list somewhat, Eustace."

"Gentlemen... charge your glasses," Will Draper says. "Let us toast the passing of a most noble lady... I give you... Queen Jane."

"The queen," they mutter, and down their cups to the dregs.

"There will never be another like her," Pru says with a far away look in her eyes. "God save a motherless child, son and no son, prince and no prince."

"My wife tells me you are travelling north soon," Will says to John Beckshaw. "There is much business to be done there."

"I have only just returned, Will," Beckshaw says. "It is odd that your wife should need Pru away so quickly. What of my King's Examiner duties here?"

"Your first duty is to your wife, man," Will replies. "Take her away, John, until it is safe for her return."

"The king would not let…"

"The king is not the enemy," Will replies sharply. "Take Pru away."

"It feels like I am running away," the younger man says to him, "and that is not in my nature, sir."

"None of us are running, John," Will Draper says. "We are simply regrouping, and assessing the best way ahead. When the time comes, as always, you shall be by my side."

9 Preparations

The plans of mere mortals are often confounded by the gods, and so it is that Will Draper is forced to keep Prince Ibrahim of Kush as a house guest until after Queen Jane has been buried with all due honours. It is an onerous task, as the two men, who seemed destined to be friends grow to dislike each other's company. Whilst Ibrahim loafs about the big house, Will goes about his business, leaving his most faithful servant, Adam, to keep an eye on things at home.

"It is not that I distrust you, my love," Will explains to Miriam, "but that I find this foreign prince's manner to be grating, and his observations on women to be most un-gentlemanly."

"I do not take offence, my love," Miriam assures him. "For I find the fellow to be most arrogant. I pray you will get him from under my feet as soon as you can?"

"I shall." Will leaves Draper House with regret these days, but must serve the king's business whenever it arises, or resign his lucrative post. He goes down to the jetty, and asks one of the boatmen to row him down to the Tower of London, where he has prisoners to question. As they slip out into the current, another boat appears, coming upstream, and makes for the Draper's private jetty.

"Will… is that you, my friend?" The loud hail floats across the intervening water and causes Will to turn and look to the oncoming craft.

"Richard, what is it?" he calls back. The two boats glide past one another, a dozen feet apart.

"I have come to ask you out for a drink," Richard Cromwell says. "It is so glum at Austin Friars these days thatI fear to smile."

"I am for the Tower," Will replies, "though my royal guest is at home. You might wish to take him out carousing, and have him turn his attentions to a woman other than my poor wife."

"Ah, then the fellow is nought but a dirty scoundrel," Richard says. Miriam is a fine woman, and he thinks any sane man would want her, so bears the Blackamore no real ill will in the matter. "I shall take him to Madam la Zouche's gentlemen's whore house in Cheapside, and let him take his pick of her lovely wares."

"Stout fellow… I knew I could rely on you. I shall defray your costs, if you send me an account." The boats have become further apart, and the conversation ends with them shouting distant farewells. It is only when Will is out of earshot that Richard thinks about where his friend is going. He is off to the Tower, to see his prisoners, and Richard realises that he is remiss in not explaining that he has already spoken with them.

*

The arrangements for the funeral are well in hand. As custom dictates, Henry leaves the arrangements for Queen Jane's burial to the Duke of Norfolk, in his capacity as Earl Marshal of England, and to Sir William Paulet, who is the Treasurer of the Royal Household. Jane's burial is planned for the 12th day of November. Thomas Cromwell, though not officially an executor of the proceedings, keeps a close eye on matters, and ensures that no expense is spared.

The King himself has, according to the Duke of Suffolk, '*retired to a solitary place to see to his sorrows*', and will not show his face at court until the unpleasant part of things are done with. He has always been this way, and thinks it natural to shut himself away from all those things that displease him.

The two appointed grand functionaries have to send for the

Garter King of Arms to study the precedents, since no '*good and lawful*' queen has been buried in England since Queen Elizabeth of York, back in the year 1502. Despite Jane being the king's third wife, the previous two are not considered to have been fit for the purpose, one because she was not considered a legal wife, and the other because she was, in the king's eyes, at least, a most traitorous whore.

It falls to Cromwell to arrange for the wax chandler to fulfil his roll as royal embalmer, and to see that the Queen's corpse is sealed in a lead lined casket by the same plumbers who had done such a fine job of installing Miriam Draper's new privies at Draper House.

After this is done, ladies and gentlemen of the court, now in mourning, parade about with white kerchiefs hanging over their heads and shoulders, and keep a perpetual watch around the royal hearse in a beautifully draped '*chamber of presence*'. The chamber is lit by twenty-one wax tapers, night and day, until the 31st day of October.

Then it is the Feast of All Saints, and the entire Hampton Court Chapel and the great chamber and galleries leading to it, are hung with white mourning silks, and decked out with images of Henry, and his late queen.

Having dutifully performed the menial tasks, Thomas Cromwell is pushed aside by Norfolk, who sees that the hearse is drawn, by torchlight, to the Hampton Court Chapel where the Lancaster Herald, in a loud voice, asks all present to pray for the soul of the beloved Queen Jane.

After this, Cromwell must see that the priests watch in the chapel by night, and the Queen's ladies guard her by day, until the 12th day of November when the hearse is to be taken to Windsor, borne on a chariot drawn by six white horses, and accompanied by nobles, and heralds with the royal banners. White is the accepted colour of mourning, and it can be seen hanging in every window on the way.

Cromwell is busy conferring with the king, and manages to gain permission for Princess Mary to play out the role of chief mourner. The young woman has recovered from the first flush of grief, which had prostrated her, and will ride at the head of the procession on a horse with exquisite velvet trappings.

At the last, it is Cromwell who has made the final choice of resting place. He understands that though he loved Jane more, the king also loved her, though in a less honest way, and he suggests that the coffin is installed within St George's Chapel, and buried in a vault beneath the centre of the choir. It is the same vault that awaits Henry and, one day, Jane will lie with him forever.

"Her body, but not her soul," Thomas Cromwell tells himself.

*

"What is that you say, fellow?" Mush Draper staggers away from the door of the inn, and seems incapable of standing due to his intoxicated state. The bigger of the two men who he has just jostled is about to sneer, and walk on, but his friend whispers to him. They are both Norfolk men, and here is a Cromwell man, alone, and in his cups. It is a chance far too good to miss, and will earn them a reward.

"I said, watch where you are going... turnip head," the big man replies, and winks at his friend, who slides behind the young Jew. "Or I will give you a fine drubbing."

"Oh, you would think to drub me … you fat bastard?" Mush lurches to one side, and looks ready to throw up, and the smaller man draws his knife from his belt. It will be just another casual stabbing outside a low drinking house. No witnesses, and all over in a moment of time.

He is right, of course, and he errs only in his idea of the actual victim. Mush has seen the move, and lashes backwards with his left hand. The dagger goes into the man's gut, and rips up towards his heart.

"Dear Christ …. murder!" the big man cries, but no one cares to interfere. Mush lets go of the dagger in his left hand, and strikes with the one in his right. The tip goes up, under his enemy's chin, and into the brain. The big man falls to his knees, already dead. Mush retrieves both weapons, wipes them clean of blood, and saunters away from the blood soaked scene.

*

In Arundel, Peter Lackland, one of Norfolk's stewards, is riding with the local hunt. As senior man present, he is allowed many liberties, and uses his position to brow beat the inn keeper into serving them without payment. After downing a half dozen bumpers of free ale, the steward pulls one of the younger serving wenches aside, and forces himself on her.

A few regulars see, and turn away their eyes. It is never safe to get between a Norfolk man and his desires. One drinker watches with revulsion, but the steward has over a dozen armed men with him. The man drains his mug, and slips away from the scene of rapine. He leaves the inn, and runs towards the forest.

His immediate passions satisfied, Peter Lackland leads the hunting party away, and into the edge of the woodlands. Hounds bay, and find a scent. A deer, startled by the sudden presence of the pack, leaps away into the thicket, and they all give chase.

The steward gallops into the copse, after the fleeing deer, and does not come out. It is not until early evening that he is finally missed, and a search is instigated. The steward is found, beside his horse, with a quarrel from a hunting crossbow sticking from his left eye. Someone recalls a man with a crossbow in the inn, earlier, but he is not a local, and there is now no sign of him.

*

There is nothing more dreary than being the mistress of an old man, and Cat Morley longs for more than the Duke of Norfolk's old hands on her body. He is generous enough, but lacks the youthful vigour to keep her satisfied. Because of this, she is wont to accept dinner invitations from other gentlemen, and find some solace in their company.

That evening, she dines with Richard Cromwell, who promises her a special surprise. She arrives at a discreet address, to find the younger Cromwell in the company of the most magnificent man she has seen for some time. The tall, handsome black man is, Richard claims, the eldest son of Prester John of Kush, a famous African king.

After a few glasses of wine, Cat Morley finds herself climbing the stairs with the handsome fellow, and feels the rush of a passion she does not have with old Norfolk. Prince Ibrahim ushers the girl into an empty bed chamber, and guides her over to the waiting bed.

"Oh, sir… would you have your way with me?" she asks, and the fellow grins and pulls the dress from her plump white shoulders. "I see you will." He pushes her back down onto the mattress, and begins to run his hands up, under her skirts.

Below, sitting alone at his table, Richard Cromwell listens to the rhythmic bumping of sexual congress coming from above, and smiles to himself. Norfolk's mistress is a lewd sort of wench, and can refuse no man with gold in his purse. It is a wonder that, until now, she has not come down with some awful thing.

During the course of the day, Ibrahim, who is boastful of his many sexual conquests, has admitted that he is recently poxed by a 'noble' Spanish lady. Though of only minor consideration, the infection causes a most irritable itching at times, and defies all forms of medical treatment.

Norfolk cannot be killed, for the king would not approve of such a crime, but he can be discomforted. Apart from those of his men now lying dead, the old duke will find, to his horror, that he has a painful itch, donated by Prince Ibrahim, through the medium of a shared woman.

Richard drinks off his mug of beer, and considers how well he has taken revenge on Norfolk. Cromwell will nod at the unexplained deaths, and smile, but the nephew will not mention about the cleverly passed on pox. Uncle Thomas can be so prudish about such things, Richard Cromwell thinks.

*

The cost of burying great people is considerable, and Thomas Cromwell understands how easy it is for those left behind to become resentful of the expense. Because of this, he has drawn up two sets of accounts; one for the treasury, and one for the king.

In his wisdom, the king's minister has had Sir William Paulet approve, and sign the one, and the Duke of Norfolk put his seal to the other. In the event of the king ever asking, it will seem that Norfolk has presented a padded account to the treasury, and creamed off the difference for his own coffers. It is a small thing, but it will add to the reckoning, if the duke should ever come under suspicion.

"Two hundred and ninety four pounds, seventeen shillings and four pence?" Henry examines the individual outlays, and nods his head in approval. "Tom Howard has been careful with my money, Thomas."

"I am sure the duke has your interests at heart ... ever since you spoke with him about me," Cromwell says.

"Yes, he was most rude about your parentage," the king says, without realising the offence he might cause. "He quite forgot himself, and called you a 'jumped up butcher's boy'. I was forced to remind him that it was Cardinal Wolsey who was the son of a butcher, and that you were from honest blacksmith stock."

"Most kind, sire." Cromwell presses the point. "How did he take your warning to him?"

"To behave himself with you?" Henry has, as usual, failed to adopt the strong approach demanded. Instead, he has used so many euphemisms with Norfolk, that the duke thinks he has been given the word to prick Cromwell at every turn. "I think he will be more circumspect from now forward, but if not... you must come back to me, Thomas."

The fellow is a bloody coward, Thomas Cromwell thinks to himself. Norfolk will never let him be, unless told to cease his disruptive, and infantile, behaviour.

"Let us hope the duke will see sense," Cromwell says. "Now that you have spoken to him so harshly."

"Strongly... as a king should," Henry says. "Not harshly, Tom, for that is not my way. I wish all my subjects to respect me."

"They all love you, sire," Cromwell replies.

"I should think so," Henry concludes. "Now, what am I to do about taking another wife?"

"Perhaps Your Majesty might

wait until the period of official mourning is over?" Cromwell speaks without thought, for the first time in many years.

"Good God, yes," the king tells his first minister. "I do not mean at once... but in the future?"

"There are several likely candidates, sire," Cromwell says.

"A nice French princess... or a frisky Italian royal."

"Sire, I doubt either the French king, or the Bishop of Rome would be favourably disposed to let one of their women marry so firm a Protestant king." And that is that, Cromwell thinks. Trapped by his own vanity, and with only princesses from enemies of Roman Catholicism available to wed. Good luck with that one, Your Majesty.

"Never the less, we will put out feelers, Master Cromwell."

"Yes, sire." Oh dear, Cromwell thinks, now I am back to Cromwell, and Thomas is reserved for another day. "I shall write to our ambassadors today, and instruct them to make enquiries amongst those places where we are well respected."

"Excellent." Henry wonders where Lady Mary Boleyn is these days, and considers selecting her for the position of royal mistress again. "How is the realm?"

"Quiet, sire."

"No more problems over the Boleyn affair?" Ah, here it comes, Cromwell thinks. The king has something sticking in his mind.

"None, sire. The people love you."

"What of the innocent members of that family?"

"Are there any, sire?"

"I always felt Lady Mary was a loyal subject," the king muses. "She was ever kinder to me than her sister. Is she keeping well these days?"

"I believe she has retired to the country, Your Majesty."

"What... she has married?"

"Not without your permission," Thomas Cromwell says. "No, I believe it is for reasons of ill health."

"Oh, that is unfortunate," Henry says. "Perhaps the country air will help her recovery?"

"I fear not, sire," Cromwell lies. "The doctors recommended her complete absence from court ... in case it was catching."

"Of course... she must obey the doctors," Henry says. "What about Lady Rochford? Is she recovered from her husband's death?"

"Lady Jane Rochford, I fear, is

gaining a certain reputation, sire," Thomas Cromwell replies, more truthfully. "She might wish to return to court, but ... the scandal ..."

"Scandal?" Henry lives a cosseted existence, and seldom hears of the outside world, unless it suits his ministers.

"Yes, sire. Rumour has it that the lady is so ... active, that Tom Wyatt has penned a poem about her affairs."

"A poem?"

"The Ballad of A Lady is said to be most ribald, and names her lovers in a series of comic verses," Cromwell lies.

"Quite disgraceful!" Henry crosses the beautiful woman, who is Richard Cromwell's current mistress, off his list and suggests the name of another lady.

"Recently widowed, sire," Cromwell says, then strikes his hand against his forehead, as if he has just had a thought. "Oh, fool that I am!"

"What is it?" Henry is quite alarmed at his minister's action.

"Forgive me, but I was wondering if two bereaved people might be allowed to console one another ... if in private?"

"I do not see why not," Henry says. "Are you suggesting that this lady might find comfort in my company?"

"Lady Meg has spoken of you in glowing terms, sire," the Privy Councillor says. "She is mature enough, at thirty four, to know that you cannot offer anything more than a few moments of comfort, and a small estate. Shall I broach the subject, sire?"

"Why not?"

Bastard, Cromwell thinks. She is not yet cold, and you seek to find a new bed warmer. He recalls his times with Jane, and finds himself welling up. He wipes a hand across his eyes, and Henry frowns at the gesture.

"Tears, Master Cromwell?"

"Forgive me, but I do so miss Queen Jane," he says with a boldness that takes the king by surprise.

"As do we all, Thomas," he says. "I know she was like a dear niece to you… and that your son is wed to her sister … but we must move on. There is a great realm to rule."

"One final thing, sire." Cromwell thinks he might as well speak about Will Draper's odd guest, and give the king something to occupy his mind, other than other women. "It seems we have a foreign prince amongst us. The Prince of Abyssinia is currently lodged with your Royal Examiner, Will Draper."

"Should I receive him?"

"I believe he has a strange and wonderful tale to tell, sire."

"Arrange it." Henry smiles to himself, and tries to recall where Abyssinia actually is.

*

Will Draper's prisoners are gone. The gaoler, an old childhood friend of Thomas Cromwell, shakes his head and holds out the relevant paperwork. It shows that all five men have been transferred from his custody, and given into the hands of a far worse keeper.

"Given over to Master Abraham Wake, this very morning," the gaoler says. "By order of Tom Cromwell."

Abraham Wake is the Tower's prime torturer, and with some justification, for he knows ways to make men talk that would shame the devil himself. Fortunately, he is also on Will's payroll, and the King's Examiner will have no trouble in gaining access to Walter Tall and his men.

The short walk between towers is along a cobble-stoned path that is flanked by exquisite green lawns. It is a prisoner's last glimpse of beauty, before he descends into the Tower of London's torture chamber. The underground room is designed to strike fear into a man's soul, and the roaring of wild animals from the king's zoo, situated on the floor above, adds to the horror.

"Master Wake, if you please," Will asks of a stunted, one eyed man at the door.

"Who's askin'?" the grotesque assistant demands.

"Colonel Draper... the King's Examiner." The man grunts, and steps aside. It is a name he knows, and he dare not bar the fellow's entrance. As Will steps inside, he drops a penny into the man's hand. "Fetch him for me." The man smiles and lopes off, only to return in a moment with his master in tow.

"Colonel Draper... a pleasant surprise. How might I help you, sir?"

"Ah, Abraham, good day to you." Will holds up his warrant, as a formality. The man is in his pay, as are almost a third of the Tower's staff, and will do his bidding. "You have a man called Walt Tall, and four of his band, I am told. Pray show me to them."

"They are gone, sir," Wake says, with a note of surprise in his voice. "At your orders... or so I was led to believe."

"Gone man?" Will shakes his head in frustration. "Where?"

185

"Above," Abraham Wake explains. "To the animals."

"To the... dear Christ... you are feeding them to the lions?"

"Well, they *are* all dead, sir," Wake says. "It saves on meat costs if we use them as food for the lions."

"All dead... how... why?" Will is struggling to understand, when Abraham Wake produces a signed receipt, for submission to the treasury.

"Five souls at four shillings a head," the King's Torturer tells the colonel. "That is a pound, for but an hour's work, sir."

The receipt, which must be surrendered to a treasurer, in return for his fee, is signed and authorised by Richard Cromwell. It only then that Will Draper begins to understand.

"Cromwell's nephew came here?"

"With the men. He had just removed them from the gaoler's domain, and wanted them to be broken, quickly."

"Which, I am sure, you did."

"I never fail, sir... save on purpose." Wake is alluding to the time he prolonged a man's slow torture, to give time for the colonel to send help. "I trust Master Marsden is well?"

"Well, married to an heiress,

and living in London, much against his wishes," Will says, and smiles. Marsden, a genial country bumpkin is married to Richard Rich's sister, much to the great man's horror. "Now, you must tell me what came about."

"I hung up the first fellow… a rogue without ears… and Master Richard asks if he has a name for him. The fellow shakes his head, so I run my big knife down from his balls to his…"

"Spare me the details," Will says. "He did not speak?"

"No, nor did the next three. Other than to swear they knew not who employed them. Each one went painfully, and un-shriven, into the next world. Then your fellow had the last man hung up, and bid me remove his eyes."

"That sounds very like Richard," Will mutters. "What then, Master Wake?"

"Walter Tall let out a shriek, as would wake the dead, and begged to be spared. Master Richard asked him for a name… and he gave it up. Then I cut his throat, and chopped the corpses up for the lions. You should see the relish with which they…"

"The name, Abraham," Will asks, and Wake repeats what he has overheard.

"The rogue said he was approached by a Welshman, called Williams... as are they all... and that he worked on an estate just outside the town of Hereford. The landlord of this estate ... his master... is a certain Sir Adrian Ball. Does that help?"

"It does, though I am shocked that Richard thought to twit me over this."

"He claimed to be doing it in your name," Wake says, "and I did not doubt him."

"You did your duty, as you see it, and I cannot blame you," Will says. "Here, take this for your loyalty." He drops five shillings into Wake's hand, and the torturer bows.

"You are a better master than the Attorney General," Abraham Wake says. "He does not know how to treat a loyal servant, sir. Why, just the other day, he warned me to be prepared for a number of women in a month's time."

"Women?" Will is nonplussed.

"Witches, he says." Wake sniffs to show his disdain. "I asked for a list, but he just shrugs, and says he has not yet *picked* them."

"Then he means to arrest innocent women," Will Draper guesses. "I must speak with Tom Cromwell."

"I dare say he already knows,"

Wake says, and jerks a thumb over towards the gaoler's tower. Yon fellow is a Cromwell creature, and has been told to ready enough cells."

"It seems that the new Attorney General of England is finding his feet," Will mutters. "Is he really that brave, or has someone greater put him up to this?"

10   A Council of War

"This is a pleasant surprise," Thomas Cromwell says, as he escorts Will into his old library. The books, which were transported to the chambers Queen Jane had given him, are beginning to return, and the shelves do not look too desolate anymore. "How are Miriam and the children keeping, Will?"

"Well, sir. And you?" Will knows his old master is in mourning for Jane Seymour, but does not know the real depth of it.

"Well enough. The king bids me find him a new mistress, Lord Norfolk is seeking to ruin my friends, and your brother-in-law is going about London, slaughtering the duke's men."

"What?" Will Draper does not doubt what Cromwell says, for Mush has been courting death ever since his wife died. It is as if he wants to meet the man who can best him. "By your order?"

"In a way." Cromwell sees he must be as truthful as he can be. "I spoke with Richard, and agreed that some of Norfolk's men might be taught a lesson. He told Mush, who took Kel Kelton and some others, and went about it with a will. To my knowledge, they have killed seven of the duke's followers in London, and another four in Kent and Suffolk."

"Dear Christ, the king will be angry."

"He does not know, and Norfolk dare not tell him… lest he is pressed for a reason. Henry knows how he means to harm us, and will not take sides. It is as if he waits to see which of his lions is the strongest."

"His own are well fed," Will says, and explains about the Tower of London business. He concludes by mentioning how Richard Rich seems certain he will have witches to torture within a month.

"I know," Cromwell tells him. "Attorney General Rich is a cursed fool. He is one moment the Lord Chancellor's man, then he is for Bishop Cranmer. I think Norfolk has whispered in his ear, that the king is worried about witchcraft, and that action might be looked upon in a favourable light."

"To what end?"

"To get at me, through you."

"How so?"

"Richard Rich will arrest a few dozen women… it matters not who they are… save for one. Prudence Beckshaw is the target. Norfolk will have Rich torture her, until she says what he wants … that your wife is the head of her coven. Miriam being in league with Satan would explain all of her immense wealth."

"This is nonsense, Master Thomas, and you know it!"

"Yes, I do, but superstitious Henry does not. Norfolk will whisper into his ear, and say Miriam is a wicked Jewess who consorts with the devil. She will be condemned to death, and her vast fortune… what ever they can find of it … stolen from her. Henry likes you, so might just about let you live. Though you would have to resign your post."

"Dear God."

"Quite. At a stroke, my strong right arm is lopped away, Will, and I am at Norfolk's mercy. Next he will go after Rafe. Oh, how close he always was with Miriam, and how she always seemed to know what the king was thinking. Henry is a fearful sort of fellow, and will react badly. Pru, her husband, Miriam, the children, Mush, Rafe and his family… all would be gone, to make Henry feel a little safer in his bed."

"What can we do?"

"I have arranged for Pru to travel, with some of my lads, which will delay matters just long enough."

"For what?"

"Oh, Will… how I envied you the first time we met," Thomas Cromwell says. "The way you made up your mind, and the way you took action reminded me of myself as a young man. It is time for that old Will Draper, my young, devil-may-care soldier of fortune, to come back."

"Then you think it is in my hands?" Will does not need to ask anymore, for he sees the solution to the predicament in Tom Cromwell's eyes. Sometimes, it is not enough to quote the law, or to do the charitable thing. Sometimes you must act, even if it is against your own conscience.

*

"Your Majesty, might I present to you the Grand Lord Absolute, Ibrahim, High Prince of Abyssinia, and eldest son of the eternal Emperor of Kush … Prester John the thirtieth of that line." Rafe Sadler is well primed by Richard, and uses every title he can conjure up to make the fellow sound impressive.

"Make him grand," Richard had said," even though he is as big a blowhard as the king already. He is good company, but likes nothing better than his own way, and he has a nasty side too!"

Now the king looks the tall Blackamore up and down, and holds out his hand for the kiss of obedience. Ibrahim studies it for a moment them comments.

"Nice rings, King Henry sir, but the diamonds in Kush are five times the size, and lay on the ground, waiting to be plucked."

"Five times the size?" Henry lowers his hand, and decides to forgive the rudeness. After all this big black man is a stranger in a strange land. He sits, and gestures towards the red carpet around his throne. Ibrahim stares, and then glances over to Rafe.

"The king graciously invites you to sit in his presence," Rafe explains. Apart from the two thrones, there is only the floor, and many a noble has had to sit on the carpeted step of the dais.

"Ah, I see," Ibrahim says, and sits on the late queen's smaller throne. "This is most cordial of you, sire. Back in Kush, we do not use such thrones. Prester John sits on a high chair carved from gold, and his people stand below. It is deemed unseemly if any should be taller than he, so we move about in a permanent crouch, lest His Majesty decides to shorten us by a head."

"Good God," Henry says,

admiringly. "Your father sounds like a great king, Prince Ibrahim."

"He has fifty thousand warriors at his back, and the reverence of his people. Because of his relationship to Jesus, his life is sacred. Not one Prester John has ever died before his time."

"His relationship to Jesus Christ?" Henry has quite forgotten that the fellow should be either standing, or sitting on the carpet, and wants only to hear all about this fabled land of Kush.

"Yes, the first Prester John was the youngest brother of Jesus Christ… or rather, half brother. His mother had several children after … and Prester John's father was a Nubian cavalry officer in the Great Caesar's army."

"I see, and how came he to be in Abyssinia?" Henry asks.

"He fled the Roman persecution with his wives, and many of his followers. They journeyed to Egypt, then on to the high plateau that is Kush… or Abyssinia, as you in Engaland call my vast country. There he conquered the local tribes … who are mostly of Nubian stock … and so made his kingdom. We are all Christians, of course, but I am the great, great, great, great, great grand-nephew of Jesus Christ. When Prester John goes to paradise, I will be the next Prester

John... the only living relative of the Son of God."

"Yet you come all this way alone?" Rafe asks, and Henry turns on him in a fury.

"Did We ask for your banal interruptions, sir?" he demands, his face glowing red with anger. "This Prester John sounds like a fine and noble king. A king who does not have to seek the advice of anyone."

"Because he is a relative of God," Ibrahim says. "Are you not also God's chosen one in this land, Henry?"

"I am king, by divine right," Henry says. "You must tell me more. What do you seek from us, Prince Ibrahim?" It is much the same question Rafe asks, but seemingly allowable when said by a king to a prince.

"Big cannon, warships, and soldiers who know how to fight the European way," Ibrahim states. "We are at the mercy of these bastard Portuguese, and would destroy them."

"Sire, a word if I may?" Rafe keeps his eyes down, and makes sure his head is lower than the king's. Henry sighs, and shrugs as if to say *'what do you do with these people?'* to the prince.

"Speak."

"Portugal are our allies."

"I *knew* that," Henry grumbles.

"In Kush, we have mountains made of gold, and diamonds lie about on the ground like *naranjas* from the tree." Ibrahim stands up , then falls to his knees in supplication. "Help us, mighty king, and Prester John will load two of your ships up with ingots of gold and chests full of jewels. We have the riches of King Solomon, and the Portuguese want it for themselves."

"Pray stand, sir... I am not a tyrant to be worshipped like a God. I know I am a mortal man, even though I am chosen by Him to rule." Henry is close to agreeing to Ibrahim's insane request, but he worries about committing so vast a force to invading the unknown parts of Africa.

"Before you speak, Majesty King... might I give you advice?" Ibrahim says. "I see you are unsure, so send me to your greatest advisor, and let him judge me."

"You mean Cromwell?" Henry says.

"I know not, but if he is your man, let me speak to him," Ibrahim says. "Let me convince him of my idea, and then let him advise you."

"A sound idea." Henry looks to Rafe Sadler. "Is Thomas Cromwell at court?"

"No, sire." Rafe has no option but to tell the truth. "Since the loss of your dear, beloved wife, Master Thomas has not been the same. These last few days have worn him out, and he is resting at Austin Friars."

"Resting?" Henry almost laughs. "I hope he does not think to retire again. I will not tolerate the idea!"

"He has quite forgotten the notion, sire," Rafe replies. "It is just that he feels safer at Austin Friars, where his young men can guard him, and tend to his needs."

"Then he can stay there, for now," Henry concedes. "On the morrow, you will have Prince Ibrahim delivered to Austin Friars, and have him speak with Cromwell. Afterwards, I shall expect a full report of all that takes place. Understood, Master Sadler?"

Rafe, who is now *Clerk of the Hanaper*, as well as a relatively new member of the King's Privy Chamber, is a little aggrieved at this off hand treatment, but resolves to keep his mouth firmly closed. He bows, as low as he can without losing his cap, and touches Ibrahim by the elbow. Henry picks up a scroll from a nearby table and opens it, to show that the meeting is at an end.

"Your king is a most pompous fellow," Prince Ibrahim says, as soon as they are back in the outer court.

"Guard your tongue, sir," Rafe Sadler warns. "The very walls have eyes and ears in every royal palace."

"He is also very fat," Ibrahim continues. "In my country, he would be considered a weak fool. Did you see how he let me ignore his hand, and how I sat on his small throne?"

"You did all that on purpose?" Rafe Sadler is outraged, and wonders what he can do about such a blatant offence to the king. "I do not understand why."

"To get the measure of the man," Ibrahim says. "I think I shall get what I wish from your real master. This Cromwell sounds like a great man."

"He is." Rafe cannot hide his admiration from the Abyssinian. "It was he who broke the power of the Roman Church, and it was he who saw an English bible in every pulpit. Master Cromwell has been the genius behind our new navy, and fended off this country's enemies. He will receive you, weigh your character, and discern your worth … all in the blink of an eye."

"He sounds like a *true* king," Ibrahim says, loudly. "I wonder he does not pull your fat fellow from the throne, and sit upon it himself."

"Who is your rather exotic, and very outspoken friend, Rafe?" Fortunately, it is only Charles Brandon, the Duke of Suffolk who has heard, and he is not likely to repeat anything against Thomas Cromwell.

"My Lord Suffolk, may I name Prince Ibrahim of Kush to you," Rafe says, formally. "Your Highness, this is the Duke of Suffolk, who is the king's brother-in-law, and best friend."

"Ah, then you must know how to crawl well, sir," the tall black man says. "It is a poor king who needs flatterers to bolster his childish pride. Do you know this Cromwell fellow?"

"Everyone knows of him," Suffolk replies, tartly. "Save for the odd savage from … Kush. What kind of a name is that?"

"It is Kush's name, sir," Ibrahim jests, and roars with laughter at his own poor attempt at humour. Suffolk offers the slightest of bows, and sets off down the long corridor that runs through the palace. He is almost alone, save for the odd servant slipping by, and he is just wondering where everyone is when a white apparition steps out into his path, and he leaps back in fear.

"Dear Christ!" he bellows, then starts to smile. The white kerchief shrouded apparition shows its face, and it is none other than the poet, Tom Wyatt, all decked out in mourning white. "Tom, you damnable rascal, what are you up to now?"

"I am hanging around, in the hope that the king sees me, and knows how deeply I mourn his loss," the poet says. "Do you think it will work, Charles?"

"Hardly. Henry is already thinking of re-marriage, and he is looking for an interim mistress. He has his eye on that buxom new lady at court …Lady Meg, who has just been widowed."

"Oh, damn," Tom Wyatt groans. "Am I to be permanently dogged by ill luck?"

"Do not tell me you *know* her?" Charles Brandon is the king's best friend, which is to say, he hates him with an almost pathetic vengeance. For years he has had to pander to his childish sulks, and listen to his dreary attempts at song writing and poetry. It raises his spirits when some pitfall looms, and Henry takes a royal tumble into it. "I mean … in the biblical sense."

"The Seventh Commandment,"

the overly licentious poet confirms. "We were two lonely clouds in a darkening sky."

"You swived her?"

"Crudely put … but yes," Wyatt confesses. "I do hope she does not mention it to the king."

"Then she might consent?" the duke asks.

"Why not?" the poet says with a broad smile. "She has never refused any other man. I am surprised you have not been to that particular well before, Charles."

"A chance missed," Charles Brandon says. "Tell me, Tom, as you are so well read… where is Kush?"

"Just to the left of Utopia," the poet replies with a smirk.

"Then there is no such place?"

"Once, perhaps. The Greeks write of it being the land where King Solomon found his fabled mines. Some say it is in Araby, and others that it lies in the heart of Africa."

"Have you not seen Henry's new visitor then?"

"No, I have been wandering about all morning, trying to look mournful," Wyatt tells Suffolk. "What of him?"

"A Blackamore," Suffolk says. "He claims to be the Prince of

Abyssinia … or Kush."

"Ah." Wyatt looks at his friend with a blank expression.

"He has spoken with the king."

"About?"

"I do not know."

"Oh, Charles, you are a veritable mine of information!"

*

"I shall not be dining at home tonight, my love," Will Draper tells his wife, and she gives a theatrical sigh. He is often away on the king's business, and she is fortunate to see him twice a week at the dinner table.

"Carousing?" she says.

"You mistake me for your brother," Will replies. "I have some business that I must attend to."

"The king demands much from you."

"It is family business," Will says. Adam comes in then, with his masters sword, buckler and freshly sharpened *Miserere*. The thin bladed dagger is so called because of its main use… which is to despatch a man 'with mercy'. "Adam shall accompany me."

"Is it dangerous?" Miriam asks, and Will touches a finger to her lips. Do not ask, the finger warns, for you might not like the answer.

"I shall be home by midnight."

"There shall be something cold waiting," Miriam says. "It seems I must eat alone, for your princely friend is off with Richard again."

"You dislike Ibrahim?"

"No, I just wonder…" Miriam dislikes the fact that he speaks better Hebrew than she, and yet, can quote from the Christian bible with ease. "He is a man with two coats."

Will Draper smiles at the expression, which is common amongst Venetians, and seems to him to be most apt.

"Kiss the children for me," he says to her, and sets out on his dark errand.

11 The Warning

Richard Rich is the youngest Attorney General of England ever to hold office, and he is overly proud of the fact. Still only in his mid thirties, he firmly believes that he will, one day, reach the pinnacle of his profession. Before that can be achieved, he realises that there are a few obstacles to be removed.

His friendship with Archbishop Cranmer, and an uneasy alliance with Bishop Gardiner promise him much, but there is the matter of the current Lord Chancellor, Tom Audley. The man is, in Rich's eyes, a buffoon, who only holds the post because Cromwell has refused it. Then, of course, there is Thomas Cromwell himself.

"Where is my damned coach?" he demands, and his secretary leaps to his feet and crosses to the window.

"It has just drawn up, master," the young man says. He is a vain, empty headed fellow, like most of those around the Attorney General. Rich likes to know he is the cleverest man in the room, and finds surrounding himself with coxcombs and idiots helps with his own self esteem.

"I am for Lincoln's Inn to speak with the Lord Chancellor, and then on to Hampton Court." Rich makes the last sound very grand, as if he is about to have a private audience with the king, but the reality is much more mundane. Rich's sister, quite against his wishes, is married to a vulgar Yorkshire fellow, who absolutely refuses to live right in the centre of the city, and Rich must speak with her about the return of certain monies he has held in trust for her… and spent on unwise investments.

She has a small lodge on the Hampton Court estate, and he fully expects a rude reception, and many angry words. Still, he cannot pay what he cannot pay, and that will be that. Her husband is a huge oaf of a man, and might well decide to give Richard Rich a drubbing, so the Attorney general has ordered that the coachman, and two big footmen are armed with cudgels.

He buckles on his sword, an ornamental Siena made thing that has never been drawn, and fastens a great fur lined cloak about himself. Rich fancies that the bulky garment makes him look bigger, and more powerful, but it only emphasises his thinness, his scrawny neck, and his pointed, pasty face. His watery blue eyes betray a certain weakness of character, which he conceals under a huge, elaborately adorned hat.

"I shall be back tomorrow," he snaps as he leaves the chamber. "See that the list of Jews and witches is completed by then."

"Sir… you have yet to give me the names of…"

"God's teeth!" Rich spits, in imitation of the king. "Must I do everything in these offices? Draw up the List of Incrimination, and leave the names blank. Then arrange for two dozen arrest warrants to be made out."

"With no names?"

"You learn fast," Richard Rich says. "We will fill in the names as they are brought to book. Though the warrants for the Jews can be made ready. One for the Draper woman, and one for the king's physician."

"Which one?"

"Theophrasus, of course," Rich tells his underling. "He has been at too many miscarriages, and deaths of queens to live. Henry will be easy to convince, once I bring him proof."

"Master Cromwell will not like it." The young man cowers under a sharp slap to his head.

"To Hell with Cromwell," Rich cries. "I do not fear him anymore!"

The Attorney General, having ordered warrants for almost thirty unknown, and therefore innocent people, strides out into the cold afternoon, and climbs into his coach.

"Lincolns Inn Fields," he calls up to the coachman, and they set off. It is only a few miles, but the state of the road makes it a slow and tedious journey. After a half hour, Sir Richard Rich snuggles down into his great cloak, and dozes off. It not until some while later that he wakes, to find that the coach has stopped. He opens the leather window flap to look out, and sees that it is growing quite dark outside.

"Driver, are we there yet?" he calls, and in answer, the coachman pulls open the door, and climbs in with him. "Are you mad... you ignorant oaf!"

"A little," the man says, and throws back his cowl. Sir Richard Rich, Attorney General of England gives a small, strangled cry. "Did you sleep well, sir?"

"Colonel Draper!" Rich cowers back into his seat. "How dare you. What is the meaning of this?" The demand comes out as little more than a frightened whisper, and Will Draper smiles an evil smile in return.

"I dare, because I must," he says. "As for the meaning ... I think you know the answer to that. I hear you have been supping with the Duke of Norfolk of late, and are of a like mind."

"That is none of your… ugh!" The slap is backhanded, but quite firm enough to snap Rich's head backwards.

"I have no time for your blustering, Rich," Will says. "So let me explain what I know to you. It will save you a few more slaps, I think."

"The king will… agh!" This time it is the left cheek that suffers, and Rich's watery blue eyes well up with tears.

"Norfolk wishes Cromwell to be gone, as do you. He dares not risk a frontal attack, so seeks a more roundabout way of bringing him down. This is also your wish. With Cromwell gone, Norfolk would be closer to Henry, and you can replace Tom Audley." Will pauses, but Rich has learnt his lesson, and remains silent and sulking. "Norfolk tried to have Cromwell assassinated some months ago, and failed. Then he sought to have me killed, and lost twenty men. I see from the look on your face that he has not mentioned these rash actions to you… so wonder what else you are ignorant of."

"Norfolk is a great gentleman," Rich says. "You would not understand the meaning of the word."

"Quite so. Do you recall how your sister met her new husband, and where?"

"At Hampton Court Palace."

"And why would she be there?" Will taunts. "Let me tell you why… as one gentleman to another… Sir Richard. She was there because she was, at the time, mistress to Tom Howard, Duke of Norfolk."

"Liar!" The third slap cuts Rich's upper lip, and starts his nose bleeding. "My sister would never…"

"You damned fool. Your sister was widowed, and under your control. She thought Norfolk was going to support her against you, and he let her down. That is why she married the very man you tried to have tortured for treason."

"All of this is of no interest to me," Rich blusters, and spits blood out onto his expensive cloak. "Why do you dare delay me, when you know I will tell the king, and have charges brought against you?"

"Poor Rich." Will smiles at his unintended jest. "Norfolk has laid information against a friend of mine, and claims her to be a witch. He seeks to ruin my wife by so doing. As a result of this, you think to hide your true intentions by starting a witch hunt across London. How many innocent women would you arrest, because they have odd dreams, or a pet cat?"

"Their guilt is for the law courts to decide," Rich says. "Your master, Thomas Cromwell knows how the law works."

"I am not concerned with Cromwell," Will lies. "He may rot in Hell for all I care. You are attacking my family."

"And mine." One of the 'footmen' appears, and it is Miriam Draper's brother, Mush.

"Hello Dick," the other footman puts in.

"Russell!" Rich feels his heart miss a beat. Sir John Russell is a childhood friend, whom he has wronged in their youth, and who now delights in upsetting his plans.

"You know Sir John, of course," Will Draper says. "He was most keen to accompany us tonight. As for Mush… I could not keep him away. It seems he knows of your scheme to discredit him and his sister, by claiming they are Jews, and he wishes to explain something to you. Mush… pray speak."

"I am displeased," Mush says. "In the last two days, I have exacted retribution on the Duke of Norfolk, by personally murdering five of his men."

"Are you mad?" Rich asks. "To confess such a thing means the gallows for you!"

"I think not." Mush Draper takes out a knife, and toys with it. "Norfolk has been punished, but you threaten *much* more. You seek to have my sister ruined, or even burnt at the stake for heresy, and that must not be."

"The law is…" Mush places the tip of his knife under Rich's chin. "Sweet God!"

"The law is of no use to you, sir," Mush explains. "You will return to your offices, and rip up your warrants. Tomorrow, you will write to my brother-in-law, and inform him that the allegations about his wife, and Mistress Beckshaw are found to be utterly false, and malicious."

"You seek to threaten the Attorney General's Office?" Rich manages to get out, but he is trembling with fear.

"No, I only promise." Mush leans forward, until their noses almost touch. "If you do not do as I tell you, I will come for you in the night, and take you off. Then I will spend a whole day removing your skin from your body. In the end, you will beg for death."

"You would not." Rich cannot

understand that there are other ways; ways that do not need the workings of the law, or the approval of society.

"Then I must kill you, if only to prove my point."

"Last chance, Dick," Sir John Russell says. "Mush is Cromwell's most trusted assassin. It was he who visited Anton Fugger." Rich has heard the story of how the banker, a foe of Cromwell, went to bed, and awoke to find a dagger embedded in the night table by his bed. "He goes where no other man can, and strikes with impunity. This *Jew* kills for the pleasure of it, and let us be clear on this point … killing a worthless turd like you *would* be a genuine pleasure."

"I have already given orders."

"Un-give them," Will Draper says. "For if Mush fails, I will see you meet with an accident. Stop me, and John Beckshaw would kill you like a dog for hurting his wife. Evade all of us, and Sir John Russell here will slip a knife into your throat."

"This is foul murder you speak of," Rich moans.

"Only if they ever find your body," Mush says, "and we have a sure remedy for that. The Tower has hungry lions, and they leave nothing to identify."

Richard Rich knows this to be true, for he actually suggested it to the Tower's chief torturer as a way to cut costs, and the thought removes his last vestige of courage.

"Is that all you wish?" he asks.

"For now," Will Draper says. "If, at some future date, you try anything against any of us… you will be killed without warning. Do you understand?"

"Yes."

"Perhaps I should have you swear an oath?" Will says, then laughs. "No, I think not. For did you not swear, under oath, that Sir Thomas More spoke treason in your presence?"

"Sir, you cannot kill me for something that benefited Cromwell as much as I."

"Careful, sir … for my dear brother-in-law is still a Cromwell man," Will sneers, "and might kill you for that insult."

"And what about you, Colonel Draper… whose man are you?" Rich asks, dabbing at his bloodied nose.

"My own, sir," Will replies. "My very own."

*

"Well bluffed," Sir John Russell says to Mush once they have thrown Rich out on his own doorstep. He looks into the young man's eyes, and shudders. "Ah... you were not?"

"Never tell a man you wish to kill him, unless you mean it," Mush replies. "Had I had my way, I would have simply killed him, and dropped his corpse into the Thames... but Will thought this way better. He says we now have the man under our thumb."

"He is a fool," Russell says. "One day, he will forget your threats, out of greed, and you will have to kill him."

"Good." Mush yawns, and pulls a flask of brandy out of his coat. "A drink to warm your soul, Sir John?"

"Jonty," Russell says as he takes the flask. "My friends call me Jonty."

"And I have been Mush for too many years," Mush replies. "My real friends know me as *Moshe*. It is Hebrew for Moses."

"Then you truly are a Jew?"

"Not enough of one," Mush says. "My grandfather was a pragmatist, and taught me to hide my true self away. Now I do not know who I am."

"Oh, bugger it. Let's go to a whore house," Sir John Russell says. "My treat."

"I cannot," Mush replies, a little

sheepishly. "I have a Venetian mistress, and she is jealous."

"I thought you to be spoken for to … *a certain lady…* whom honour bids me remain nameless?"

"Lady Mary Boleyn was my country mistress," Mush explains, "but I have news from her that she is to marry soon. Some gentleman farmer up in Cheshire."

"Then you must make do with but one mistress," Russell says to his friend. "For my part, I cannot afford one, and must sleep with those women Tom Wyatt has not yet found."

"Our poet is a lively one," Mush says, as he takes another pull of the brandy flask. "Once, I was forced to knock him on the head, and load him on a ship bound for Lisbon… all for the sake of a lady's honour."

"I wonder he does not have to fight more duels with irate husbands, or angry fathers."

"His reputation with a sword is second only to Will Draper's," Mush explains. "Few would have the courage to take offence… for life is not an easy coin to spend, Jonty." The flask is now empty, and Mush glares at it, as if it means to upset him. "Damn it, let us go to your pleasant whore house after all, where they care not if you are an infidel of Kush, an English gentleman, or a wandering Jew."

"Excellent decision," Sir John Russell says. "Though I am a little short of silver this morning."

"I have twelve shillings," Mush says, after a quick rummage in his purse. "We should have robbed Rich before we turfed him out."

"Never mind," says Russell. We need only four shillings for two pretty girls, and another two for a flask of wine. Will you stand me the treat, until the treasury pays my salary?"

"Sir, what else is money for?" Mush says, but he wonders what Isabella might have to say about this proposed adventure. "Lead on!"

*

"Hm… is that you, my love?" Will Draper is surprised at his wife's muttered words, as he has just slipped into bed beside her.

"Of course," he replies, and pats her bottom through the fine cotton shift.

"Oh good, I thought it was my husband." Miriam keeps her eyes closed tight, but cannot help but let out a giggle. Will is quite happy to join in the jest.

"Oh, that boorish fellow," he says in an effected voice. "I hear he is not a gentleman." In a moment Miriam is sitting bolt upright in the bed, and scratching a candle into life with her tinder.

"Who says that?" she snaps. "How dare they insult us so?"

"Hush, my sweet," Will says, and takes her in his arms. "It is but a jest. These courtly fellows think a knighthood makes them into something they are not. I pay them no mind."

"How many of them sneer at Master Cromwell, whilst hoping to have their loans extended?" Miriam demands. She is a spirited young woman, and thinks you should be measured by what you have done, rather than the actions of some ancestor. "How many of these gentlemen claim to have '*come over*' with William the Conqueror … yet cannot raise the price of a new pair of leather boots?"

"A few, my love," Will replies, as he strokes her hair. "Old Norfolk's grandfather claimed descent from a Norman lord."

"Stuff and nonsense," Miriam says. "The man is a shameless dog, who would hurt us, through Pru Beckshaw."

"No longer," Will says.

"Are you sure?"

"You question me, wench?" Will says, and nibbles her ear.

"Oh, I do love a big, boastful, lout," Miriam says, laying back on the bed. "They make much better lovers than gentlemen."

"And how do you know this?" Will asks, as he blows out the candle. Miriam giggles again, and seeks him in the pitch dark.

"One day," she says as her fingers find their prey, "you will be a lord, and I will be a lady."

"Would you love me more?" Will asks, and gasps at her expert touch.

"The same," she replies, pertly. "Though we would have better clothes, I suppose."

"Hush, darling," Will mutters. "Let us not think of clothes, nor waste our time on such silly things. If I have you, and the children, I am content."

"And a fine sword."

"Yes."

"And a beautiful horse… for Moll is getting old now."

"Yes, apart from a gold hilted sword, a white stallion, a ship full of gold, a castle of my own, a wardrobe of new clothes and all the jewels of Kush… I want nothing, save you."

"Your prince is going to see

Master Cromwell tomorrow, by order of the king. Perhaps I should go with him… as interpreter."

"I am sure he can cope," Will says. "He speaks reasonably good English, perfect Hebrew, and his Spanish is as good as… oh, damnation!"

"What is it?" Miriam fumbles for the tinder again, and lights the tall taper by her side of the bed. Will is on his feet, and searching for his discarded clothes.

"Oh, nothing," Will says, angry at himself. "Save that you have not married a gentleman … but a turnip headed fool!

*

"Must we?" Prince Ibrahim asks. "It is late, and I have yet to try that little red haired tart in the corner." Richard Cromwell has kept the handsome Abyssinian company all evening, matching him drink for drink, and he is now quite tired of the fellow's boastful ways.

"We must," he says. "Else how do we find the better man?"

"In Kush, it is our favourite sport, after hunting lions," Ibrahim replies. "You will lose."

"I never lose." Richard Cromwell never boasts, and he states only the facts. No man has ever bested him at arm wrestling.

"Then let us get to it," Prince Ibrahim says. "In Kush, we do not do it the dull English way. We make it far more interesting."

"How so?" Young Cromwell demands.

"Scorpions tethered to each side of the table," Ibrahim tells his drinking companion. "The loser takes the sting."

"We might find a few lice in here," Tom Wyatt jests, "but they do not bite so hard." He is out with Richard for one last time, since he is now compelled to leave court. Henry's prospective new mistress is a lively young widow with a loose tongue, and the poet fears she will disclose how she has been used by him. "What about candles?"

"Candles?" Richard Cromwell is a steady sort of a fellow, and takes a while to catch up with that which others perceive at once.

"We place a lit candle on each side of the table," the poet suggests mischievously. "The first to feel the flame loses."

"I wager a shilling on the *neygra,*" one of the other customers says, and finds himself taken by the throat. The muscular Abyssinian stands, and lifts the fellow from his feet, with one hand.

"I am of noble blood, you stinking dog," Ibrahim says into his terrified face. "You will call me Your Highness … or master." He releases his grip, and the man falls to his knees, choking for breath.

"He meant no harm," Richard says. "Your temper, or your boasting, will be your undoing, my friend."

"We are not too different, you and I," Ibrahim replies. "You pride yourself on your strength, and you bask in the glory of your master, Thomas Cromwell. Do you think your skin makes you a better man?"

"I measure a man by his cleverness, or his physical abilities," Richard replies, coldly. "As for serving my master… I do so with great pride. There is not a better man in England."

"Of course not," Ibrahim says with a lopsided grin. "Even your fat king defers to him."

"Light the candles," Richard says to Tom Wyatt, "and let us see if this fellow can squeal as loudly as he boasts!"

"Ten pounds on the prince." The room falls silent. Such a wager is reserved for the court, and represents a sum beyond the dreams of most men in

the place. The Duke of Suffolk is
pleased at the effect his words have on
them, and seats himself down by the
table. In truth he cannot afford such a
wager himself, being constantly short
of ready money, but it helps to keep up
appearances.

"Where do you have ten pounds
from, Charles?" Tom Wyatt asks, and
the room explodes into laughter. "Your
tailor will be after you for settlement if
he hears."

"I am good for it," Suffolk
replies, huffily. "Our Prince of
Abyssinia will need good soldiers for
his war, and I shall make another
fortune to replace the last one."

"You shall pick up diamonds
from the ground," Ibrahim tells him.
"Prester John will load you down with
golden chains, and give you a hundred
slaves."

"You are on, sir," Richard
Cromwell says to Suffolk. "Ten gold
pounds … against me." The two men
settle down over the table, and the
landlord, as is the accepted rule in such
contests, acts as the referee.

"The elbows must not move,
gentlemen," he says. "The hands must
remain gripped thus … and the spare
hand must be kept behind your backs.
Ready?"

Both men nod, and the landlord makes a cutting motion with his hand. They grip one another's hands, and begin to exert pressure, by centring their energy into their thick wrists. For long seconds there is no movement then, almost imperceptibly the locked hands begin to quiver. The room is so silent that a rat in the corner can be heard, scratching at a wainscot.

The hands quiver, but neither one can gain an advantage over the other. The crowd holds its collective breath as the strongest man in London battles it out with the equally muscular Prince of Abyssinia. The door opens, and Mush Draper tumbles in, arm in arm with Jonty Russell.

"By God... what a lark!" Jonty cries. "Bring us a couple of your best whores, landlord!" The two men fall silent as they perceive what is going on. Two giants, one black and one white are locked together in a monumental struggle for supremacy.

"I wager these two are well matched," Mush whispers, "and fear neither will countenance losing."

The two arms are intertwined like writhing cobras, and the huge fists are locked together in a struggle without armour, or the cries of battle. The crowd grow hushed, and they can

do nothing but concentrate upon the
two fists, and the firmly planted
elbows. A hundred heartbeats pass
without either man giving an inch, and
then another hundred and more. Still,
neither man gives ground, and their
eyes are locked in an unyielding gaze.

Richard Cromwell is a giant,
and he has killed many men with his
bare hands. He has bested the finest
wrestlers in Cumberland, disposed of
fearsome outlaws, and arm wrestled the
strongest men in twelve shires, but now
finds himself up against a true foe.
Beads of sweat form on his furrowed
brow, and run down into his eyes, until
he is all but blind, and the Prince of
Kush does not waver.

Another hundred heartbeats go
by, and palms grow slick with sweat,
yet each man holds his ground. The
huge Blackamore has done more than
any other man against Richard
Cromwell, and seems likely to do even
more. He strains, and heaves ... almost
catching his opponent off guard, but
Richard rallies, and forces them back
into a stalemate once more.

"This is almost godlike," Mush
whispers.

Richard presses hard, and feels
some give, but the prince leans into the
thrust, and matches it, until the threat

passes. The crowd are silent, sensing that only some miracle will ever end so even a contest. Outside, there is a sudden peal of thunder.

There is a loud grunt, followed by a cry of pain from the table, and the combat is over.

12 Confrontations

"You look tired, nephew." Thomas Cromwell makes the comment sound like a reproof. He often spends until long after midnight poring over state papers himself, yet is always fresh for the following day. "Working too hard... or carousing?"

"Entertaining your Prince of Kush," Richard replies.

"No prince of mine," Thomas Cromwell tells his nephew. "He is brought to us by Will Draper, and foisted on us by the king, who wishes me to make his mind up for him. Now... what of the real business in hand?"

"I questioned the rogues who waylaid Will Draper on the Plymouth road."

"Yes, he has written to me, officially, complaining about your interference in the king's matters," Cromwell says. "Though he is willing enough to let you follow up on whatever you found out."

"I am pleased to hear it, uncle." Richard takes up a slice of cold meat from the table, and crams it into his mouth. As he chews, he takes several sheets of paper from his satchel, and spreads them out across the breakfast table in Austin Friars' huge kitchen. He wipes the back of his hand across his mouth, and points at the nearest document. "A signed confession from Walter Tall."

"He could write?"

"Surprisingly, yes," Richard says. "Though the confession is in my own hand, he signed it. It says he was paid to kill Colonel Will Draper, on the Plymouth road, and that he was under the direct orders of a man called Williams... who works for a rich gentleman in Herefordshire."

"You spoke to these men?" Cromwell does not need the gory details, but he is sure that a talking to from his nephew is still a most unpleasant affair.

"I did. Bryn Williams was the land agent of a fellow called Sir Adrian Ball," Richard Cromwell reports. "This is the signed confession of Master Williams here. He was under the direct orders of Ball... and here is *his* confession. Sir Adrian confessed to have acted at the instigation of his uncle, who had been instructed by his lord of the manor."

"You have confessions?" Thomas Cromwell picks up a piece of unrolled parchment that has a bloody finger mark smudged in one of its corners.

"From them all. Williams, and the uncle, both proved difficult, but Ball pleaded to sign." Richard Cromwell has obtained these confessions by a less than subtle mixture of brutality, threats and promises. All three men, having served their purpose, are now buried in the rich Herefordshire soil. "The lord of the manor, Baron Justin Draycott, turns out to be a second cousin of Lord Norfolk's wife, Elizabeth Howard. He was most reluctant to speak to even me at first."

"Tell me you have not murdered a peer of the realm, my boy, even if he is only a lowly baronet," Thomas Cromwell says, and his big nephew smiles craftily.

"No need, uncle. I used an old warrant of the king's to gain entry. His servant could not read, but knew the seal. Then I simply showed Draycott the confessions I already had, and the contents of my bag, and he broke down and confessed his guilt. It seems Baron Warren de la Pole was at Arundel a few weeks back, visiting his relatives, and it was suggested to him, by Norfolk's secretary in person. Then Baron de la Pole went to Draycott, and he set the whole thing in motion. I tried to question the cursed traitor, but he is hiding in France."

"The damned fools." Cromwell smiles at the outcome of the investigation, which blackens Norfolk's name even more. "Will this man, Draycott, give evidence to this effect?"

"Yes, he will," the younger Cromwell says. "I have it in writing, and he knows that if he reneges ... he dies, most horribly."

"Well done, nephew." Thomas Cromwell gathers up all the documents, and slips them into his own satchel. It is only as his nephew is taking his leave that he thinks to ask what was in the bag that so frightened the poor baron into a confession.

"Oh, just Sir Adrian Ball's severed head," Richard replies. "It had a most salutary effect."

*

It is a busy day for Thomas Cromwell, and appointment follows appointment with a briskness that gives him no time to languish over the loss of his dear Jane. No sooner is Richard out of the door, than Ned Seymour calls. He is shown into the refurbished library, and served with wine and a tray of morsels to pick at.

"Good morning to you, Ned," Cromwell says, as he makes his appearance. "I see you are fed and watered. Excellent." He takes a seat behind his desk, and steeples his fingers in a way that says 'proceed' to his guest.

"What are you playing at, Cromwell?" Ned Seymour demands. "How dare you remove the prince from my care. The king shall hear of your actions, and no mistake!"

"The Prince of Wales," Cromwell muses. "Such a grand title for so small a boy. Why, the king might make him more than that yet. Henry speaks of his son with the greatest love, and would grant him estates, and titles, beyond the scope of most men."

"Is that why you stole him from me?" Ned Seymour barks, and two of Cromwell's young men appear at the door, as if ready to pounce on him. The Privy Councillor holds up a hand, and waves them away.

"Pray, do not anger my fellows, Ned ... for they are likely to beat you for your rudeness." Seymour is open mouthed at the sheer insolence of the man, and the crudity of the threat. "I suggest you temper your speech, and lower your voice."

"You would threaten me?" Ned Seymour knows that whoever holds the new prince, holds power over the king, and can gain much for themselves.

"Return the prince, or face the consequences."

"The very words I was going to use to you, had not my nephew acted as he did," Thomas Cromwell replies. "He saw the danger you were in, and acted. You should thank him."

"Danger… me… what are you saying?"

"Prince Edward has been loaded with titles, and each one brings a dowry. The Principality of Wales earns some forty thousand pounds a year, whilst lesser titles bring in ten or twenty thousand a year." Cromwell consults a document on his desk. "The guardian of the prince would have control of two hundred thousand a year. A tidy sum for Henry to consider."

"What do you mean?" Ned Seymour seeks to gain power through his nephew, Edward, and had not thought of any accrued income. "Two hundred thousand pounds… my God!"

"The king would not care for any other man to be so rich, or so powerful, Ned. You would come under suspicion, eventually, and I would be forced to investigate you."

"Investigate me?" Ned is alarmed at the thought. "For what?"

"Treason, theft, kidnap, fishing without a licence… what matters it? Do you know how many cases I have investigated, where the accused survived?"

"You threaten me again, sir."

"I warn you. Play the good uncle all you wish, but do not presume to take on roles not yet delegated to you. Edward is safely back home, and I have told the king that you sought only to care for the dear boy for a few days... until he was ready to assume full parental control. I did not mention the money."

"I had no intention..."

"I know that, Ned. Are we not related? My only beloved son is wed to your dear sister... and we are bound to one another. It only remains for you to understand who is *head* of this extended family."

"How do we benefit?" The Seymours are a grand old family, who really did come over with the Conqueror, but their family fortunes are at a low ebb. Ned and Tom Seymour are masters of little more than Wulfhall, a couple of smaller manors, and a few hundred acres of sheep pastures.

"I do not seek to benefit, but to serve," Cromwell says. "As must you and your brother Tom. I shall suggest to the king that you are both useful men, and recommend positions for you.

These placings, in charge of a
dockyard, or as master of the king's
chandlery, will pay a couple of hundred
a year a piece. With a dozen such
positions, you will soon have over a
thousand a year each."

"That is a start, I suppose," Ned
Seymour concedes.

"Of course. As Edward grows,
you will have to assume more and more
responsibility. With each new placing,
you will become richer. Why try to
steal the whole loaf, when you can
have it, a slice at a time, in complete
safety?"

"What you say makes some sort
of sense," Ned says with a grudging
nod of the head. "It was never my idea
to take little Edward, you understand."

"Of course," Cromwell says,
and has to suppress the urge to laugh.
The suggestion that the younger brother
is to blame is entirely ridiculous, and
the remark shows how loyal the
Seymour siblings are to one another.
"Pray, counsel your brother Tom to be
less headstrong in future, and we shall
all prosper to our heart's content. Be
content, and all will come good."

"One day, Henry will…" Ned
starts, but Cromwell slams his hand
down on the desk and makes him jump
in terror. To even speak of Henry's

ultimate death is forbidden, and idle speculation could see them all ruined.

"You are one word away from uttering treason against the king," Cromwell warns him. "Good day, sir."

Ned Seymour leaves, and wonders how it comes to pass that Thomas Cromwell always has the say over him? He considers all that has come to pass, and fears that the king's minister has saved his hide, and guided him truly. Even though it is for his own benefit, Cromwell's intervention grinds on his nerves, and he resolves to keep his future options open.

*

"Make a note," Thomas Cromwell says to one of his young men. "See that Edward's guards are always our men, and that the Seymour brothers are given posts that keep them away from court as much as possible.

"Good posts?" the young lawyer asks.

"Yes, lest they grow foolish and greedy," Thomas Cromwell decides. "Is the Duke of Norfolk here yet?"

"He sent word that it is for Cromwell to call on Norfolk, as he is the greater man of the two."

"Did he, by God." Cromwell chuckles at the man's audacity.

"So, we did as you said, and

hinted that it was a matter of great concern, that would benefit him greatly. He asked what, and our messenger hinted that you are preparing to retire, and wish his help to smooth the way with the king."

"And he fell for it?"

"He did, sir." The young lawyer smiles at how simple a deception can fool even a clever man. "His greed betrays him, and he thinks to help you out of office. Our agents inform us that he is on his way from Chelsea, and will be with us by midday."

"Then we must feed him," Cromwell says. "Have cook send in a couple of chickens, and a flagon of beer. His Lordship likes strong ale to wash down his meal, as I recall."

*

"When do I get to meet your marvellous Thomas Cromwell?" Ibrahim asks Rafe Sadler.

"Soon," Rafe replies. "He must see Ned Seymour, and the Duke of Norfolk first. We shall eat, and see him in the afternoon."

"Why am I made to wait?" Ibrahim asks. "Am I not a royal prince?"

"It is because you are a royal prince," Rafe says with great diplomatic skill. "Master Cromwell does not wish to fit you in, and so restrict the interview. He honours you by this action."

"Really?" Ibrahim considers this to be a reasonable answer, and in truth, he is in no hurry to come into the man's presence. His mission is not so urgent that it cannot wait an hour or two. The outcome, he reasons, will still be the same.

"Does it hurt?" Rafe gestures to the blister on the back of Ibrahim's hand. The prince scowls, and slips his hand under his cloak.

"I underestimated Master Cromwell's big nephew," Ibrahim says. "It will not happen again... I assure you."

"Ah, Richard is a one for his trials of strength," Rafe Sadler says. "If ever I was to challenge him, it would be to something he does not excel at... like thinking quickly."

*

The Duke of Norfolk is here, Master Cromwell."

"Ah, at last. Show him in at once, and do not let us be disturbed," Cromwell says.

"Colonel Draper is also here."

"Damnation... what now?" Thomas Cromwell considers for a moment, then decides. "Let him wait.

The King's Examiner can examine my wall hangings for a while. Send in Norfolk."

Cromwell arranges himself behind his desk, and eases open the right hand top drawer. Inside it, there is a beautifully ornate Turkish dagger, a gift from Mush after his recent trip to Corfu. It is unlikely that he will need it, but the nobility can be quite unpredictable, when cornered.

"Ah, my dear Lord Norfolk... do take a seat." Cromwell does not rise, and the blatant discourtesy angers the old duke. He glares at the king's first minister, then flops down into the chair nearest the fire.

"No shilly shallying about, Master Cromwell," Norfolk says with his usual bluntness. "Your man seems to think you are ready to step aside. Is this so?"

"Well, I have become aware of some bad feeling towards me, and my position of late," Thomas Cromwell replies. "Perhaps the best way to stop all this, is to ask the king to allow me to retire."

"He refused once... so why not again?"

"You might impress upon him the urgency of the matter," Cromwell says, and Norfolk scowls deeply.

"And have my ear chewed off again?" Norfolk asks. "I think not, Cromwell. If you wish to go, then go, and be damned to it."

"If I give the king good enough reasons… he might relent."

"Are you serious?" Norfolk asks. Cromwell nods his head, and gestures to the scattering of papers across his desk top.

"I am. It has come to a pretty pass when certain people conspire to murder a King's Examiner. Why, I ask myself, would they stop there? Would they not then be emboldened to strike at ever higher flying targets?"

"You must do as you choose." The Duke of Norfolk has no intention of being a Cromwell scapegoat again, and will not speak with the king.

"Yes, I must. The king must be told about this latest plot."

"What plot?"

"It seems a fellow paid some dangerous rascals to attack Colonel Draper on the Plymouth road," Cromwell says. "It was a perfidious Welshman … called Williams."

"Good luck with that," Norfolk snipes. "Wales is full of men called Williams."

"This one was living in Herefordshire," Thomas Cromwell

explains, "so was somewhat easier to find. He implicated his master, before he died. The master then implicated his, and he his. Until we find ourselves at the top of the tree."

"What are you saying?" Norfolk sees that his careful chain of command has been unravelled, and starts the process of absolving himself of any blame. "That some fellow is bearing false witness against me?"

"Did I mention you, sir?"

"I am here, am I not?" Norfolk replies, tartly.

"I have a sworn statement, from a close family member, My Lord Norfolk. What say you to that?"

"Lies."

"How can you say, when I have not yet told you what it contains?" Cromwell watches Norfolk squirm, but is aware that he has a busy day ahead, and needs to finish with the man quickly. "It seems you have been suggesting wicked things to this relative."

"Then he misunderstood," Norfolk says. "How often does the king make a casual remark... only for some overly eager idiot to misinterpret it? I might say *'oh, but that such a fellow is a thorn in my side'*, and they think that to mean something quite dark and sinister. So they go to someone else and say 'Lord Norfolk wishes such a thing'. Soon, some village idiot thinks he will be richly rewarded for killing someone."

"Of course," Cromwell concedes. "It can happen so very easily, My Lord. However, in this case, we have the very man who first spoke with you. My nephew has spoken with him and, without any torture, extracted the most amazing confession. In short, your wife's relative implicates you in a plot to murder the king's men, and undermine the king's peace. He also swears ... on oath... that you consort with the Bishop of Rome to bring his church back to England, and put a Roman Catholic on the throne."

"You mean Princess Mary?" Norfolk shakes his head. "This will not run, sir. Henry has a son... a legitimate son. Mary cannot rule."

"Not whilst Edward lives," Cromwell says, softly. "Our witness will say that you plotted to have Edward kidnapped by his uncle Ned, so that you could get at the child. Henry will believe this, because he already knows how the Seymour brothers tried to misappropriate the Prince of Wales."

"Your man lies."

"He is a nobleman, sir... and

has not been tortured. He came
forward, and laid information against
you, for the good of the crown.
Because of this, he is exempt from
prosecution. His lands will not be
forfeit, and his life will be spared. You,
on the other hand, will come under
grave suspicion."

"You scurrilous bastard!"
Norfolk clenches his fists, and glowers
at his old enemy. Then a thought occurs
to him. "You are a liar, sir... for Baron
de la Pole is in France."

"Really?" Cromwell sighs at the
ease with which the man is so
completely undone. "I did not mention
Warren de la Pole, did I?"

"Oh." Tom Howard sees that he
has as good as confessed his
involvement, but not in front of
witnesses... thank God. "My cousin
Henry will not believe a word of it."

"Nor will I," Thomas Cromwell
says. "I will defend your honour, My
Lord. I shall go to the king, and insist
on a full investigation ... during which
you will be lodged in the Tower of
London, for your own safety. I shall ask
that the King's Examiner be appointed
to investigate, and let him get on with
it. How long, I wonder, before he traces
back from our traitorous baron, to
Master Williams... and to the very

rogues who attacked him."

"I might have said something ... untoward," Norfolk concedes. "You know how things can be misconstrued after a few drinks, Cromwell. Though ... upon my oath as a nobleman ... I never meant any real harm to come to anyone."

"If only there were no signed confessions," Thomas Cromwell says. "If only your wife's relative had not mentioned the Bishop of Rome... whom he called 'Pope', or the royal succession to the throne of England. I have it all down in writing ... undated, of course... and would be forced to put it in as evidence. Now, let me see how it would appear on the charge sheet ... attempted kidnap of the royal heir should be enough, but then we have the attempted murder of the king's man, colluding with the Pole family and the Bishop of Rome, and plotting to remove the legitimate heir, and replace him with Princess Mary. Dear God, My Lord Norfolk ... had you a dozen heads to cut off, there would not be enough."

"Your case is an absolute tissue of lies, you loathsome son of a whore." Norfolk makes as if to stand, and Cromwell drops a hand to the knife in his open drawer.

"Sir... you slight my dear

mother's memory. Shall I also add that to the list of charges?"

"What do you want?" Norfolk demands. "Were it just my death, I suspect I would be in the Tower already."

"Most shrewd, Lord Norfolk," Cromwell admits. "As much as I would like to see your head on Traitor's Gate, I desire something else far more."

"Name it."

"You must stop your slanders against the Draper household."

"Ah, then I am right. She is of Jewish blood, and so is her damned brother. Very well, consider it done."

"Then you must stop these ridiculous witch trials."

"That is for the Attorney General's Office to decide."

"Sir Richard Rich has already folded, sir," Cromwell tells the flustered duke. "It seems his will is weak when it comes to burning innocent women."

"I see. What else?"

"You must write to Reginald Pole, and arrange for him to return to England, secretly."

"So you can have him killed?" Norfolk sneers. "By Christ, Cromwell, we are cut from the same cloth, you and I. The man is doing you no harm in

Italy."

"He is in France, sir," Cromwell replies. "You will write what I tell you. If he returns to England, he will receive a fair trial."

"I could tell you to go swive yourself, and take my chances," the duke says. "Henry is as wary of you as he is of me, these days."

"Then please leave." Thomas Cromwell reaches for the bell on his desk., and Norfolk holds out a restraining hand.

"No... wait." He considers the chance he runs in going up against Cromwell at the moment, and sees that he is at a disadvantage. It is Cromwell who has the king's ear, it is Cromwell who arranged the marriage to Jane Seymour, and it is Cromwell who has helped provide an heir to the throne. Then there is the small matter of him actually being as guilty as sin, and the papers being there to prove it. "Is that all?" he growls.

"You will cease to meddle in my affairs," Tom Cromwell concludes. "I bear you no personal ill will, My Lord. You hate me, because I am a commoner, but I help to rule well, do I not? This country is rich, in part, because of me. Your wool fetches the best price it has ever done, because I know how to deal with the Flanders weaving houses. In short, I do all the work. Stay by Henry, and hunt with him. Tell him funny stories, and swap tales of great battles to your heart's content, but leave me to run England efficiently. Is that clear?"

"Yes." Norfolk can say no other. Henry is so fearful of treason, and attempts to undermine him, that Norfolk would be an easy mark at the moment. Cromwell need only point out that a traitor's estates, and his wealth can be confiscated, as soon as the axe falls, and he is a dead man. "It is clear that you think more of yourself than others do. Might I go now?"

"Of course, My Lord, and thank you for your gracious help in these matters. I know you hold me in low esteem, but might I offer you a word of advice?"

"Go on."

"You have a new mistress, I believe?"

"What of it?"

"Have you slept with her during this past week?" Cromwell asks him.

"It is none of your bloody business …" Norfolk snaps, "but no, I have not had time."

"Good. Then do not. For your own sake, give the whore a bag of silver, and send her packing. Heed my warning, sir."

"Why, what do you know?" Norfolk does not expect the answer he gets, when it finally comes.

"E v e r y t h i n g ," T h o m a s Cromwell says to the astonished duke. "*Absolutely* everything."

13 The Wild Rover

Andrew McCloud is that peculiar mix of Scots father and French mother that proliferates north of the borderlands, and gives him so clear cut a view of the world. There are but two factions for him to consider … those he likes, and those he does not. This philosophy has served him well over the years, and his taste in friends ranges from clever street urchins, to grand lords.

Of all his friends, he considers Miriam Draper to be one of the finest, and so accords her the honorific of *Milady*, and treats her, as closely as possible, like he would a man. It is to her that he has come over the matter of his missing passenger, and wonders if she can be of some help.

"A Spaniard, you say?" Miriam furrows her brow, and tries to recall any such instruction. "I wrote to you, and bade you give a Spaniard passage on your ship?"

"Just so, Milady," the captain says. "The old fellow came to me with a letter, bearing your seal. He claimed to be a good family friend, and was related to you through the Coventry branch of the family… though he looked, and sounded, more Spanish to me."

The allusion to Coventry reminds Miriam how few people know of her Jewish blood, and the fake papers that prove she is from the midlands town, provided by Thomas Cromwell.

"So, you effectively smuggled some Spaniard into England, thinking him akin to me?" The captain of *The Wild Rover* looks suitably abashed, and twists his cap in his hands in anguish. He is just coming to realise that he has been taken advantage of, and that his actions might reflect badly onto his employer.

"I thought to do you a favour, Milady," Captain McCloud replies. "He seemed to be such a gentle old soul, praying all the time, and I saw no harm in it. Only now, he has vanished from the ship… and we cannot find him anywhere."

"Then he is here without permission," Miriam replies. "That seems to indicate that he is up to some mischief. This man is nothing to do with me, Captain McCloud, and I cannot understand why he should play so strange a jest on you. I will mention it to my husband, and ask his advice."

"The man knew personal details about you, and your family, Milady," the captain persists. "It can mean nothing good. He knows what your seal looks like, and certain confidential matters concerning your business. I have made a serious mistake. I can only now think that he is a dangerous enemy… and I … damned fool that I am… have brought him to your very door."

"Pray calm yourself, my dear Captain McCloud," Miriam says. "What possible harm can one elderly man do?"

*

"Where is he?" Eustace Chapuys is almost white with anger, and does not know how to react. His secretary, a young man from his own home city of Annecy, is agitated at his master's dismay and gestures to the closed study door.

"I answered the door, and the fellow started talking about how tired he was from his long journey. Before I could think, he was past me. He was in the house almost before I knew it, sir," Antoine Desailles reports. "It seems he came here by ship, and has entered the country without any legal papers. He also claims you were expecting him."

"Mother of God!" Chapuys throws open the door, and is confronted by a slightly built man in his late fifties, who is dressed in black, and wears a bishop's ring upon his finger. "My dear Bishop Sanchez ... is it really you?"

"In the flesh," Sanchez says, and holds out his hand for Chapuys to kiss the ring of office. "I come in the utmost secrecy, my old friend, and hope you have kept my coming to you private?"

"I have told absolutely no-one... not even my most devoted servants," Chapuys says to the small prelate. "Which is why my secretary was taken so much by surprise." Alonso Gomez knows, of course, but is away for a couple of nights, visiting an agent in Norwich. "I do not understand what is..."

"Going on?" Bishop Sanchez says. "Of course not. You are not privy to the workings of the Grand Inquisition."

"Mother of God!" Chapuys crosses himself. The Inquisition exists for one reason alone... to bring those lost souls back to the fold. "You are here on their business?"

"I am their representative." The bishop gestures for Eustace Chapuys to take a seat in his own study. "The Grand Inquisitors have decided that, for religious reasons that do not concern you, someone must die. I need to get as close to this heretical enemy as possible, and you are well placed to offer me some help afterwards."

"How so?" Poor Chapuys sees he is enmeshed in some vile murder plot, and does not know how to extricate himself without offending the Inquisition. "I am a diplomat, my dear bishop… not a trained assassin. What use can I possibly be to you in this matter?"

"Afterwards, you will provide immunity to us, because of your status as an embassy. We, in your company, can leave England inviolate. In short, Ambassador Chapuys, you are our perfect escape route; our one chance to fulfil our mission, and escape with our lives intact."

"But why?" Chapuys asks. "Surely, if God wills this death, he will ensure the safety of his chosen instrument?"

"God moves in mysterious ways. It might be that he has put the idea of using you into my head. Even the most dedicated of assassins must have some hope of escape," Bishop Sanchez replies. "You offer us that hope, Chapuys. Their king will not risk violating your ambassadorial position for the sake of a petty revenge. He will fear the emperor's displeasure, and let you slip us safely out of England. With such a strong chance of getting away with it, a hardened man will take the opportunity."

"The opportunity to do what?" Chapuys asks, but he is already beginning to suspect the awful truth.

*

Thomas Cromwell has had a busy day of it, and would like nothing better than to sit down with a fine wine, and a good book to read. He has just received a copy of *The Castel of Helth* by Sir Thomas Elyot, which purports to be a veritable almanac on healthy living, and how to keep the body's humours well balanced.

Elyot is an acquaintance of Adolphus Theophrasus, and claims to be a self taught physician. The book, the author claims, is a model for sensible diet, and explains the worth of regular exercise, and balanced bowel movements. In a rare moment of weakness, the privy councillor endorsed the work as a favour to his friend, Doctor Theophrasus, and the free copy is a thank you from a grateful Elyot who now has orders for a hundred copies.

It is with regret that Thomas Cromwell puts the small cloth bound volume aside, for he realises that he can put the next task off no longer. The king demands that he meets with the fabled Prince Ibrahim of Kush, and discusses the likelihood of launching a military attack against the kingdom of Portugal, for the promise of some vast imagined treasure. He looks about the library, to ensure that all is in readiness, then rings the small bell on his desk. A young man puts his head around the door.

"Master?"

"Is the Prince of Kush still without, Jonathan?" he asks of the young man.

"Yes, Master Tom," the lad replies. "He arrived here with Master Richard. I took them some wine, and beer about an hour since. Now, the big *neygra* is declaiming for all to hear. He is entertaining the scullery maids with tales of lion hunts, and far off, magical, lands."

"Very well… have him come in."

"Alone, sir?" the lad asks. He is aware that security about Austin Friars has tightened since the attempt on the master's life by Beresford and Sir Francis Weston before their execution, and this command does not fit the usual routine.

"Yes, alone," Thomas

Cromwell says. "Have Richard sent off to the kitchens. I am sure he is quite famished with all this lion hunting." Jonathan Cox grins at the thought of his master's nephew wrestling with so wild a beast.

"Master Richard could probably overcome the *Nemean* lion of the famed Herakles," he replies.

"Providing he has eaten well," says Cromwell. "Now, do as I bid you, and send in my black prince."

"Yes, master." Jonathan bows to Cromwell's will, and is backing out of the library when he recalls something else he has to relate. "Ambassador Chapuys has just arrived, and is with a friend of his."

"Am I expecting him?" Cromwell knows his own diary well enough, and there is no mention of his friend coming ... not even in the hope of a dinner invitation.

"No, Master Thomas."

"Who then is with him?"

"A clerical gentleman, by the cut of him," the young man informs his master, "though not of the English faith, sir. He has the sharp pointed beard of a Spaniard, and a rather spectacular jewelled crucifix about his neck."

"He is attired entirely in

black?" Cromwell enquires.

"Yes, master, but with purple velvet at the neck and on both of his cuffs," the lad observes.

"A Roman Catholic bishop then?" says Cromwell, and the youngster is forced to shrug at his own sad lack of ecclesiastical knowledge.

"Old enough to be one, perhaps?" he offers.

"Very well. Have them wait, at least until I have the measure of this magnificent Abyssinian prince." Thomas Cromwell flicks an imaginary speck of dirt from the sleeve of his new otter skin doublet, and prepares to be amazed. "Show him in."

*

Jonathan Cox does not like the idea of his master giving interviews without at least an armed secretary taking notes behind a screen. He goes in search of his law tutor, Barnaby Fowler, whom he finds in the kitchen, and begs him to warn a couple of stout guards to be on hand.

"This Abyssinian is as tall as Master Richard, and looks like he can handle himself," Cox explains, and Barnaby astutely nods his understanding. The young man returns to the main hall, where Prince Ibrahim is still entertaining Richard, the newly arrived ambassador, and his friend, with a ribald tale of a curious little monkey, and a sleeping snake.

The prince sees that his time is come at last, and he stands up. Richard also rises to his feet, and holds out a big restraining hand to Ibrahim, who looks blankly at him, then nods, as if in sudden realisation. He unbuckles his belt, and hands over both sword, and knife to Cromwell's cautious nephew.

"A most admirable precaution, my friend," Ibrahim says to him. "Wish me luck, my brothers... for I am charged with saving my realm this day."

"Good luck, Prince Ibrahim," Ambassador Chapuys says, with a lavish bow. He is here under orders from the bishop, and does not know how to warn them that the old prelate seems intent on murder. Now this amusing prince is leaving, the ambassador might get the chance to whisper to Richard, or to one of his young men, so that the dangerous old man can be stopped, and searched for weapons.

It is important that Chapuys is not suspected of betraying the Grand Inquisition's man, lest he finds himself suddenly called back home, to face charges of treason.

Then, quite unexpectedly, the Bishop of Alghero steps up to the big prince, and hugs him. It is a comical sight, as there is almost two full feet between them in height.

"May God Almighty aid your blessed endeavours, sir," he says, and steps back. The prince bows, and makes for the closed library door. He half expects that Richard Cromwell will cry out, or have his progress halted, but nothing happens. He puts a hand on the heavy iron knob, and pushes the door back. The knife, which the clever Spanish bishop has slipped into his doublet hangs heavy at his breast. It is a neat trick, and ensures that he does not have to face Cromwell unarmed. He could, of course, break the fellow's neck, or strangle him, but the ancient dagger of Saint Longinus is razor sharp, and will do the job most efficiently.

He steps into the room, lit by four long tapers set in the walls, and moves towards the great oak desk. It is occupied by a single man, busy scratching at a parchment with a penknife, as if trying to eradicate some earlier mistake. His hand goes to the opening in his doublet, and his fingers curl about the ornate hilt of the blade within. The figure hunched over the

desk pauses, then looks up, and
Ibrahim pulls his hand clear of the
concealed weapon.

"Ah, Prince Ibrahim... how are
you this fine day?" Will Draper puts
down his quill, and sprinkles sawdust
over the warrant he has just completed.
"Forgive me, but it is an arrest warrant,
and it is most urgently needed."

"Colonel Draper... I did not
think to see you here." The big
Abyssinian casts a glance about the
room. "Where is your famous Master
Cromwell today?"

"Called away on more pressing
matters," Will says. "Pray, take a seat,
and try some of this rather delicious
wine."

"Your king *assured* me that I
would meet with Thomas Cromwell,"
Ibrahim says, sharply.

"Yes, but not *when*," Will
Draper tells him. "First, I must speak
with you, and clear up a few small
things that have come to cloud my
mind."

"What is it you wish to know?"
The big black man sits down, warily,
and reaches for the wine.

"How comes it that you speak
such fine English?"

"I am quite sure that I have
mentioned this to you before, when we

first met. Your language was taught to me as a child, by my father's ministers and various wise men," Ibrahim replies. "I found it hard to master."

"And your Spanish?" Will asks.

"Picked up during my travels," Ibrahim explains. "I was over a year in Spain… either in prison, or travelling. You might say I was self taught… but out of necessity."

"And your Hebrew?"

"The tongue of my people," Ibrahim replies. "When we fled Israel, after the fall of the temple, it was all we had of our culture."

"Yes, my dear wife, who knows these things, remarked on how well you spoke Hebrew," Will Draper says. "Though she did think it rather odd that you spoke it without a classical, or pure, pronunciation."

"Is she then really of the Hebrew race?"

"Are you?"

"My people are Christians, and they left the Holy Land almost one thousand six hundred years ago," Ibrahim says. "We speak the tongue that has evolved amongst us."

"Clever." Will pours himself a glass of wine, and drains it down in a couple of deep swallows.

"What do you mean?" Ibrahim

begins to feel uneasy, and wonders where all this is leading to.

"You sailed from far off Abyssinia, to England... and overcame many hardships... to ask for our help in defeating the Portuguese."

"Yes."

"Yet you know we are allies."

"Yes, but I have hopes that our fabulous treasure will change your minds," Ibrahim says. "My father, Prester John, wishes us to be friends, and promises a fortune in return for your help."

"Prester John... ruler of Kush." Will shakes his head. "Yet when I spoke with Adolphus Theophrasus, a learned Greek at the court, he said that the title was invented by an Italian charlatan several centuries ago. He put it in a forged letter, which he hoped to sell to the then Pope."

"You doubt my father's title now?" the black man blusters.

"Oh, I doubt everything, Ibrahim," Will says. "It is my nature. At first, I simply assumed you to be a fraudster, intent on some financial gain. Then I thought you might wish to dupe the king out of a great fortune. I even considered that you might, indeed, be a royal prince, and that you are telling me an approximation of the actual truth."

"What do you think now?" Ibrahim puts down his wine glass, and brushes his hand against the place where the knife hangs inside his doublet. The touch reassures him. He is bigger than Will Draper, and he thinks himself able to overcome him in a fight.

"Now, I *think* nothing," Will says. "I *know* the truth. You are not from the land of Kush… or Abyssinia. You are merely a Spanish Moor. One of those thousands who became Christian, and so were able to carry on living in Spain. I suspect that is why you were chosen. Someone in Spain wishes to put you inside our court, and get you close to the king, and to Thomas Cromwell. They must have spent months inventing your tale."

"I am Prince Ibrahim of …"

"Enough of this!" Will bangs his fist on the desk. "You are a Spanish spy, sent to murder Thomas Cromwell. When you did not make any attempt against the king, I wondered why not. Then it finally came to me… that Cromwell is the real target. It is Cromwell who opposes the Bishop of Rome's doctrine, and it is he who supports protestant causes across the Holy Roman Empire. Your master, whomsoever he might be, wishes him dead … yet could not get anyone close enough to do the wicked deed. Why, even our own lords have tried, and they cannot kill my old master!"

"You think I would…"

"No more lies," Will says. "Let the truth be known, my friend. Your fabulous tale was invented, purely to get you noticed. It was important that the king met with you, and then sent you to meet with Thomas Cromwell. Once in his company, you were meant to kill him… and escape… but how?"

"You seem to have all the answers."

"Enough of them. To kill Cromwell, or even attempt it, means certain capture, and a terrible death. Yet you chase after whores, drink to excess, and lust after my own dear Miriam. You do not seem the sort of man to martyr himself for the sake of his adopted religion, Ibrahim."

"Nor am I," Ibrahim says. "What makes you so sure I am not who I claim to be?"

"It was on the road. I can only imagine your horror at falling in with me at Plymouth, when what you meant to happen was so different. You had yourself landed away from London, so that you might spend the time in making a slow progression. As you approached London, your fame would spread far and wide, until you would be feted as the novelty of the year. Under such circumstances you would have soon found yourself in noble company. Great lords do so love to have their *natural fools* and mountebanks around them. It makes them feel superior, you see… and it lowers their guard. Once close to the court, and accepted as a harmless novelty, you could seek out and kill Thomas Cromwell, then make your escape."

"Nonsense."

"Not so. The letter was a clever move. It added authenticity to your claims, and put the local pastor in your camp. Unfortunately for you, he involved me. By chance, I came to visit poor Reverend Craven on an entirely different matter, and he saw a chance to pass you on to someone else. So, I and Kel came upon you, unexpectedly on your part, and you had to fall in with my immediate return to London. To do otherwise would have raised my suspicions. There was now no chance for you to build up your fanciful tale. Instead, you spun me your fabulous yarn, and hoped I would place you inside the court, upon our return. Like a complete fool, I obliged."

"You believed me," Ibrahim tells him. "What evidence have you that I am other than a royal prince of Kush, my friend?"

" It was only the other night that I recalled a conversation we had on the way, in which I mentioned the Spanish ambassador to you. You referred to him, by name, as Chapuys. How came a wild Abyssinian to know that particular gentleman's name? From that moment, the scales fell from my eyes. Then Richard mentioned how a secret Spanish agent had been discovered, and taken a few days ago. I regret that he was killed for his trouble. Before he died, the man gave Richard Cromwell an unfamiliar name: The Bishop of Alghero."

"Ah." Ibrahim holds his hands up as if to say... there you have it. "I see I am quite undone, Colonel Draper, and must hope you treat me with some degree of civility still."

"Then I am right." Will Draper sits back, and smiles at his own cleverness. "This Bishop of Alghero was to be your salvation?"

"Yes, you are right, my friend," Ibrahim confesses.

"I knew it. That same gentleman who is now sitting outside, waiting for you to strike." Will sighs.

"Once Cromwell was dead, you would rush into his arms, and the two of you throw yourselves onto the ambassador's mercy. Chapuys claims your souls, and the king is powerless. Am I right?"

"Perhaps, but as none of these things have come to pass, I wonder where you think this is all going?"

"Then you admit it?"

"Admit what?" Ibrahim smiles at his inquisitor. "That I am Spanish, and of Moorish descent? That I am educated enough to speak Hebrew, English and Latin? Of course. Let us imagine a poor soldier for hire, who has a chance to make his fortune. He is approached by a powerful cleric, but is unwilling to die for a cause he does not altogether believe in. The man who kills this Thomas Cromwell will not live… or will he? A plan is formed. Let some clever mummery be played out, so that I might get near my prey, yet also let me have a chance of living."

"Then the bishop is sent to shield you, and bring you safely back to Spain… thanks to Eustace Chapuys."

"Poor Chapuys," Ibrahim says. "A vain dupe, used without having any idea of his true involvement. Bishop Sanchez was to ensnare him into the plot, but the suddenness of my progress made him have to rush things. Your little Savoyard diplomat is like a blindfolded man... blundering around, arms held wide. I dare say they will recall him now, and he will be a ruined man."

"And you?" Will asks. "I cannot arrest a man for only wishing to kill Cromwell, nor can I arrest a bishop of Rome without proof. Will they welcome you back to Spain?"

"Oh, I am probably a dead man," Ibrahim says. "The bishop must blame someone for this pathetic failure... so why not me?"

"You might wish to consider your options," Will says. "Why not turn your back on Spain, and work for me?"

"For you?" Ibrahim wonders what trickery is afoot. "Or do you mean for Thomas Cromwell?"

"Cromwell wants nothing to do with you," Will says. "Once I told him of the plot, he washed his hands of the whole affair. You, and your ultimate fate, are my concern now. What say you?"

There is a sudden commotion in the outer hall, and a flurry of shouts and curses. Will Draper leaps to his feet, and crosses to the door. He throws it open, only to find Eustace Chapuys

sitting on top of a cursing Bishop of
Alghero. Thomas Cromwell has
entered the hall, and Chapuys, fearful
for his friend's life, has finally thrown
caution to the winds.

"Take him!" Chapuys cries. "He
means to kill Master Cromwell!" Two
young men appear from behind a
screen, hoist the ageing prelate to his
feet, and hastily search him for any
concealed weapons. Bishop Sanchez
slaps at their hands, his arms fluttering
like a small bird's wings, and protests
his complete innocence. Then he sees
Ibrahim grinning at him, and realises
that the game is up. The man has failed
him, and Thomas Cromwell is standing
within ten feet of him, and he is very
much alive.

"Damn you, Chapuys," the
bishop spits. The Savoyard diplomat
has made an outrageous choice,
between the English, and the Roman
Catholic faith, and favours a dangerous
protestant in front of the will of God.
"How dare you accuse me… a bishop
of the true faith, of murder? They
warned me that you were dangerously
close to these English heretics, but I
waved aside their stories, and avowed
to them that the Eustace Chapuys I
once knew is a staunch supporter of the
Holy Roman Empire, and of Pope

Paul."

"My Lord Bishop," Chapuys replies, "I seriously doubt that Pope Paul gave his blessing to such a vindictive act. You are wrong to blame Thomas Cromwell for all the ills of this world."

"He is unarmed, sir," one of the men set to guard Cromwell observes. "What are your orders?"

Thomas Cromwell has been watching this odd little mummery play itself out, and glances across to Will Draper, so that he might shed some light on things.

"It seems there has been a misunderstanding," Will tells him, without a flicker of expression on his face. "This saucy fellow, who calls himself a prince, came here to trick you in some way. I think he meant to dun you for money... to fight the Portuguese. It was a silly ruse, which I saw through at once. I was admonishing Ibrahim, when we heard the commotion."

"Which was the Holy Roman Ambassador, losing his wits, and leaping on a bishop," Tom Cromwell says. "This much I understand, but why attack Bishop Gomez, Eustace?

"I... I thought him a threat to you, Cromwell," Chapuys replies, hesitantly. He has nothing to offer but his word that the bishop spoke of some high ranking fellow's death. He was sure, once he spoke out, that they would find a knife on the man, or some other damning evidence. "You are disliked back home, and I feared they meant to do away with you."

"Disliked me, you say? They are a clever lot, for they sought to use a sixty odd year old bishop who hobbles about on a stick as an assassin." Thomas Cromwell says. "How was he to do it, my dear old friend... read me extracts from the *Book of Ecclesiastes*, and so bore me to death?"

"Blasphemer," the bishop mutters.

"Come now, bishop," Cromwell says. "I seek to clear your name, and you abuse me? Perhaps I meant only that the way you read it was what bored me?"

"I came to pay my respects," the Bishop of Alghero says, stiffly, "and am attacked for my troubles."

"Not by me, sir," Cromwell replies, with a wry smile. "Nor by any of my young men. They sought only to raise you from the floor, after Eustace knocked you over."

"Then I am free to leave?"

"Sir, you have only just come,"

Cromwell says. "Have you letters of introduction for me from your masters?"

"No… they were lost… at sea." The bishop finds himself hemmed in by his own lies, and is at a loss as to how he might extricate himself. At any moment, he thinks, the black mercenary might confess all, and get them both killed, or thrown into a dungeon.

"Ah, yes. I believe the crossing of *The Wild Rover* was a little choppy," Cromwell concurs. "Perhaps you might consider more conventional ways to visit us in the future?"

"I know not what you mean." The little bishop wonders just how much his enemy knows. As if in answer, Thomas Cromwell pulls a sealed document from under his doublet.

"Here, sir. Passage back to Cadiz… courtesy of His Majesty the King. Henry does not like foreign priests running about England unsupervised, and advises you to be aboard ship as soon as is practicable."

The bishop takes the proffered papers, and offers his hand for the usual kiss. No one stirs, and after a moment, he leaves the chamber to the sound of his own footfalls. The second the doors swing closed behind him, Thomas Cromwell grins.

"Oh, Eustace… you saved my life… you ass!" he says, and several of the company chuckle. "Why would that scrawny old fellow think he could murder me?"

"He spoke of it, almost as a done deed," Chapuys admits.

"Yes, but not by him," Cromwell replies. "Rather by *him*."

Ibrahim sees the pointing finger, and returns an ingratiating smile as if in his own defence. He reaches into his doublet, and draws out the dagger given to him by the bishop.

"I mean you no harm, sir," the big black man says. "See, I have brought you a wonderful gift. It is the very dagger used by the wonderful Saint Longinus… who was the…"

"I know my bible, Master Ibrahim," Cromwell says. "Now, must I have you deported back to Kush… or will you accept Colonel Draper's kind offer?"

"Kush is too warm at this season," Ibrahim says with a sly smile. "Besides, I find myself out of funds, and unable to even buy myself a glass of beer. It seems that I cannot return to Spain, for fear of losing my life, and England offers me a new home and easier pickings. I have travelled far and wide, and I can say, without any hesitation that the girls here are much prettier than anywhere else in the world!"

"Very well... you may live," Cromwell says. "Use him well, Will, and make sure he keeps out of my way."

"Then every one is happy," Eustace Chapuys says, sulkily. "I have saved your life, and for what? I can never return home now."

"Poor Chapuys," Thomas Cromwell says. "You make too much of things."

Perhaps, the little Savoyard thinks, but he can still hear the words the bishop uttered to him when he protested at the would be murder: *"Cross us, Chapuys, and you shall answer to the Grand Inquisition!"* Once the bishop reaches Toledo again, he will blacken the character of everyone concerned, if only to make his own failure seem all the less. The emperor will have no other option but to strip him of his rank, and recall him to face an investigation.

The Inquisition is a heartless machine, and he doubts he would survive its grinding justice.

14   The King's Fool

"The Bishop of Durham has written to you, sir," one of Cromwell's young secretaries says.

"What does old Tunstell want now, Cedric?" Thomas Cromwell asks. "Did I not reward him enough for his help with the recent rebellion?"

The bishop was a great help in swaying Henry towards the right course, and owes his position in life to being in Cromwell's good offices. He is that rarity amongst priests... an honest man. By duping the king into doing right, he feels completely at one with his conscience, and still able to act in a manner befitting a true servant of God.

"It is not a begging letter," Cedric answers. "At least, not on his own behalf. He addresses you as a man of law, and seeks your expert opinion on a legal matter which is much vexing him at the moment."

"Really?" Thomas Cromwell sighs, and gestures for his young man to continue.

"He writes of '*an innocent, and quite natural fool*' whom has spoken words of great malice against the king. This fellow says the king is an ass, and not worthy to rule England. Instead, he capers about, and claims the title for himself. He is half witted, and most folk simply laugh at his antics, but it seems that the Earl of Cumberland seeks to hang him for it. Out of compassion, the bishop wants him spared. He writes to you, hoping you will explain the finer points of the law to His Lordship."

"Henry Clifford is a good servant of the king," Thomas Cromwell says, "and earns his keep by guarding our northern borders against the Scots, but he is a dunderheaded fool when it comes to the law. Write to him, and explain that the law provides for natural fools, and places them under the specific guardianship of the king. As such, no true fool can be tried for utterances against the crown, or the king."

"As you wish, sir."

"As the law wishes, Cedric," Cromwell replies. It is so much a part of his life, that Thomas Cromwell can no longer act outside it without causing himself many sleepless nights. "This *natural* fool is considered innocent, because his condition is natural, and not put on to gain some advantage. He is touched by angels."

"Like Will Somers?" the secretary says. "There is a fool that knows nothing of the natural."

"Just so," Cromwell tells his young man. "Will Somers is, by reason of his razor sharp wit, considered to be the finest ever King's Fool. The fellow is made a fool, but not a true one. He knows how to twist his words about, and make them sound witty. Because of this, he is not a natural fool ... or idiot. Were he to slander the king, he would have no real defence in law."

"Because he feigns his foolishness, sir?"

"Just so. The Fool is no real fool, and must stand trial, but the innocent fool is a true fool, and is to be helped and pitied. Now, be off, and let me ponder in peace."

The secretary bows to his master, and slips out of the well stocked library. The shelves are adorned, once more, with those precious books that had to be moved to Cromwell's chambers at court. Now, with Queen Jane dead, the king has consented to his return to Austin Friars, along with his precious library.

"You make a good point, Bishop Tunstell," Cromwell mutters to himself. "Can a man be condemned, simply because he is a fool? Or must we favour those who are too infirm of mind to see the wrongs they do to others?"

"Uncle... are you..." Richard Cromwell pauses in the doorway, and glances around the chamber. "My apologies. I thought you were speaking with someone."

"My conscience," Cromwell says. "Come in, Nephew, and let me use you as the Devil's voice."

"You wish some advice from me, sir?" Richard is wise enough to know that only an Erasmus, or a Thomas More could fulfil such a role with any success. "I fear my wit is not up to the severity of the task."

"You are wiser than you think," Cromwell tells his huge nephew. "You speak without thought... and that removes the possibility of guile. What am I to do about this Prince of Kush you so like to arm wrestle with?"

"He has lied to us, and tried to deceive us," Richard says.

"That is what *he* has done, not what I should do."

"He meant to kill you."

"He failed," Cromwell objects. "Besides, he did not even try to kill me. Will Draper says he had a dagger hidden in his shirt, yet made no attempt to use it."

"Had you been present..."

"Ah, you give me an *if*." Tom Cromwell sighs. "*If* he had not met

Will, or *if* the king had not sent him to me… I can go on all day long … *if* you but wish, my dear nephew."

"Then what will you charge him with?" the younger Cromwell asks. "He pretends to be a prince, and seeks to fool us all."

"Then he is a true fool," Cromwell says. "For his part was doomed once he met Will Draper. His guise was seen through, almost at once. Can we really punish a man for being a true fool?"

"You want to find a clever reason to let him go," Richard discerns. "Some trick of the law that will save him from the hangman's noose?"

"The law says he is guilty of trying to dupe us," Cromwell says, "but the penalty for that is not death. Does not the King's Fool, Master Somers, dupe the king on many occasions?"

"In jest, sir!"

"I never found him that funny," Cromwell mutters. "No, the false Prince of Kush will not hang at my behest. I was resolved to send him back to his masters with a curt note, so as to make them feel foolish, but Will Draper has other ideas."

"Then Will Draper decides for us?" Richard is jealous of his friend's influence, and speaks without thinking.

278

"Would you have me spurn his suggestions?" Cromwell shakes his head, wearily. "He has the king's ear, and his wife is making our fortunes for us. Why is there nothing to find against us when the royal accounts are audited?"

"Because of Miriam."

"Just so. We use her as a filter for our wealth," Cromwell says. "We trust her, and she makes us richer by the day. We have no need for petty corruption, when that sweet girl can turn our honestly earned shillings into pounds. Of course I listen to her husband!"

"What does he want?"

"The prince," Cromwell says. "In return for his life, the man is bonded to the Drapers... for life."

"Then he is to be their slave?" Richard shrugs. "Just as long as he does not come weaving his silly stories to me anymore. He is little more than a great oaf."

"I doubt we will see him again," Cromwell says. "At least, not for many years. Now, what about my dearest friend, Eustace Chapuys? Pray give me your views on the fellow."

"He did a very brave thing," Richard says. "Though it was a foolish act. It seems that the bishop spoke of your death, and he thought that Bishop Sanchez was to be the actual assassin. He says that he wished to tell us, and warn us of this fellow, but had no chance. At the end, when you entered the outer chamber, he thought you were about to be struck down. That is why he threw himself on the bishop, and started to shout for help."

"Then his intention was most certainly pure," Cromwell says. "Eustace Chapuys is the most honourable, and noble creature I have ever come across. It is a pity that his career… and quite possibly his life… is coming to so sad an end."

"How so, sir?" Richard is fond of the little Savoyard diplomat, and considers him to be almost part of the Austin Friars family. "There is no real harm done, and the Bishop of Alghero suffered nothing but a blow to his pride, and a bruised arse."

"Would that all men were as forgiving as you, my dear nephew," Thomas Cromwell replies. "The bishop's master is to be the next Grand Inquisitor of Spain. Such men never forget a slight, and he will be sure to exact vengeance for his minion."

"But uncle, Eustace only sat on the pompous old fool."

"And announced him to be an

assassin," Thomas Cromwell says. "The good bishop is, of course, quite innocent. In so far as he did nothing overtly aggressive towards us."

"What of the knife in the Blackamore's coat?" Richard is vexed that he did not realise the trick, and is made to look like a dunderhead. "Does that not show clear intent to murder?"

"The bishop simply denies ever seeing it," Cromwell explains. "He claims to be here on a visit to Ambassador Chapuys, and wished only to meet with me. The law is with him, Richard."

"Then poor old Chapuys is in a sticky position," Richard says. "For this bishop must answer to his master in Toledo, and will not care to stand the blame. If the Moor is nowhere to be found, then our Eustace must fill the martyr's shoes."

"That is the way with politics," Cromwell muses.

"Will they recall him?"

"Certainly."

"Might they arrest him?"

"Probably."

"Could they punish him?"

"Of course," Cromwell confirms. "Eustace Chapuys is one of the finest diplomats this sorry world has ever seen, and he has served his master, the Holy Roman Emperor, with zeal, and fortitude. Unfortunately, he is not a Spaniard. He is a Savoyard, and his first language is French. It will be an easy matter to frame false charges against him. They will claim he has had his head turned by our protestant ways, and that he is now a heretic."

"That is a damned shame, sir." Richard Cromwell ponders the difficulty, and will do for some time, for he is not the equal of his uncle in wit or wisdom, and needs more time to think. "A most damnably damned shame."

"I am summoned to Whitehall Palace," the older Cromwell says, after a lengthy pause. "The king claims to have a weighty matter to discuss with me. He has the getting of another wife on his mind, and there is little room for anything else."

"Already?" Richard shakes his head. "The king is not one for letting the daisies grow beneath his feet, is he?"

"I fear not," Cromwell says. "Still, a new wife would keep him from being under ours. Have an escort readied, and send word to Will Draper. Tell him … tell him the prince is his, and remind him that I do not wish to see our royal Abyssinian friend again, ever!"

"As you wish, Uncle Thomas," the younger Cromwell replies. "Good luck with the king." He envies the close relationships his uncle has with Henry and the more senior lords at court, and wonders if he will ever be able to move in such heady circles. For the moment, he must deal with lesser men, and help tidy up their messes. Chapuys is a friend, and must be saved in some way.

Cromwell hints at it, and expects his nephew to carry out his unspoken wishes.

*

"A charlatan you say?" Henry is in his privy chamber, surrounded by his barber, his doctor, his Master of the Stools, and Charles Brandon, the Duke of Suffolk.

"I regret so, Your Majesty," Thomas Cromwell says. "After an investigation by Colonel Draper… your Royal Examiner, he is found to be no more than a natural fool who does not understand the difference between truth, and lies."

"Then we must stretch some truth into the rogue," Henry snaps. He has been taken in by the man, and was looking forward to sharing in the riches of the land of Kush. "Have him hanged, but slowly."

"You cannot do that, Hal." All heads turn to the Duke of Suffolk, who has the temerity to gainsay the king. "You heard what Cromwell said. The fellow is a *natural* fool... a simple minded creature that can recite tall tales in the manner of a parrot."

"Is this so, Thomas?" Henry asks. "I *cannot* hang the fellow?"

"Sire, you are king of this realm, and so can do anything you wish... however... to hang this particular knave would be against the law. Natural Fools are protected, by order of the king. You would be seen to be going against your own sound judgement, and certain people might wonder at your actions."

"Then the man is unfit of mind?" Henry is loath to excuse someone who has hoodwinked him so perfectly.

"Mad as a Nottingham goose," Suffolk puts in. "Why, who but a madman would believe such ridiculous claims? Even Tom Wyatt, a man of wild fancy, knew that it was all nothing but a silly prate. Jewels lying in the streets, and a king who is Christ's great grand nephew... I ask you!"

"Of course, I saw through him at once," Henry replies. "That is why I sent him to Thomas. If I let him live, what will become of him? I pay a fair pension to my King's Fool, but cannot support every addle-pated bumpkin who wanders into my court."

"Mistress Draper has taken it upon herself to look after the fellow's needs," Cromwell says. "She is setting up houses for the poor, and those who cannot think, and will find him a place within their walls."

"Poor Houses?" Henry shakes his head in wonderment. "Is there a need for such places?"

"Your people are, on the whole, prospering, sire," Cromwell tells him, "but one cannot avoid the odd widow, orphaned child, or maimed ex soldier. Rather than have them beg in the streets, Mistress Miriam sees they are fed and sheltered, in return for an honest days work."

"She is a fine woman," Suffolk adds. "It is a pity that she is not a man, else you could elevate her in some way."

"Yes, that would be just." Henry's mind churns slowly, then spits out an idea. He has been led to like a horse to water. "Might I not improve her standing with this court by elevating her husband?"

"Would that I had your clever mind, sire," Cromwell says, "so that I could be a better servant to you. You see, where we are blind. Of course, you are right. Colonel Draper's elevation to the status of knight would make her Lady Miriam."

"Have it done… and grant them some land," Henry says. "What have we to spare?"

"Nothing, sire," Cromwell replies. "Though I am currently looking at Reginald Pole's holdings around Shrewsbury and Stafford."

"Does the swine then still blacken my name in Rome?"

"Yes, sire. His last public letter claimed you to be an illegitimate king, and an usurper of the throne." Cromwell enjoys passing on this perfectly true piece of gossip. "He says your new church is false, and your bible nothing more than a distorted fable."

"Did it, by God?" Henry slams his fist down onto his dressing table. "Strip him bare, Tom… and deed a few hundred acres to Will Draper."

"As you wish, sire."

"This rogue wishes to shave me now," Henry says. "Then good Doctor Theophrasus wants to look at my piss, and read the omens. All I want to do is speak on the matter of my new wife."

"Once mourning is done, I shall

be happy to present you with several options, sire."

"No ugly ones," Suffolk says, and the king laughs at the jest.

"She must be clever, but not too clever," Henry says, "and she must not be of a displeasing nature. I might travel to Calais, and meet a few prospective brides."

"Pray, do not do that, sire," Cromwell warns. "The French will mutter that you are desperate for a wife, and spread ugly rumours. Because they resort to strangling and poisoning their unwanted queens, they think we are the same."

"Bloody French," Henry curses. "Can we not put our army in the field, and take Normandy from them?"

"With you at their head, our men would sweep the field of Frenchmen, sire," Suffolk says, excited at the thought of plunder.

"And lose ten thousand men," Cromwell says. "We have no need of their land, when we have their wealth. They need our wool, our leather and fine silks, and they need our timber. We sell it at a high price, and put import taxes on the wine and furniture they sell to us. We do not need to take over a poor country... for fear of having to support it."

"That makes sense, though I would love to…"

"Why not pick a fight with the Scots?" Cromwell says, with an ingenuous smile. "They are always raiding our border towns, and need to be taught a lesson. Let My Lord Suffolk raise ten or twelve thousand men, and ride north to harry them in their own land. Why, you might even ride into battle at the head of your own great army."

"Cromwell!" Suffolk is appalled. To risk the life of the king so blatantly is a thing not to be contemplated. "You wish the king to put himself in mortal danger?"

"Danger?" Henry is incensed. "Was it not I who charged the French at the famous Battle of the Spurs?"

"Well… yes." Suffolk dare not speak the truth, as the king has, many years since, convinced himself of his heroic deed.

"Then I can route a few thousand ragged arsed Scots, can I not?" the king asks.

"Bravo, sire!" Cromwell encourages the king to this great act of folly for two reasons. He knows that if Henry falls in battle, there is a legitimate male heir to take his place and, more importantly to Cromwell, he deeply resents how the king has treated his late beloved Jane. His loyalty to the king is overcome, temporarily, by his dislike of the man, and he wishes to do him some small harm.

"Then make it so," Henry declares. "Issue a warning to their king. Tell that weak jawed James to desist, or face my mighty wrath."

"He will back down," Suffolk says.

"I hope not," Cromwell says, "for I have a mind to travel, and would gladly ride alongside my king."

"Oh, dearest friend!" The king is in full flow, and will not be thwarted of his dream. "Your courage will shame my great lords, and spur them into action. Cumberland will raise his troops, and Warwick too. Even old Uncle Norfolk might answer the bugle call, one last time. If not, then Will Draper shall be my general."

"Hail to Henry... King of England, Wales, Ireland... and soon... Scotland!" Thomas Cromwell almost laughs at the insanity of it all, and pictures the king, gout ridden and obese, being hoisted into the saddle. Then he thinks of him, charging into twenty thousand wild Highlanders and being hacked to pieces. "May God guide us, and grant us victory!" he cries.

"When?" Henry demands.

"Why, as soon as young King James cares to pick up the gauntlet," Tom Cromwell replies with mock enthusiasm. The veil of his dislike shifts, and the minister sees how destructive his advice might be to England. He continues to show enthusiasm, but tempers it now with genuine advice. "Though we must be careful who we leave behind to guard our backs. With us in Scotland, the French are sure to try their hand against us. Still, once we have done with James, we can return south, and drive the French back across the channel. We might leave Norfolk behind, to hold London … if he can."

"This will take much careful thought," Henry says. Once his fervour dies, he sees why such an expedition might prove fatal to both himself, and his dynasty. "I do not want the French at my throat. Put it down for discussion at the next council meeting, Master Cromwell. A king, even one with my own martial fervour, must always be guided by prudence."

"Yes, at once, sire." Henry will never ride into battle again, Cromwell thinks. Instead, he will spend the rest of his days eating, drinking, and searching for a new wife. "With regards to your impending re-marriage... might I suggest we look to those royal states who have also thrown off the heavy yoke of Rome?"

"You have mentioned this to me before," Henry says. "Have you already chosen me a bride, Thomas?"

"Not I, sire," Cromwell says. "I wish only that you find happiness, and a mother for little Edward. The ladies of Flanders, and the cities of the Hanseatic League are every bit as lovely as the French or Italian women, and the Spanish girls are far too pious."

"Pious... yes, just so." Henry leans back, and the barber starts to scrape at his stubbly cheeks. "Find me a girl with a love of life in her, Thomas. Young, but not too young. Fair of face, and shapely of form. Find me a woman fit for a king's bed, my friend!"

*

Rafe Sadler wonders why he has allowed himself to become so useful to the king. The man's demands are constant, and he is almost at his wits end over the latest task he has been given. The great ledger set before him contains the names, and details, of every eligible woman in Europe, and he has been carefully editing it for the past two days. Each name is considered, and rejected for a variety of reasons. Some ladies are too old, and some are far too young. The king cannot wed a twelve year old, Rafe thinks, if only for decency's sake.

Then there are those noble women who are Roman Catholic, and will not renounce their faith, even for the promise of a royal wedding. These are mainly Spanish, Italian, or French, and their love of the Bishop of Rome would make for an uncomfortable marriage with the protestant Henry.

One princess, of a suitable age, and with a fine dowry, has refused to even speak with the English ambassador, because she believes the awful stories she has heard about the king. The tale goes that, once he takes their virginity, the king beheads his bed mates, personally. The ambassador protests that such a tale is both unfounded, and decidedly wicked. The girl does not wish to risk her neck, and so stands her ground. She would choose a lifetime spent in a nunnery, rather than occupy King Henry's bed, she insists. So Rafe Sadler sighs, and scratches her name out with his quill.

After considering the flowers of Flemish womanhood, and removing all those who are too old, or have a known infirmity of either mind or body, he finds the cupboard to be quite bare. There is the nineteen year old Princess Theresa of Luxembourg, a lady of dubious lineage, and a Burgundian duke's daughter, suspected to be of doubtful morals already on his sparse list, but he must find the king more names to consider.

He realises that he must cast his net further a field, and begins to look at the small city states, who form volatile leagues amongst themselves, to help stave off the intervention of either the emperor, or Pope Paul.

Even here, he finds few dukes, princes or electors who are willing to ally themselves to a man who discards wives so readily, and uses the protestant church for his own ends. They are dour, pious fellows, and seem to cherish their daughters every bit as much as their sons. Name after name is considered, and struck off.

At last, Rafe lights upon a small duchy on the north western border of Flanders. It is a part of those Germanic states, which are fiercely Lutheran protestant, and it trades, almost exclusively, with the larger English mercantile houses. The people are a mixture of German, Flemish and Low Dutch, who call their prosperous little state *Kleef.*

The Duke of Kleef, John III, has a twenty three year old daughter, who is unmarried, protestant, and fairly rich. Rafe Sadler considers all these points, and wonders what the girl looks like. It seems to him that a visit to the place would soon establish if this girl, Anne, is a suitable partner for the king.

After some deliberation he transfers the details to a separate short list he is compiling for Thomas Cromwell to peruse. He places the information to one side, then retrieves it. He reads through it once more, then picks up his quill. He dips the sharpened nib into his freshly ground ink, and draws a line through the name Kleef. Above it, he writes '*Cleves*'.

"There… that will roll off the tongue better," he mutters to himself. "*Anne of Cleves*. May God help her if she is successful!"

15   Terra Nuevo

It is a quiet evening at court. The king is in a foul mood, and does not want any, save a few favoured friends to share dinner with him. This means that a hundred hangers on must fend for themselves, and beg a free meal where they may. Suffolk is an ever present, of course, along with a dozen hunting friends, and as many ladies... chosen for their looks, rather than their conversation.

The king's minister, Rafe Sadler slips in to the long dining chamber, and makes his way towards the king's seat. One of Jane Seymour's ladies sees his approach, and slides away from Henry, whose immoral interest she has been trying to cultivate, but in vain.

"Sire, the Holy Roman ambassador is here," Rafe Sadler whispers into the king's ear. Henry grunts, and tosses down the capon's leg he has been gnawing at.

"Good for him. What does he want?"

"He demands an immediate audience, sire."

"He *demands*, does he?" The king's already florid features grow redder, and he lurches to his feet. The leg, which he injured in a joust, spasms, and sends a shooting pain into his groin. "By God, but I thought that little Frog bastard had more sense than to annoy me like this!"

"He is most certainly incensed about something," Rafe Sadler replies. "Though I can get no real sense from him. He is swearing that we are trying to cheat his master over the Americas."

"Are we?" Henry is aware that he cannot be aware of every minor detail of his own foreign policy, and expects his current favourite advisor to know the answer for him.

"Not that I am aware of," Rafe Sadler answers, truthfully. "I think the poor fellow has been misled in some way. Eustace Chapuys is a most honest fellow … for a foreigner… and would not make complaint without some just cause."

"Can we afford to anger the emperor just now?" Henry is alluding to some delicate negotiations which are to be started, in regards to him seeking a new bride. The girl might well come from a domain over which Charles has some say.

"Your Majesty may do as he pleases," Sir Richard Rich puts in from further down the long table. He is Attorney General, and seems to insert himself into the king's company more and more these days. "You are the king, sire."

"Thank you for that, Sir Richard," Henry says without turning his head. He enjoys the base, overblown flattery of the fellow, but finds him to be unpleasant company at other times. Not for the first instance, he regrets appointing him to so high a position, without first asking Tom Cromwell's advice.

"Rich is right, of course... you *are* the king, but if we wish to find a wife amongst those states who owe the emperor some allegiance... I fear we cannot afford to upset him." Rafe is thinking of the handful of names he has found for Cromwell, and where they lie in relationship to the emperor's sphere of influence. "Might I suggest you proceed with a note of diplomatic caution, sire?"

"You may, my dear Rafe," Henry says, thankful for such sound advice. Rich would insult the man for no good reason, the king thinks, other than to show off his stature at court. "Let us have the good fellow in, and see what is sticking in his little froggy throat."

"I think..."

"Shut up, Rich, for you plainly do not," Henry snaps, and the man slinks away to a corner, like a kicked dog.

Rafe Sadler raises a finger, and signals for the king's guards to admit the ambassador. The court chamberlain announces his presence in a stentorian voice, and there is a loud flourish from one of the gallery sackbut players. The strange new instrument gives of a mellow, ululating sound, thanks to its unique sliding arm.

The little Savoyard bustles in, brushes the startled chamberlain aside, and almost forgets to perform the royal bow, before launching into an extemporised speech.

"Your Majesty… I am here to express my absolute horror at the actions of your people, in regards to my master's rights of ownership in the Americas. Your Majesty's action is a flagrant flouting of … of … of the friendship between our two great realms!" There, it is out, and be damned to the English king's feelings, Eustace Chapuys thinks. What kind of a ruler behaves in so underhand a manner? The king, who is already standing approaches the ambassador with a hurt expression plastered onto his face, and shakes his head, as if in misery at his words.

"My dearest Chapuys," Henry

replies, and slips a comforting arm about the smaller man's shoulders, "what are you talking about? What have we done to offend your emperor so?" He hugs, and then gently pushes the man away from him. Chapuys is taken aback at such familiarity from a king, and has to pull his disordered thoughts back into some semblance of order.

"Why, Your Majesty, you seek to steal my master's new world from him," the ambassador says. "You intend invading the emperor's new found domains, and plundering them of those great riches which belong ... by international law... to the Holy Roman Empire."

"I do?" Henry shakes his big head in vexation, and looks to Rafe Sadler for some explanation. "Sadler... is any of this true? Are we doing as Master Chapuys claims?" Rafe shakes his head, emphatically, and asks where such a tale has come from.

"News has come to me that ships are being fitted out, even as we speak," Eustace Chapuys complains. "The London and Bristol docks are being scoured for sailors to man the expedition."

"You have seen this?" Rafe asks.

"Well… not exactly seen…" Chapuys can see that the king has no idea about what he speaks of, and Rafe Sadler, whom he trusts, also appears rather confused by it all. His voice loses some of its confidence. "There are … rumours."

"Ah, rumours," Rafe Sadler says. "Rest assured, my dearest Eustace, neither the king, nor I, have any knowledge of such an action. Your emperor's gold mines are safe from us. I fear your agents have misinformed you. If our navy is active, it is only because of the sudden rise in Portuguese shipping movements. We think it wise to keep a grip on the Iberian shipping lanes."

"Then you are not moving against the emperor?" Chapuys realises that he is questioning the king's word, and looks at Rafe instead.

"Charles is like a brother to me," Henry says, with finality. "I hold him in the greatest esteem, and I hope you will make him fully aware of that, Master Chapuys. At some future date, it may be that we can be of great service to one another, and I would not upset him for the world… not even his 'new' one!"

"A thousand apologies, sire," Eustace Chapuys mumbles, and backs from the king's presence. He feels like a fool for believing foundationless rumours, and hopes the matter goes no further. It is already likely that he will be recalled, and even punished, once Bishop Sanchez returns to Toledo, so this small fiasco will do even more harm to his career. In the space of a few days, his well ordered and comfortable life has started to fall apart, and he can only wonder what fate still has in store for him.

*

"Eustace, how are you?" Cromwell is on his way in to see the king, and smiles at so happy a meeting. "You must come to dine with us soon. Austin Friars is empty without all my old friends in it, and you only live next door!"

"Thank you, Thomas," Chapuys replies. "I am occupied just now, with matters of a delicate nature. I spend all my spare time composing a suitable, and grovelling, apology to send to Bishop Sanchez. The Bishop of Alghero is in an unforgiving mood, and he says he will have me up before the Inquisition, once he is safely back in Spain."

"Oh, the silly fellow is all piss and wind," Thomas Cromwell says. "I shall write to him also, and beg him to excuse your rather odd behaviour."

"Odd? I sat on him," Chapuys says, with a tremble in his voice. "Now, I have just offended the king. My stupid agents have played me false again."

"Come to supper tonight," Tom Cromwell insists. "Things will look better once you have had a good meal, and we can talk about the king's desire for a new wife in his bed."

"I doubt I will be of any use to you there," Eustace Chapuys says. He is feeling sorry for himself, and is not to be consoled with mere words, or the promise of a nice supper. Thomas Cromwell bids him farewell, and slips into the dining room. The king has left, and is to be found in the throne room, where he and Rafe Sadler are poring over some freshly drawn sea charts. Cromwell bows low, and saunters over to join them.

"Ah, Thomas… what news of the Portuguese?" Henry asks.

"They still stink of herrings, sire," Cromwell says. "Other than that, they are quiet enough."

"Then why are we readying ships?" the king asks.

"Why, for the proposed expedition to the New World," Thomas Cromwell replies. "It is almost ready to sail."

"Great God, man!" Henry swears. "I have just *promised* Chapuys that I know nothing of this."

"Nor did you, sire," says Thomas Cromwell. "We spoke about leasing some of our warships to the Draper Company, some time ago ... but that is all. Now, it seems they intend staking a claim on the northern shores of America."

"The Spanish will not stand for it," Rafe says. He is astounded that Cromwell has kept this to himself, and wonders why he has been treated so shabbily. "They will protest, and make ready for war."

"The Spanish have no legal right to bar us from that land," Cromwell says. "Thanks to your blessed father, Your Majesty."

"What has my father to do with this?" Henry senses that Cromwell has something up his sleeve, and wonders at the magnificent guile of the fellow.

"Why, it was he who commissioned the great expedition of 1497, sire." Cromwell takes a charter from under his arm, and spreads it open before the king. "He contracted for an Italian fellow called Giovanni Caboto to sail from Bristol, and chart the northern coasts, in the hope of finding a passage to India."

"By God... John Cabot... I recall the name," Henry says. "I do not recall anything coming of it though, Thomas."

"Caboto sailed up the coast, and charted lands *never* before visited by Europeans. He named it *Terra Nuevo ... or New Found Land*." Cromwell indicates where he means on the map attached to the old charter. "See here. Giovanni Caboto is contracted by the king, and anything new is to be charted, and is then to be claimed in His Majesty's name."

"I knew nothing of this," Rafe complains.

"Thank God, or you would not have been able to support His Majesty's rebuttal of Señor Chapuys' angry claims. The king had no knowledge of these plans... so spoke the absolute truth."

"You cunning dog," Henry mutters. "I spoke the truth to Chapuys when I said I knew nothing. Now, after the fact, you may tell me what is afoot."

"The Draper Company have chartered four ships from us, sire," Cromwell explains. "The contract says they will use them for exploration, and for the transport of timber. It does not mention where this timber is to be felled."

"Oh, you clever rascal," Henry mutters. "Then the scheme you spoke of is not some mere dream?"

"No, sire. If we do not find a passage to India, we will establish a fort in this New Found Land, and build a new town. In years to come, the new colony will furnish us with timber, ships, furs, and gold. The entire cost of the expedition will be born by the Draper Company... and the profits shared."

"How much will this venture realise?" Henry has no qualms about deceiving the emperor anymore, and seeks only to establish what his portion will amount to.

"Nothing in the first year, of course," Thomas Cromwell tells him. "Then about twenty thousand a year, rising steadily, as more land is brought under our sway."

"A tidy sum," Henry says. "Though the emperor will be angered with us, and might even go to war."

"He will not care, because we take only that which he does not want," Cromwell points out. "Why fight for that which you have shunned for the past forty years?"

"The emperor always sets a

great deal of store by his reputation," Rafe puts in. "He might still wish to display his annoyance in some way."

"How?" Henry is willing to stand some discomfort for twenty thousand a year, and a vast new land to rule.

"He might impose new trade tariffs," Rafe suggests.

"And so might we," Cromwell replies with a shrug.

"Might he seek to bar His Majesty from choosing a new wife from amongst his realms?" Rafe asks.

"Ah, yes… that would be most unfortunate," Henry says.

"Sire, if the emperor was single, and asked for your daughter Mary's hand in marriage, would you grant it?"

"Of course. It would tie us closely together and… ah, I see what you mean. If I marry into the Holy Roman Empire, it can only benefit Charles. Once again, you seem to have everything in order, my dear friend."

"I seek only to do my duty, sire," Cromwell says. He bows, and retires to the outer court, where Rafe Sadler catches up with him. Before he can speak, Cromwell holds up a hand and halts the coming complaint.

"Yes, I kept it from you," he says. "It was vital that Henry put

Eustace Chapuys' mind at rest, and he is such a poor liar. This way, he was able to aid our cause. I told you nothing because it is a private matter, between the Draper Company and myself. If things go awry, you can plead your innocence to the king, with utter conviction."

"I wish you had trusted me, Master Thomas," Rafe replies, somewhat haughtily. "You know where my loyalties lie."

"I do, and would not presume on that loyalty... unless absolutely necessary." Cromwell places a hand on his old pupil's shoulder. "You are like a son to me, Rafe, and I seek only to keep you safe. Whilst Miriam Draper, Will and Mush can slip away to Flanders, if anything goes amiss, you, Richard and I must stay behind to pay the piper."

"How might this new escapade bring danger to you?" Rafe asks. "If I understand, then I might be able to help."

"Four ships on a journey into the unknown," Cromwell tells him. "A sudden squall at sea, or unfriendly natives, and the expedition might flounder. Then Henry would want recompense for his men o' war, and would set the price high. He might also wish to punish those who fail him. You know how he can be, these days."

"I see. Then what of this Portuguese business?" Rafe knows that Lisbon has outfitted six thirty gunned warships, and sent them off to sea. "Is that anything to worry us?"

"Not at all," Cromwell says. "It seems that a part of Ibrahim's wild tale has come to pass. The Portuguese intend setting up trading posts on the African coast, and seek to send priests into Abyssinia. I pray the streets are not paved with precious jewels, or the king will have my head!"

*

"You dislike me, madam," Ibrahim says softly. "I can sense it in your voice, and see it in your eyes."

"A gentleman does not look into a lady's eyes, without her consent," Miriam replies, coldly. "I do not need to like you, to employ you, sir. My husband owns you, and thinks you will be of great service to us."

"I can kill with dagger or sword, and I respond well to the tinkle of silver coins in my purse," Ibrahim taunts. "What would you have of me?"

"I wish you to be my commander, sir."

"Of what?"

"Fort Henry in the king's New

Found Lands."

"The Americas?" Ibrahim grins at the audacity of this woman, and curses his luck that she is not available to him. "Why, that is further away than Kush, madam."

"As if you would know. I intend establishing a trading post and fortress," Miriam says. "It will be stocked with provisions and trade goods for a year, and manned by as many hard reprobates as I can find. Can you govern two hundred murderous ruffians, sir?"

"I can." Ibrahim has captained a company in several conflicts, and knows how to keep men loyal to him. "Though it will be a harsh world to master. What about weapons?"

"A hundred muskets, two hundred pikestaffs, crossbows, swords, fifty barrels of black powder, and what ever number of cannon we can spare from the ships."

"And women?" Ibrahim touches upon the one comfort most men cannot live without. "Did not Noah pair the creatures of God off in his ark? Men work harder, and fight better, if they have a woman to come home to."

"Women from my Poor Houses might choose to go with you, if

promised honourable marriage," Miriam replies. "They are tough women, who have lived through many trials. I think many of them are well suited to start a new life in a strange land. Most would go willingly."

"And if there are not enough of these good ladies?" Ibrahim knows that the lack of women makes men fractious, and ready to fight over those few they do have.

"The docks, and the streets around Putney and Wapping, are infested with prostitutes. They are so numerous that most earn but a penny or two for their favours. You might wish to contract some of these whores for the voyage. Be completely honest with them, Ibrahim, and only choose the hardiest. Tell them how hard the life will be, and make no rash promises. Many will go as wives, and even more as paid company. These last must be paid their worth, of course, but need not demand marriage for their services."

"Dear God, but you are a shrewd one, Mistress Draper," the Moor says. "Might we not be better calling this new English outpost Miriam's Land? Dominated by a woman, and managed by her husband's slave."

"You are under no compulsion to go," Miriam tells him. "We are not the Inquisition, and we do not seek to force you to it. If, however, you accept, you will be entitled to a hundredth part of the profits, and be given the rank of Colonel General."

"How much would that come to?"

"Two hundred a year."

"Which would be of little use in my new kingdom," Ibrahim responds. "Instead, let me have a portion of land, deeded to me by the king."

"How large a portion?"

"Oh, let me think. As far as I can walk in a day, by as far again in breadth … let us say twenty miles by twenty miles?" Miriam frowns, and glances over to Pru Beckshaw, who is working away at her abacus.

"Four hundred square miles," the girl announces, "at six hundred and forty acres to the mile. That is…"

"A little over two hundred and fifty thousand acres," Ibrahim confirms."

"You may cut out *ten* thousand acres of wilderness," Miriam bargains. "You shall have the timber felling rights to your own land, but must pay for the working of it out of your own purse. You will also be able to sell some of your land to the other men, so that they might farm it. You may build a saw mill, of course, but it will belong to the Draper Company. If we make this adventure profitable, the king will leave us to our own devices, and we shall all become very well off."

"And if I refuse?" Ibrahim has a fair idea, but wishes to hear the words from Miriam's own lips.

"Then you will receive a free passage back to Spain," Miriam says, sweetly. "*The Wild Rover* sails from Wapping on the evening tide. Once in Cadiz, you may leave the ship, and do as you please, sir."

"You drive a cruel bargain, Mistress Miriam," the big black man says. "We *conversos* are not loved by the Spanish church. They suspect we will revert to our Muslim or Jewish faith, if only given the chance."

"Would you not?" Miriam asks. She is, in her own way, a *converso*, having concealed her Judaism to save her own life.

"It is no sin to wish to save yourself," Ibrahim replies, and for the first time he lets his mask of indifference slip. "Do you know what an *Auto-da-fe* is... no? Then pray, let me explain, my dear Miriam, for I once witnessed one in Toledo."

"An act of faith... *auto da fe*," Miriam whispers.

"Just so. The final, brutal, public ceremony of the Spanish Inquisition. I once watched as the crowds gathered in the public square, facing the great cathedral. In the centre of the square, there were at least a dozen wooden stakes, where the so called heretics were to be burned alive. Then the cardinal... a foul creature of the Grand Inquisition... named Juan Pardo de Tavera... came out, and shouted out the names of all those whom the Inquisition had condemned. Then the heretics were led out, wearing black robes, decorated with red demons and flames. Officials of the Inquisition, all dressed in plain black robes, tied them to the stakes, with the vast crowd surging forward, and baying like hungry wolves."

"Were they Jews, or Muslims?" Miriam asks. She knows the tales of ancient persecution, and has heard how some Christian states deal with those they label Christ Killers, and heretics. Each religion seems to have its own way of murdering in the name of their own particular God.

"Mostly Jews who had recanted... but a few of my faith, and one poor protestant... a simple minded

313

Flemish woman who had not the wit to swear on the bible, and so save herself. Then Cardinal Tavera spoke up. '*Do you give up your heresy against the holy church?*' he cried to those poor wretches tied to the thick wooden stakes. Two frightened young men, who repented at the last, were strangled to death before the fires were lit … as a sign of God's divine mercy. Most, however, stood silent, or defiant. The fires were lit with firebrands, and the square echoed with their terrified screams, and wild, animal-like cheers from the crowd. You should watch a man burn, madam… if only to understand how wicked men can be to one another. The smell of roasted flesh stays in the nostrils forever."

"Such wicked things, done in the name of God," Pru Beckshaw says, and puts a contract before the handsome Moor. "Go and build a new world, sir… where all are equal before Him."

Ibrahim nods, and scratches his name onto the parchment.

"Let this new world of ours offer freedom to every man," Miriam says, "be he Muslim, Jew, or Christian. Judge a man by what he does, rather than by what he is."

"If I succeed, thousands more

will wish to follow," Ibrahim says. "How will the king see that?"

"Leave the king to me, and to Master Cromwell," Miriam tells her false Abyssinian. "We will keep him content, until the new land is completely established. What do you see, Pru?"

"A land of milk and honey," Pru promises. "Where the lion shall lie down with the lamb."

"Ah, another promised land," Miriam Draper says with a smile. "Perhaps I should scour England for all its hidden Jews, and send them hence?"

"A land of Jews, ruled by a Moor. This all sounds most wonderful, ladies," Ibrahim says, "but I fear our promised land will be a Godless place for the nonce. Your Israelites might be safer taking their chances with English law courts, or the Spanish Inquisition!"

16   Portrait of a Lady

The King's Examiner in Chief is a well known face these days, and the dockyard workers all know him, and think him a decent sort of a man. They know how he started life as a private soldier, and how he rose to his current high position, and admire him for it. If one can do it, so can they all, they reason.

They clear the way for him, and direct him to the Draper cog, which has just tied up at the dockside. He steps around a steaming pile of horse muck, and stands on the quay, ready to greet an old friend.

"It has been a while, Master Holbein," Will hails.

"Will Draper... is it you?" The stolidly built Flemish artist throws his arms wide in greeting, and steps down from the narrow confines of the ship's gang plank. "How long ago is it since we fought together now?"

"Six years," Will replies, as he recalls a skirmish with some Welsh bandits. "See, I have another old comrade with me. You remember Barnaby Fowler, do you not?"

"A h ,   B a r n a b y ...   h o w prosperous you both look." Holbein slaps the smaller man on the back, and he almost tumbles over. "How is the wound these days?"

"It rarely troubles me, save in wet weather," Barnaby replies.

"In England, that is most days," Holbein jests. "You two look more prosperous than I. How so?"

"Sir Will Draper is now the General in Chief of the King's Royal Examiners," Barnaby boasts, "and I am a Master at Law, with my own house in the country, and over three hundred pounds a year."

"*Sir* Will Draper!" Holbein is grinning like a schoolboy up to mischief. "Why, you were a half starved mercenary when we first met, not a knight of the realm. Now it is I who am famished, and looking for sustenance. Is Richard still with you, or that scrap of a boy, Mush?"

"You shall meet up with each of us again," Will promises, "for Master Cromwell is laying on a supper for us all tonight. Where are your bags, old friend?"

"My servant will see to that, and my pupil will fetch my canvasses and drawing materials," Hans Holbein says.

"Your servant … your pupil?" Barnaby Fowler laughs. "I see you have also progressed well in the world, my friend."

"After painting the king, I was able to command large fees from my patrons," Holbein explains. "I never pick up a brush these days for less than a hundred pounds."

In truth, the young Holbein has faded away, and he no longer seeks to upset people with his scurrilous illustrations of the famous, and the infamous. His illustrations, produced for a wicked satire on modern society, called *In Praise of Folly,* and written by the great philosopher, Erasmus, will remain amongst his finest, but most obscure, works.

Still, the painter thinks, sketching rude illustrations that are both hilarious, and irredeemably satirical, does not put food and drink on the table. Better by far to paint obvious poses, and pocket the cash.

"A hundred pounds for one painting?" Barnaby gives out a low whistle of appreciation.

"Then I fear to ask what you will charge me to paint my family," Will Draper says. "I thought to have a portrait of my wife and children from you."

"I am indebted to you, Will," Hans Holbein says. "Your Miriam shall sit for me free of charge."

"That is most gracious of you," says Will. "In return, I shall give you some sound advice. Drive a hard bargain with Master Cromwell this evening, for he means to keep you busy in this coming year."

"Then I am not merely summoned to paint the king again?" Holbein asks. It is a few years since his last portrait, and he has assumed that Henry wishes nothing more than an updated vision of his own personal majesty.

"The king wishes you to travel across Europe, and paint several ladies for him," Will says.

"Ah, a wife hunt," Holbein says with a wry smile. "Am I to be honest, and paint in every dimple, or ever so slightly drooping eyelid… or does your Master Cromwell wish me to *enhance* these ladies?"

"That is for you to ask of him," says Will. "As far as I know, Henry seeks a pretty, not too clever, young woman, to adorn his bed chamber."

"How long do I have to complete these portraits?" Hans Holbein can paint with an almost unheard of speed, when pushed, but he prefers having the time to do his sitters some justice.

"Three women in nine months,"

Barnaby puts in. "By then, the mourning period will be done, and the king can choose his new wife at his leisure."

"His fourth, is it not?" Holbein is, at heart, still a Roman Catholic, and he frowns on the king's casual sounding profligacy with his wives. "Let us hope this one fares better than her poor predecessors."

The painter breathes in the cold air of London, and looks out, across the vast city. He wonders why he ever returned to Augsburg, and resolves to try and make his life, and his living, in England from now on. The Tudor court can, he thinks, provide enough subjects to keep him in work for the remainder of his life, and he hopes that Master Cromwell can ensure he still has the king's royal patronage.

"After supper, you must come and stay with Miriam and I at Draper House," Will enthuses. "It will be nice to spend time with someone who has no axe to grind, or career to push. The children will love to see you."

"Children?" Holbein smiles. It has been several years, and his memory of the young Miriam is fresh in his mind still. Of course there are children. "How many?"

"Three now." Will is

inordinately proud of his growing brood, and wants nothing more than to show them off to an old friend.

"God has blessed you, my friend," Hans Holbein jests. "I must prepare a bigger canvas than I first thought!

*

"Be careful with that box, you clumsy dolt!" The Bishop of Alghero curses. "It contains my finest vestments." His new servant bows low, and apologises for his ungainly actions. The man, a Spanish sailor without a ship, seeks only to please. He is, as he explains it, stranded in England after his ship sailed from Tilbury without him. The man was obviously too drunk to rejoin his own ship, and he wants nothing more than to serve the bishop, and earn a safe passage back to Spain. "Stow it in my cabin, then bring aboard the rest of my belongings. Keep an eye open for any strangers loitering about the wharf, and tell me. My enemies have spies everywhere."

"*Si Señor,*" the servant replies, and scurries away to do as he is bidden. Bishop Sanchez watches him at his labours, and ponders over how so slow witted a fool can best serve him. After the fiasco at Austin Friars, he feels safer with a compatriot at his service, and curses the ill luck that has foiled his murderous plans.

"Chapuys," Sanchez grumbles. "I will see you hanging by your wrists for the way you treated me." He recalls the sudden attack, and the ridiculous position he found himself in, with the treacherous little Savoyard sitting on his chest. That Chapuys had cried out against him, and announced him to be an assassin, only added to the ignominy of the situation, and made him all the more determined to exact vengeance.

"Master?" The servant cocks an ear, as if he thinks he is being spoken to. "What is your wish?"

"Nothing, but to be away from this unwholesome island," the bishop replies. "I long to be back in Toledo, amongst friends."

"Ah, Toledo."

"Have you ever been there?"

"No, master, but I once met a man from Toledo," the servant says. "He claims it to be the finest city in Spain. For myself, I am from a village close to Bilbao. It is very poor."

"Close to Bilbao, you say?" the bishop asks. He once spent a few happy weeks in the city, where he was entertained by a skilful young lady who did not mind what his calling was, providing he could pay in gold coin.

"What is it called?"

"*San Vincente del Burro*," the slow witted fellow replies, with a hint of pride in his voice. "We have a great feast day each October to celebrate the man who lent his ass to Our Lord Jesus."

"Fascinating," Bishop Sanchez says, in a voice rich in sarcasm. "Get on with your work, and make sure my bed is made up before we leave port."

"Of course, Señor Bishop."

"*Your Grace*," Bishop Diego Sanchez tells the man. "One must always address a bishop as Your Grace, or … My Lord Bishop."

"Oh, I see." The servant nods his understanding, and goes about his duty. Everything is stored away, and the bishop's bunk made up, just as the ebb tide catches at the heavily laden Spanish merchantman. The crew, a mix of Spaniards and Spanish Sardinians, are well trained, and move about their assigned duties with consummate ease. Lines are cast off, fore and aft, and sails unfurled to catch at the gentle breeze. The captain stands beside the local river pilot, and watches as he guides them past the mud flats just off the Wapping shore.

"God's speed," the pilot mutters, as he climbs down a rope, and into the small skiff that will return him to the Wapping coast. "I hope you are safe home, before the devil knows you are under canvas," It is an old saying, meant to send a ship on its way with a blessing, and the Spanish captain nods, and crosses himself. If God sends a favourable wind, he will be in Cadiz before the week is out, and rid of the frightful Bishop of Alghero, who threatens with every word he utters. At least, he thinks, with Sanchez on board, there is no need for the devil to come calling in person!

*

The deck hands work in shifts, and half the crew is below, eating their last hot meal for the next few days, a savoury stew of fish and rice. Once at sea, a cooking fire is forbidden, and they must live in hard tack and sour wine. The bishop sits to one side, and eats his fill, before giving the crew a hasty blessing, and retiring for the night. The ship is not as sturdy as the English vessel he was first given passage on, but he feels safer under Spanish sails.

He ascends the wooden ladder from below decks, and makes his way to the poop. Climbing the four steps up, he enters the rear cabin, usually reserved for the captain. Once inside he recites a few prayers, by rote, and undresses himself for bed. His new servant fusses about him, and sees that the goose feather pillows are well plumped up, and his mattress pummelled into an acceptable shape.

Once he has attended to these duties the man crosses himself, and mutters his own short prayer of atonement.

"God forgive your humble servant for this wickedness."

"What is that?" Sanchez asks, as the Spaniard crosses himself again. "Lord forgive you for what, you oaf?"

"For what I must do, sir," the servant says. "I hoped you would leave England, and spare my master, but Richard Cromwell tells me otherwise."

"Cromwell?" Bishop Sanchez is suddenly alert. "What do you know of that vile fellow?"

"Only that you came here to kill his beloved uncle," the servant says.

"What is this?" Sanchez slips a hand under his pillow in search of the knife he keeps hidden there. It is gone, of course, and he begins to sweat in fear. Something is truly amiss, and he cannot think what to say, or do.

"Master Richard tells me you

wish to have Eustace Chapuys recalled, and punished... for saving Thomas Cromwell."

"Get away from me!" The bishop is suddenly frightened, and lurches up in his bed. His new servant, presented to him so conveniently, thrusts him back down, and snatches up the feather filled pillow. For a moment, the bishop cannot understand this action, then the awful reality strikes home. He is about to meet his maker, some years before he intended.

"Murder!" Sanchez cries.

The word is stifled by the pillow, and Alonso Gomez leans into his task. The bishop struggles for a few moments, but he is frail, and no match for his attacker. He gives one last desperate shudder, before going limp. Chapuys' faithful servant keeps the pillow in place until he is sure, then returns it to its rightful place. He goes about the room, and makes sure that everything is in its place, and that all signs of a struggle are tidied away.

Richard Cromwell has chosen his man well, for he knows how much Alonso Gomez loves his master, and how much he would do to preserve his life. So it is Gomez who waylays the bishops old servant, and makes him disappear, and it is this same Gomez who presents himself to the bishop at the last moment, as a lucky replacement for the 'lost' man servant.

In the early hours of the morning, the Spanish merchant ship will come out into the open sea, and the crew will be busy trimming sails, and setting themselves onto the right course. It will be mid morning before someone thinks to see why the old bishop has not emerged from his stateroom, demanding to be fed.

They will find the bishop dead, ostensibly from a heart seizure, and there will be no sign of his oafish servant. Gomez sneaks up onto the top deck, and slips over the side. It is still only a matter of fifty strokes to the river bank, where dry clothes, and a fresh horse await him. By dawn, he will be back at his master's side, ready for the day to come.

*

"May Almighty God in Heaven be thanked for this divine deliverance," Ambassador Eustace Chapuys says. "I shall pay for six masses to be said in Annecy… to help his soul on its way." He crosses himself, and hands the message over for his old friend to read. Thomas Cromwell takes it, and glances at the few scrawled lines from one of Chapuys' agents.

"A heart attack they say?" He folds the paper and hands it back. "It seems you are not to be recalled after all, my friend. Almighty God moves in mysterious ways, his wonders to perform."

"Indeed." Eustace Chapuys frowns. "This is none of your doing, is it, Thomas?"

"You think far too much of my powers, old friend," Thomas Cromwell protests. "The Bishop of Alghero was on a Spanish owned merchant ship, sailing down from the dock at Wapping, to the open sea. How could even I strike the damned fellow dead under such difficult circumstances?"

"I suppose not... and forgive me for doubting your word, my dearest old friend..." Chapuys feels the need to apologise, yet still has his suspicions. "Whatever the actual cause of the bishop's demise, I am to be spared a recall and investigation. I doubt the Grand Inquisition would have allowed me any mercy."

"Perhaps not." Tom Cromwell wraps his cloak about himself, and stares out across the frost covered gardens. "The emperor has no finer ambassador in Europe, Eustace, and I look forward to many more years of dealing with you."

"We should speak of the king's new wife," Chapuys says.

"The mourning period is not yet up," says Cromwell.

"No, but we both know your royal master's mind on the matter, and he will not wish to dawdle," Chapuys replies. "I believe Master Holbein is to paint the three favoured ladies?"

"That is so. We signed the contract over supper the other night." Thomas Cromwell has little heart for the business, but knows he must show some enthusiasm. "With a portrait to view, and a list of each lady's advantages, His Majesty should be able to make a most informed choice. Once he has his mind set on a particular lady, I must begin the negotiations."

"Then let us pray King Henry favours the same candidate as the emperor," Eustace Chapuys says. "In this way, our two realms might come to grow ever closer."

"Am I to know who your Charles favours?" Cromwell asks his friend. Eustace Chapuys smiles, bows forward, and whispers a name into Thomas Cromwell's ear. The king's most favoured minister nods his head, and grins with pleasure. It is a good choice, he thinks, and one that can only benefit both the Holy Roman Empire, and the realm.

*

The west country port of Bristol is mainly used for trade with the Irish, and along the Welsh coast. Its distance from London, and the difficulty of accessing the rest of the more prosperous parts of the kingdom gives it a satisfactory air of seclusion. Because of this the Draper Company decide that it is the ideal place from which to launch its colonisation of the New Found Lands, mapped out by Cabot decades before.

Miriam Draper is not one for overly emotional farewells, so has watched the departure of her small fleet from the distant sally port of Bristol's dilapidated castle. The view across the River Frome from the old Norman fortification is uninterrupted, and the sails of her five ships can be seen clearly in the afternoon light.

To one side, Hans Holbein is running his charcoal over a freshly stretched canvass, attempting to catch the historic moment for all time. He works fast, and will have the broad outlines finished before the sails disappear from sight. Later, in the seclusion of his workshop, he will recall the finer details, and the subtler hues, and block in the finishing touches.

Will Draper is stood behind his left shoulder, amazed at such skill. He turns from his close study of the artist's deft working, and notices that Miriam is shivering, even though the day is not too cold a one.

"Am I being foolish, my love?" she asks. Her husband takes off his fur lined cloak, and drapes it about her slender shoulders. She settles into the his arms, and allows his strength to lift her spirits once more.

"Were I a single man, I would long to be on one of yon ships," Will says, with a faraway look in his eyes. "Imagine it, my love. An entire new land, with great forests, lakes, and rivers. If your captain can get them all safely there, Ibrahim will establish an empire with a handful of men."

"And if he does not, and I fail?" Miriam asks. It is always the way in any mercantile endeavour. You can invest, choose the best men, and provide the finest ships available, but then you must sit back, and wait. The fates will decide if you see a return on the investment, or find yourself under the displeasure of a king.

"Then the king will want paying for those four of the five ships that are his," Will Draper says. "It is, as always, only a matter of money. Let Henry profit, and he will forgive the failure, perhaps even jest about it at our expense. Let us succeed in all our endeavours, and he will take the glory, and as much of the profits as he can."

"There is a time coming," Miriam murmurs, "when things will not go so easily, and the king will not be appeased so readily. If the Duke of Norfolk ever regains his nerve, or if Master Thomas chooses the wrong bride for him…"

"Enough of this idle chatter, my love," Will Draper says to his wife. "Master Cromwell has never put a foot wrong, and he is not about to start now. He has the sharpest wits, and the finest mind in all Christendom."

"Yes, you are right. I should have more faith in his judgement," his wife agrees. "Though *you* sometimes doubt him, husband."

"It is only his methods I doubt," Will says. "He has a happy chance of everything working out in his favour, but the means he uses are sometimes opposed to my own thinking. It seems, as the years go by, that I have become more morally inclined, whilst he has sometimes encompassed evil ways to gain his own way. His decisions are never selfish, and he seems to have

England in mind at every step of the way."

"Great men must make great decisions," Miriam tells him.

"If I were to cast you off, then murder you, I would be taken up, and punished. Cromwell arranges the death of Anne Boleyn and her brother... with my help... and he is rewarded. The king promotes me for my sins, provided they are done in his name."

"Enough of all this foolishness, my love," Miriam says, soothingly. "We are pawns, and must move as our masters dictate we should. The only way we shall ever be free of this world you seem to despise so much, is through great wealth. We must amass so great a fortune, and hide it well, that our futures are safe from the Henrys, Norfolks and Poles of this land."

"What then?" Will is feeling melancholic, and finds it hard to see the way ahead. "Must we become so rich that the nobility fear to meddle with us?"

"No, we must hide what we can from them, and live lives of quiet prosperity," Miriam replies. "Leave it to me, husband, and we will both die of old age, surrounded by our many grandchildren."

"And what of Tom Cromwell?"

Will asks. "How can a man of such ability, and position in court, ever hope to end his days quietly in his bed?"

"He must tread carefully, and hope to become less useful to Henry over the years. He must allow lesser men to assume power, whilst he slips away into retirement."

"Will they let him?" says Will.

"Why not?" Miriam wonders if she believes her own words, even as she speaks them. "Sir Richard Rich will gain power, because evil men do, but so will Rafe Sadler, and even slow thinking Richard. Perhaps the Austin Friars camp will continue to administer through them, and afford Master Thomas a happy old age. All he needs to do is make the right choices for another year or two, and all will be well."

"I pray you are right," Will concludes. "Cromwell loves England, Austin Friars, and the law… in that order. Let us hope none of these three let him down."

"He loves little Edward too," Miriam says, with unconscious irony. "He sees Henry loves himself too much, and has little time for the boy. Master Tom would be like a father to the prince, if given the chance."

"Why not, after all … he is

already like a father to half of England," Will replies. "He feeds the beggars, pensions the widows, and employs the orphans. He even took me under his wing when I was nothing more than a wanderer."

"He saw that within you that I did," Miriam says.

"Should I leave?" Hans Holbein says. "Then you two might better enjoy your sweet talking."

"Just get on with your work, Hans," Miriam retorts. "I want this moment captured in time."

"I could draw you, in your husband's arms, just as well," Hans replies. "The subject is a sweeter one."

"You should get a wife of your own," Will says.

"I have one," Holbein mutters. "Why else would I be hiding here, in Bristol?"

"Do you have children, also?" Miriam asks, bluntly. "For every man should be a father."

"Yes," Holbein says, but adds nothing more. Not everyone can be as lucky as his friend, Will Draper, and not everyone can be as sure of his own child's parents.

17   Swan Song

"When will Hans Holbein be ready to travel?" Thomas Cromwell does not look up from the warrant he is writing, and his nephew sees that it is for the arrest of yet another Roman Catholic cleric, in England without permission, and who is thought to be travelling somewhere in Hampshire.

"By the end of this week, I think," Richard replies. "Once he is back from Bristol, he is all ours, uncle. I have arranged a line of credit with the Antwerp bankers, and another in Augsburg. Hans will have a hundred pounds advance, and enough expenses for six months. By that time, he should have painted all three candidates for us, and be on his way back to England."

"Excellent. The sooner, the better." Cromwell raises his duster pot and shakes fine sawdust over his signature. "Here is an arrest warrant for the renegade priest Angelo Caetani. Use it to ensure there is no protest over his arrest, and convey him to Portchester Castle."

"Is he to be tried there?" Richard Cromwell asks his uncle.

"No trial." Thomas Cromwell finally looks up, and a glance at his nephew is enough to convey what is to happen to the hapless priest. "These renegade foreign priests are becoming a trouble to the state. They are caught, and condemned, and each one becomes a martyr after his trial and execution."

"Yes, heaven must be overflowing with new saints, uncle," the younger Cromwell jests. "Peter will have to widen his pearly gates to get them all in." The Privy Councillor fails to even smile, for he has decided that Father Angelo Caetani is to be taken prisoner, interrogated, and disposed of, without the need of a jury.

"This fellow must disappear, without trace," Cromwell insists.

"I shall speak with him, discover who his patron is, and bring you the name," Richard replies, dutifully.

"Pray, do not bother," Tom Cromwell says. "These people proliferate like rats, and spread their poison far and wide. Find out a name, by all means, even who his helpers are, but do not clog up the courts with more arrests, nephew. Do you understand?"

"Yes, uncle." Richard Cromwell bows, and turns to leave the study. This Sardinian priest is a dead man, and so too shall be his foolish patron. Some hunting accident will suffice for the priest's confederate, and save the cost of a long, drawn out legal action. It is a change of policy for Thomas Cromwell, who perhaps realises that his love of the law is not enough to keep England safe from a sudden papist backlash.

"Oh, and there is one more thing … which I almost forgot to speak of, nephew." Thomas Cromwell stands up, and comes from behind his broad desk. He steps close to his nephew, and drops his voice to little more than a whisper. "It is about Hans Holbein. You are close friends with him, are you not?"

"We fought together in Wales," Richard says. "He is a man after my own heart, and I love him like a true brother, Uncle Thomas." Cromwell raises his hands, as if to ward off a blow from his nephew.

"Do not misunderstand me, my boy," he says. "I hold Master Holbein in the very greatest respect. As a loyal friend of yours, he can rely on my patronage. It is just that I require a certain favour of him, and do not feel able to ask it outright. We have only a working relationship, you see. I thought it might come best from an old friend. Perhaps you might do me the favour of meeting with him, on my behalf. You might care to drop a word in his ear?"

"Oh, I see." The younger Cromwell is relieved that his uncle means the man no harm, for he feels a certain amount of loyalty towards Hans, who once saved his life in a violent mêlée. "What word would that be, sir? What do you want of him?"

"These portraits he is to paint for the king... the three contestants for Henry's royal hand in marriage... do worry me somewhat." Tom Cromwell clasps his hands together, almost as if in prayer. "What if the prettiest one of these girls is not the most suitable candidate for our purposes?"

"That is for the king to decide, I would suppose," Richard replies. He is not quick on the uptake, and fails to see what his uncle is asking of him. Cromwell sighs, and comes right to the point.

"This marriage may cement the relationship between England, and the Holy Roman Empire ... if only Henry chooses well." He pats his giant of a nephew on the arm. "One of the three suit's the Emperor Charles, and ourselves, more than the other two ever could, and it is *this* lady we wish Henry to choose."

"Then let us hope she is the best looking of the three girls, my dear Uncle Thomas, for ... ah, I see." The penny drops at last, and Richard Cromwell sees what is required of him. "I shall whisper into Hans Holbein's ear, sir. He is a decent sort of a fellow, and will grant me this favour. Though another hundred in gold might better convince him to our way of thinking."

"Promise him another two hundred, if King Henry chooses as we desire," Cromwell concludes.

"As you wish, sir." Richard is almost out of the door when he pauses, and turns back, somewhat confused. "But uncle, which of the three ladies is to be painted in the most satisfactory light?"

"Why, Anne of Cleves, of course," Cromwell says. With the daughter of an ally on the throne, and with Charles, the Holy Roman Emperor in full agreement to the marriage, the king will prove to more manageable, and easier to direct, he thinks.

"As you wish, sir," Richard says with a broad grin. "Let us hope the king finds her as pleasing in the flesh."

"Once here, Henry will be too eager to notice the odd blemish," Cromwell says with assurance. "With a staunch Lutheran queen by his side, Henry will never turn back to Rome. England will be safe from the tyranny of Roman Catholicism, and all our futures shall be assured. May God speed Anne of Cleves to us!"

"Amen to that," Richard says, and sets off about his new tasks with a happy heart.

*

"Be honest… what do you think of it?" Holbein stands back from the easel, and allows his eager patron a look at the finished work. Will is speechless. The image of his wife looks back at him, and he almost swoons with pride. Holbein has captured the inner beauty that seems to radiate from her, and makes her entire being glow with an inner light.

"Stunning, quite stunning," Will mutters at length.

"Mistress Miriam's sweet face was made to paint," Hans Holbein says. "She has a rare sort of beauty that lends itself to the medium. I have had some magnificent women sit for me before, but your wife is the best, by far."

"She will be pleased." Will is fascinated at how the light seems to dapple along the edges of her lace collar, and pick up the richness of her olive skin. "You make her look like a Spanish queen."

"I do not do justice to her, my friend," Holbein replies. "I still fail to catch the warmth of her skin, or the elusive half smile that plays about her lips."

"No man could ever do a better job," Will tells him, sincerely.

"Rare praise indeed, my friend. You must hang the portrait in your great hall… but not over the fire, where smoke will darken her into obscurity," the artist explains. "Put her on the east wall, where she may catch the light, yet the sun cannot fade her."

"Thank you, Hans," Will says. The portrait has been completed inside a week, and he is pleased with the outcome. "You must let me pay you for your skill."

"There is no charge for a labour of love," Holbein replies, with a gallant bow towards the door, where Miriam has just appeared. She crosses the chamber, and gazes at her image.

"Do I really look like that?" she says.

"No, you are more beautiful," Will tells her, seeing her through the eyes of a love that seems undiminished for the passing years. "Hans has caught your soul, and painted it onto this canvas."

"Oh, you talk such rubbish," Miriam says, "but I am content to listen to your lovely lies, my husband."

"Upon my return, I shall paint

your children for you," Holbein says. "Once these tiresome foreign portraits are done with, I shall settle in London for good."

"Then you shall have one of our houses," Will says.

"You own other houses?" the artist asks.

"Miriam is most secretive, but I know about the land she has been buying up, and the houses she has built on it," Will discloses. "I am right, am I not, my love?"

"You are." Miriam smiles at how confident he is with her as the maker of their fortune. "We own four mansions along the river, and will find you one… for either a good price, or a modest rent, my dear Hans."

"Then I shall return," Holbein promises.

"With your wife and family?" she asks.

"We shall see," Holbein replies, and the matter is dropped.

Miriam is happy. Her future, and that of her family, hangs on the return of her ships from the New World, and there is, for the first time in years, no dark cloud to threaten their lives. Ibrahim will make them a fortune in America, Henry will settle down with a new wife, and his son, and she shall see her family fully accepted into the world of the court. Sir Will Draper shall progress through the courtly ranks, and Lady Miriam will be on his arm, as they move into a brighter tomorrow.

*

The chambers, at the rear of a dilapidated tavern on the Southampton road are, at least warm. A log fire roars in the grate, and the two rooms serve well enough as a bedroom, and dining room for the lone priest.

He has been waiting in his makeshift quarters for three days and nights, for a courier who will never arrive. The man, sent by well wishers, and with gold for him, lies dead on a heath somewhere to the north.

Angelo Caetani is not the usual sort of a priest, and he comes to England with a particular mission to complete for his masters. He is not here to spread the word of Christ, or gather support for the Roman church, but to perform a task that will bring his own advancement and, quite possibly, a bishop's mitre.

He pokes the fire until it roars at him like the very maws of Hell, then crosses to the small table, where he has had laid out a veritable feast of cold meats, cheese, fresh bread, and wine.

The table is set for two, and there is a knife and goblet placed beside each pewter platter. The priest nods his satisfaction.

"Father Caetani?" The big man fills the door of the cottage, and blocks out the sunlight. You do not look much like a lord's messenger, the priest says to himself. What is afoot, and who is this fellow?

"You are mistaken, sir," Angelo Caetani replies without blinking. "I know no one of that name."

"I am Richard Cromwell," comes the sure reply, "and you are the Italian priest, Angelo Caetani. Do not think to deny it, sir, for I have met with, and disposed of, your expected visitor. The gold you wait for will never come, and there is no possibility of escape. I have here, a warrant for your arrest. You are to be taken from here, to a place of confinement where…"

"You will break my bones until I confess?" Angelo Caetani chuckles, and waves Richard into the seat opposite. The table is laden with food, and set for two places. Richard sees that the messenger he waylaid has missed out on a fine repast.

"For your expected guest, priest?" he says.

"Please, call me Angelo… and I

shall call you Richard," the priest says. He sits, and mutters a quick grace over the meal. "I take it that I have been betrayed?"

"We watch the harbours, and you were seen coming ashore," Richard tells his prisoner. "You priests never learn. When will you see that England has no need for Rome, or its old ways?"

"Ah, you think I am here to preach?" Father Angelo Caetani smiles. "That is not my intention, sir. Pray, be seated… and join me in this… my *last supper* as it were. Here, try this smoked ham. It is in the most delicious apple sauce."

Richard is about to refuse, when the priest picks up a slice with his fingers, and puts it in his mouth. He chews for a moment, then swallows, and reaches for another piece.

"See, my son. It is not poisoned," the priest says. "It was meant as a reward for the man who was to bring me my gold."

Richard grins sheepishly. He feels foolish at having been seen through so easily by Caetani. so takes up a slice on the point of the very knife he will later use to make the priest speak.

"Very good," Angelo Caetani

says, and reaches for the wine jug. He pours out two goblets full, and gestures to the honey roasted fowl. "Shall we attack this bird ... as a sort of last meal, my friend?"

"Why not?" Richard says, and waits for the priest to dismember the fowl and bite into a plump breast. Caetani sees this and grins.

"I admire your caution, sir," he says, "but I am a man of God... not a black hearted assassin. I sway men with the holy word, rather than the sword."

"Then I will eat with you," Richard tells him.

"After which you will torture me for information," Father Caetani says. He pulls off a chicken leg, and nibbles at it. "You English are so blunt in your ways. Why not offer me money... or some other inducement, to make me turn my coat?"

"Would you?" the younger Cromwell asks.

"For money?"

"Yes."

"No, you do not have nearly enough gold to bribe me," the priest says. "I have been promised that which you cannot give me. Once my mission is successful, I am to be made into a bishop... and then, God willing ... into a cardinal."

"For preaching your nonsense at a few dissident Roman Catholics?" Richard finishes off his fowl and eyes the goblet of wine, still untouched, and gestures to the priest's own drink. "Last chance, Father Caetani," Richard tells him. "Drink up, and then you must come with me."

The priest picks up his goblet, and drains it of wine in two swallows. Richard sees there are no ill effects, and downs his own goblet.

"Eat up, and then you must come with me," Richard announces.

"I regret that I can do neither," Father Caetani says. "You see, I was expecting a messenger, bringing me money. Warned of his coming, I had this sumptuous meal readied. It is a sad world where you do not know who to trust, and I could not allow the fellow to go off, and reveal my whereabouts for a few pieces of silver. True, he might have been faithful… but why should I even take the chance?"

"What's this?" Richard is puzzled. "You meant to kill your own messenger?"

"I did, Master Cromwell," Angelo Caetani reveals. "I intended poisoning him, taking the gold, and going about my mission. Instead, you turn up in his place. Your fame goes before you, of course, my dear fellow. My people know how you kill for Thomas Cromwell, and torture honest men. The food, *and the wine*, is to be your last meal... not mine."

"Brave words for an unarmed man," Richard says.

"Oh, but I am very well armed, my dear Master Cromwell," Father Caetani replies. He stands up, and Richard tries to emulate him, but his legs are numb. "You have a knife, whilst I use another weapon. I regret that I must leave you now, but I have a sacred mission... may God guide me."

Richard Cromwell lurches upwards, but his legs fail him, and he crashes to the ground. There are pains shooting down his arms, and his chest is constricted. He finds himself on his side, with his legs drawn up to his chest.

"Poison," Caetani explains.

"In the wine?" Richard manages to gasp, and Caetani laughs.

"Nothing so crude. You saw me drink, did you not? No, I was a little rushed for time, so used a crude potion. I painted it on the inside of your goblet, and let it dry. It will, I fear, take some time to kill you. Thank you for the horse, Richard Cromwell. It will speed me on my way."

"Dear Christ," Richard Cromwell gasps. "What kind of priest could…" He chokes, and feels his stomach constricting.

"Do not fight it," Caetani says. "Death is but the next step, my friend. Close your eyes, and I will help you on your way." The priest kneels beside the big man, and traces a finger across his forehead, in the sign of a cross. *"Per istam sanctan unctionem et suam piissimam misericordiam, indulgeat tibi Dominus…"*

The words tail of into a mumble, and Richard sees a cloak of darkness closing about him. His limbs are numb, and his eyes are becoming misted over. The priest stands, and Richard sees him pass outside, a black raven against the sunlight. The pain sends spasms through him, and he wonders if God is ready for his soul. He sees the faces of all the men he has killed, and wonders if they will be waiting for him in Hell.

There is a white shape in the doorway, and Richard fancies it is an angel, come to take him to his maker. She is robed in white, and there is a glow of light about her soft blonde hair. The face is that of a sad Madonna, and her eyes glow with concern.

He tries to speak to this ethereal

creature, but no words come out of his constricted throat. The angel kneels, and touches his brow with soft, cold fingers. Then she moves a hand to her snow white wing, and seems to pluck a feather from it.

"Leave him be, my lady," another voice says. "He is already a dead man."

"Are you, sir?" the angel asks, softly, her voice full of concern. "Are you ready to meet your God yet?"

Richard Cromwell is not, and so he begins to cry.

~The End~

Afterword

Whilst the reader must realise that these stories are works of fiction, they are built around a strong thread of historical presumption, and fact. The feud between Norfolk and Cromwell is well documented, and the details of Jane Seymour's death and funeral are drawn from contemporary accounts.

*

Whilst little exploration of the Americas took place under the reign of Henry VIII, it is a fact that his father funded an expedition to discover the fabled North West Passage to India.

John Cabot, a Genoese explorer, is accepted to be the first European to map out mainland North America in 1497, and his claim to this 'new found land' was the basis for the later English justification of colonisation rights.

*

The Abyssinian, himself, is a work of fiction, but Ibrahim's easy presence in England can be supported by many other black visitors to the Tudor court. Both Henrys' had musicians at court, of Moorish origin, as did Elizabeth I in later years. In addition, many towns about England have men and women of African origin listed amongst their rolls of 'freemen', or as merchants, slaves, musicians and general labourers. Though hardly a significant part of the Tudor population, there were several thousand foreigners domiciled in England during that period, for one reason or another.

Some, undoubtedly were brought here as slaves, but many more were here as parts of foreign embassies, visiting merchants, or simply mariners who decided to stay. Though something of a novelty, there is little evidence of racial discrimination against people of any colour.

The Tudor court discriminated against those who offered a threat, and so it was that Spaniards and Scots were considered in a poor light. The threat of a militant Islam was as great then as it seems to be now, and Europe was united in turning back the military advances of the Ottoman Turks, who were camped at the gates of Vienna. Though posing no military threat, the Jewish race was still persecuted, for no other reasons than the rather flimsy excuse that they 'killed Christ', and that they were good bankers.

*

There is also some documentary evidence that the next Queen of

*England, Anne of Cleves, was a
'ringer'... put in place by the anti
Roman Catholic faction in court. As
leader of this protestant clique, Thomas
Cromwell would have been
instrumental in pushing forward Anne's
claims.*

*Holbein's involvement has
always been known, but it is for the
reader to decide how complicit he was.
The fact remains that Henry viewed the
list of proposed brides himself, and
chose Anne of Cleves. How much he
was influenced by others is a matter for
conjecture.*

*

*Upon the death of Jane
Seymour, the future of her infant son,
Edward became of paramount
importance. His uncles, Ned and Tom,
were keen to bring the boy up, and
certainly pressed their claims, as
relatives.*

*

*Miriam Draper's undertaking to
set up 'work houses' for the benefit of
the poor might seem to pre-date similar
early Victorian institutions, but such
establishments were in operation as far
back as the twelfth century, in York, and
Winchester. The element of giving
'alms' to the poor, or having them work
for their keep was not new in Tudor*

times, but it was left to the church, or rich individuals, rather than the state to make provision.

*

From the moment that Henry became 'defender of the faith'... the new Church of England was undermined by Catholic lords, foreign monarchs, and the Roman Catholic church. Many priests were infiltrated into English daily life, where they were meant to give succour to those who remained loyal to the Pope.

Anne Stevens.

Other books by Anne Stevens.

The Tudor Crimes Series

Winter King*
Midnight Queen*
The Stolen Prince*
The Condottiero*
The King's Angels*
The King's Examiner*
The Alchemist Royal*
A Twilight of Queens*
A Falcon Falls*
A King's Ransom*
Autumn Prince*
The Abyssinian*
A Cardinal Sin
Traitor's Gate
Mercy of Kings
This Crown of Thorns
Rose Without a Thorn
Katheryn, the Quean
The King's Siege (due March 2018)
This Death of Kings (due June 2018)

Other Reading….
King's Quest* (Bk1 in the Georgians)

All novels are available in e-book format, and those marked with an * are also out in paperback.

23531264R00211

Printed in Poland
by Amazon Fulfillment
Poland Sp. z o.o., Wrocław